INC

fugitive knew what was happening. He could
the monstrous undead creature's fingers grop-
g in his brain, fumbling among all his secrets. Also,
knew he was a dead man. The black zombie's
gers had gone into his head effortlessly, flowing
nto flesh and bone and painlessly mingling – but
ey need not come out the same way. And it could
e just as slow as the monster wished it. What was
at for a way to die?

he fugitive filled his mouth and spat straight into
torturer's blazing eyes!

he fingers at once shifted their position in his
, solidifed, were withdrawn through his eyes,
g the eyeballs with them. Blood and brains
red in twin jets. Still clinging to the palings like
ch, the thing jerked the fugitive's head up and
kly back down, impaling it on one of the spikes.
ms and legs flew outwards, jerked spastically,
k loosely. And his corpse twitched . . .

*Also by Brian Lumley in New English Library paperback*

Necroscope: The Lost Years – Volume 1
Necroscope: The Lost Years – Volume 2
Dagon's Bell and Other Discords
The Second Wish and Other Exhalations

*About the author*

Brian Lumley is the internationally bestselling author of the *Necroscope* and *Vampire World* series. A career British Army Military Policeman for over twenty years, he has been a full-time writer since leaving the army. He lives in Torquay, South Devon.

# The Compleat Crow

Brian Lumley

NEW ENGLISH LIBRARY
Hodder and Stoughton

Copyright © 1997 by Brian Lumley

First published in Great Britain in 1997
by Hodder and Stoughton
A division of Hodder Headline PLC

A New English Library paperback

ISBN 0 340 69544 7

British Library Cataloguing in Publication Data
A CIP catalogue record for this title is available from the
British Library.

Typeset by Avon Dataset Ltd, Bidford-on-Avon, Warks

Printed and bound in Great Britain by
Clays Ltd. St Ives plc, Bungay, Suffolk

Hodder and Stoughton
A division of Hodder Headline PLC
338 Euston Road
London NW1 3BH

# DEDICATION

This one is for John the Balladeer, Jules de Grandin, Dr
Laban Schrewsbury, Carnacki, John Silence, Van Helsing,
and many other members of a fraternity too long to list
here. Nor may we forget Prince Zaleski, Nayland Smith
or Sherlock Holmes; except that in their case, despite
bordering on the supernatural more than once, their
deductions were not so much paranormal as 'elementary'.

# ACKNOWLEDGEMENTS

From THE CALLER OF THE BLACK, by Brian Lumley, published by Arkham House, Copyright © 1971 by Brian Lumley: *The Caller of the Black, The Mirror of Nitocris, De Marigny's Clock.* Also from the same collection: *Billy's Oak*, from THE ARKHAM COLLECTOR, Winter, 1970, Copyright © 1969 by August Derleth, and *An Item of Supporting Evidence*, from the ARKHAM COLLECTOR, Summer, 1970, Copyright © 1970 by August Derleth.

From THE HORROR AT OAKDENE & Others, by Brian Lumley, published by Arkham House, Copyright © 1977 by Brian Lumley: *The Viking's Stone, Darghud's Doll.*

From WEIRDBOOK 17, edited/published by W. Paul Ganley: *Lord of the Worms*, Copyright © 1983 by Brian Lumley.

From KADATH, July, 1982, edited/published by Francesco Cova: *Name and Number*, Copyright © 1982 by Brian Lumley.

From WORLD FANTASY CONVENTION 1983: Sixty Years of Weird Tales, edited by Robert Weinberg, Published by Weird Tales Ltd.: *The Black Recalled*, Copyright © 1983 by Brian Lumley.

# CONTENTS

# CONCERNING TITUS CROW

FROM ONE POINT of view: 'No man ever knew Titus Crow better than I did; and yet his personality was such that whenever I met him – however short the intervening time since our last meeting – I would always be impressed anew by his stature, his leonine good looks, and by the sheer weight of intellect which invariably shone out from behind those searching eyes of his . . .'

And from another: 'He was tall and broad-shouldered and it was plain to see that in his younger days he had been a handsome man. Now his hair had greyed a little and his eyes, though they were still very bright and observant, bore the imprint of many a year spent exploring – and often, I guessed, discovering – along rarely trodden paths of mysterious and obscure learning . . .'

Mysterious, obscure learning . . .

Titus Crow is an occult investigator, a psychic sleuth, an agent for Good in the detection and destruction of Evil. During WWII, as a young man, he worked for the War Department; his work in London was concerned with cracking Nazi codes and advising on Hitler's predilection for the occult: those dark forces which *Der Führer* attempted to enlist in his campaign for world domination.

Following the end of the war, and from then on right through a very active life which encompassed many 'hobbies', he fought Satan wherever he found him and with whichever tools of his trade were available to him at the time. Crow became, in fact, a world-acknowledged master in such subjects as magic, specifically the so-called 'Black Books' of various necromancers and wizards, and their doubtful arts; in archaeology, paleontology, cryptography, antiques and antiquities in general; in obscure or avant-garde works of art – with particular reference to such as Aubrey Beardsley, Chandler Davies, Hieronymous Bosch, Richard Upton Pickman, etc. – in the dimly forgotten or neglected mythologies of Earth's prime, and in anthropology in general, to mention but a handful.

As a collector, particularly of strange *bric-à-brac* and *outré objets d'art*, Crow had few peers in the years before . . . before his transition. But of that latter – *change* – sufficient has already been recorded elsewhere.

A one-time writer of macabre short stories, he occasionally chronicled his own adventures; at other times such work was undertaken by his lifelong friend Henri-Laurent de Marigny (son of Etienne, the world-famous New Orleans mystic), while others of his adventures were reported by mere acquaintances.

All of the Titus Crow adventures, in short story or novelette form, are here collected for the first time in one volume. They are presented chronologically, as best as may be determined, and along with *The Burrowers Beneath* and the 'post-transition' novels, they complete the Crow canon.

In addition to the tales in which Titus Crow is a primary actor, there are three other closely related stories: *The Mirror of Nitocris*, the one and only personal chronicle of Crow's apprentice and fellow traveller, de Marigny; *Inception*, in which Crow plays only a cameo role; and lastly *The Black Recalled*, in which nothing of Crow appears at all!

... Or does it?

Only one thing remains to be said. In the light of Titus Crow's fascination and lifelong affair with matters of dark concern, much of this volume is naturally taken up with narratives of relentless horror. Therefore – it is not a book for the squeamish.

You have been warned!

Brian Lumley
Brixham, Devon,
England
May 1985

# INCEPTION

*THE TITLE OF this first story speaks for itself, but without giving too much away – I hope! Another funny thing about the story is this: it **is** the first Crow tale – but it was written last!*

*I 'blame' this story on Paul Ganley; when we were talking about a Crow book, he said: 'What about Crow's early years? Why **exactly** was he the way he was?'*

*I could see what he was after, and so answered: 'No, no – we already have Titus Crow's origin in **Lord of the Worms**.' But Paul's questions had been sufficient to set the wheels turning in my head, and damned if I could stop them! I became immediately caught up in the new story, so much so that the novel I was writing had to wait. It waited for three days, at the end of which time I wrote **Finis** – a very satisfied **Finis** – on Titus Crow's beginnings.*

December 1916. One week before Christmas.

London, in the vicinity of Wapping, an hour before dawn . . .

Mist-shrouded façades of warehouses formed square, stony faces, bleakly foreboding with their blind eyes of boarded windows; Dickensian still, the cobbled riverside streets rang to the frantic clatter of madly racing foot-steps. Except for the figure of a man, flying, his coat flapping like broken wings, nothing stirred. Just him . . . and his *pursuer*: a second male figure, tall, utterly silent, flowing like a fog-spawned wraith not one hundred yards behind.

As to who these two were: their names do not matter. Suffice to say that they were of completely opposite poles, and that the one who feared and ran so noisily was a good man and entirely human, because of which he'd been foolish . . .

And so he fled, that merely human being, clamorously, with pounding heart, tearing the mist like cobwebs in a tunnel and leaving a yawning hole behind; and his inexorable pursuer flowing forward through that hole, with never the sound of a footfall, made more terrible *because* of his soundlessness.

London, and the fugitive had thought he would be safe here. Panting, he skidded to a halt where a shaft of light lanced smokily down from a high window and made the cobbles shiny bright. In a black doorway a broken derelict sprawled like a fallen scarecrow, moaned about the night's chill and clutched his empty bottle. Coarse laughter came from above, the chink of glasses and a low-muttered, lewd suggestion. Again the laughter, a woman's, thick with lust.

No refuge here, where the air itself seemed steeped in decay and ingrown vice – but at least there was the light, and humanity too, albeit dregs.

The fugitive hugged the wall, fused with it and became one with the shadows, gratefully gulped at the sodden, reeking river air and looked back the way he had come. And there at the other end of the street, silhouetted against a rolling bank of mist from the river, motionless now and yet full of an awesome kinetic energy, like the still waters of a dam before the gates are opened —

The guttural laughter came again from above, causing the fleeing man to start. Shadow-figures moved gang-lingly, apishly together in the beam of light falling on the street, began tearing at each other's clothing. Abruptly the light was switched off, the window slammed shut, and the night and the mist closed in. And along the street the silent pursuer once more took up the chase.

With his strength renewed a little but knowing he was tiring rapidly now, the fugitive pushed himself free of the wall and began to run again, forcing his legs to pump and his lungs to suck and his heart to pound as desperately as before. But he was almost home, almost safe. Sanctuary lay just around the next corner.

'London' . . . 'home' . . . 'sanctuary.' Words once full of meaning, but in his present situation almost meaning-less. Could anywhere be safe ever again? Cairo should have been, but instead, with the European war spilling over into the Middle-East, it had been fraught. Paris had been worse: a seething cauldron on the boil and about to explode shatteringly. And in Tunisia . . . In Tunisia the troubles had seemed endless, where the French fought a guerilla war on all sides, not least with the Sahara's Sanusi.

The Sanusi, yes – and it was from the secret desert temple of an ancient Sanusi sect that the fugitive had stolen the Elixir. That had been his folly – it was *why* he was a fugitive.

Half-way round the world and back their Priest of the Undying Dead had chased him, drawing ever closer, and here in London it seemed that at last the chase was at an end. He could run no further. It was finished. His only chance was the sanctuary, that secret place remembered from the penniless, friendless childhood of a waif. It had been more than thirty years ago, true, but still he remembered it clearly. And if a long-forsaken God had not turned from him entirely . . .

Wrapped in mist he rounded the corner, came out of the mazy streets and onto the river's shoulder. The Thames with all its stenches, its poisons, its teeming rats and endless sewage – and its sanctuary. Nothing had changed, all was exactly as he remembered it. Even the mist was his friend now, for it cloaked him and turned him an anonymous grey, and he knew that from here on he could find his way blindfold. Indeed he might as well be blind, the way the milky mist rolled up and swallowed him.

With hope renewed he plunged on across the last deserted street lying parallel to the river, found the high stone wall he knew would be there, followed it north for fifty yards to where spiked iron palings guarded its topmost tier against unwary climbers. For immediately beyond that wall at this spot the river flowed sluggish and deep and the wall was sheer, so that a man might easily drown if he should slip and fall. But the fugitive did not intend to fall; he was still agile as the boy he'd once been, except that now he also had a grown man's strength.

Without pause he jumped, easily caught the top of the wall, at once transferred his grip to the ironwork. He drew himself up, in a moment straddled the treacherous spikes, swung over and slid down the palings on the other side. And now – now, dear God – only keep the pursuer at bay; only let him stay back there in the mist, out of sight, and not come surging forward with his rotten eyes aglow and his crumbling nose sniffing like that of some great dead nightmare hound!

And now too let memory stay sharp and serve the fugitive well, let it not fail him for a single moment, and let everything continue to be as it had been. For if anything had changed beyond that ancient, slimy wall . . .

. . . But it had not!

For here, remembered of old, was his marker – the base of a lone paling, bent to one side, like a single idle soldier in a perfect rank – where if he swung his feet a little to the left, in empty space above the darkly gurgling river –

– His left foot made contact with a stone sill, at which he couldn't suppress the smallest cry of relief. Then, clinging to the railings with one hand, he tremblingly reached down the other to find and grip an arch of stone; and releasing his grip on the railings entirely, he drew himself down and into the hidden embrasure in the river's wall. For this was the entrance to his sanctuary.

But no time to pause and thank whichever lucky stars

still shone on him; no, for back there in the roiling mist the pursuer was following still, unerringly tracking him, he was sure. Or tracking the Elixir?

Today, for the first time, that idea had dawned on him. It had come as he walked the chill December streets, when patting his overcoat's inside pocket, for a moment he had thought the vial lost. Oh, and how he'd panicked then! But in a shop doorway where his hands trembled violently, finally he'd found the tiny glass bottle where it had fallen through a hole into the lining of his coat, and then in the grey light of wintry, war-depleted London streets, he had gazed at it – and at its contents.

The Elixir – which might as well be water! A few drops of crystal-clear water, yes, that was how it appeared. But if you held it up to the light in a certain way . . .

The fugitive started, held his breath, stilled his thoughts and brought his fleeting mind back to the present, the Now. Was that a sound from the street above? The faintest echo of a footfall on the cobbles three or four feet overhead?

He crouched there in the dark embrasure, waited, listened with terror-sensitized ears – heard only the pounding of his own heart, his own blood singing in his ears. He had paused here too long, had ignored the Doom hanging over his immortal soul to favour the entirely mortal fatigue of bone and muscle. But now, once more, he forced himself to move. Some rubble blocked the way – blocks of stone, fallen from the low ceiling, perhaps – but he crawled over it, his back brushing the damp stonework overhead. Small furry rodents squealed and fled past him toward the faint light of the entrance, tumbling into the river with tiny splashes. The ceiling dripped with moisture, where nitre stained the walls in faintly luminous patches.

11

And when at last the fugitive had groped his way well back along the throat of the passage, only then dared he fumble out a match and strike it to flame.

The shadows fled at once; he crouched and peered all about, then sighed and breathed easier; all was unchanged, the years flown between then and now had altered nothing. This was 'his' place, his secret place, where he'd come as a boy to escape the drunken wrath of a brutish stepfather. Well, that old swine was dead now, pickled in cheap liquor and undeservingly buried in the grounds of a nearby church. Good luck to him! But the sanctuary remained.

The match burned down, its flame touching the fugitive's fingers. He dropped it, swiftly struck another, pushed on along the subterranean passage.

Under a ceiling less than five feet high and arched with ancient stone, he must keep his back bowed; at his elbows the walls gave him six inches to spare on both sides. But while he could go faster now, still he must go quietly for a while yet. The follower had tracked him half-way round the world, tracked him supernaturally. And who could say but that he might track him here, too?

Again he paused, scratched at the stubble on his chin, wondered about the Elixir. Oh, that was what his pursuer wanted, sure enough – but it was not *all* he wanted. No, for his chief objective was the life of the thief! A thief, yes, which was what he had been all of his miserable life. At first a petty thief, then a burglar of some skill and daring (and eventually of some renown, which in the end had forced him abroad), finally a looter of foreign tombs and temples.

Tombs and temples . . .

Again he thought of the Elixir, that tiny vial in his

pocket. If only he had known then . . . but he had not known. He had thought those damned black Sanusi wizards kept treasure in that dune-hidden place, the tribal treasures of their ancestors; or at least, so he'd been informed by Erik Kuphnas in Tunis. Kuphnas, the dog, himself one of the world's foremost experts in the occult. 'Ah!' (he had said), 'but they also keep the Elixir there – which is all that interests me. Go there, enter, steal! Keep what you will, but only bring me the Elixir. And never work again, my friend, for that's how well I'll pay you . . .'

And he had done it! All of his skill went into it, and a deal of luck, too – and for what? No treasure at all, and only the tiny vial in his pocket to show for his trouble. And *what* trouble! Even now he shuddered, thinking back on those corpse-laden catacombs under the desert.

Straight back to Tunis he'd taken the vial, to Erik Kuphnas where he waited. And: 'Do you have it?' The black magician had been frantically eager.

'I might have it,' the fugitive had been tantalizingly noncommittal. 'I might even sell it – if only I knew what it was. But the truth this time, Erik, for I've had it with lies and tales of priceless treasure.'

And Kuphnas had at once answered:

'No use, that vial, to you. No use to anyone who is not utterly pure and completely innocent.'

'Oh? And are you those things?'

How Kuphnas had glared at him then. 'No,' he had answered slowly. 'I am not – but neither am I a fool. I would use it carefully, sparingly, and so dilute as to be almost totally leeched of its power. At first, anyway – until I knew what I was dealing with. As to what it is: no man knows that, except perhaps a certain Sanusi wizard. The legends have it that he was a chief three hundred years ago – and that now he's high-priest of the cult of the Undying Dead!'

'What?' the fugitive had snorted, and laughed. '*What*? And you believe such mumbo-jumbo, such utter rubbish?' Then his voice had hardened. 'Now for the last time, tell me: *what is it?*'

At that Kuphnas had jumped up, strode to and fro across the fine rugs of his study. 'Fool!' he'd hissed, glaring as before. 'How may any mere man of the 20th Century "know" what it is? It's the essence of mandrake, the sweat on the upper lip of a three-day corpse, six grey grains of Ibn Ghazi's powder. It's the humor of a zombie's iris, the mist rising up from the Pool of All Knowledge, the pollen-laden breath of a black lotus. Man, I don't "know" what it is! But I know something of what it can do . . .'

'I'm still listening,' the fugitive had pressed.

'To one who is pure, innocent, unblemished, the Elixir is a crystal ball, a shewstone, an oracle. A single drop will make such a man – how shall we say? – AWARE!'

'Aware?'

'Yes, but when you say it, say and think it in capitals – AWARE!'

'Ah! It's a drug – it will heighten a man's senses.'

'Rather, his perceptions – if you will admit the difference. And it is *not* a drug. It is the Elixir.'

'Would you recognize it?'

'Instantly!'

'And what will you pay for it?'

'If it's the real thing – fifty thousand of your pounds!'

'Cash?' (Suddenly the fugitive's throat had been very dry.)

'Ten thousand now, the rest tomorrow morning.'

And then the fugitive had held out his hand and

opened it. There in his palm had lain the vial, a tiny stopper firmly in its neck.

Kuphnas had taken it from him into hands that shook, held it up eagerly to the light from his window. And the vial had lit up at once in a golden glow, as if the occultist had captured a small part of the sun itself! And: 'Yes!' he had hissed then. 'Yes, this is the Elixir!'

At that the fugitive had snatched it back, held out his hand again. 'My ten thousand – on account,' he'd said. 'Also, we'll need an eye-dropper.'

Kuphnas had fetched the money, asked: 'And what is this about an eye-dropper?'

'But isn't it obvious? You have given me one fifth of my money, and I will give you one fifth of the Elixir. Three drops, as I reckon it. And the rest tomorrow, when I'm paid.'

Kuphnas had protested, but the fugitive would not be swayed. He gave him three drops, no more. And five minutes later when he left him, already the occultist had been calculating the degree of dilution required for his first experiment. His first, and very likely *only* experiment. Certainly his last.

For when with the dawn the fugitive had returned and passed into Kuphnas' high-walled courtyard and up the fig-shaded marble steps to his apartments, he had found the exterior louvre doors open; likewise the Moorishly ornate iron lattice beyond them; and in Kuphnas' study itself –

There on the table, effulgent in the first bright beams of day, a bowl of what appeared to be simple water – and the empty eye-dropper beside it. But of Erik Kuphnas and the fugitive's forty thousand pounds, no sign at all. And then, in the corner of the occultist's study, tossed down there and crumpled in upon itself, he had spied what seemed to be a piece of old leather or perhaps a large canvas sack; except it was the general *shape* of the thing that attracted the fugitive's attention. That and the question of what it was doing here in these sumptuous apartments. Only when he moved closer had he seen what it really was: that it had hair and dead, glassy, staring orb-like eyes – Kuphnas' eyes – still glaring a strange composite glare of shock, horror, and permanently frozen malignance!

Innocence and purity, indeed!

That had been enough for the fugitive: he had fled at once, with nightmare gibbering on his heels, and with something else there, too. For to his knowledge that was when he had first become the fugitive, since when he had always been on the move, always running.

Nor could he scoff any longer at the idea of an undead guardian of that Sanusi temple he'd robbed; for indeed the thing which had followed him, drawing closer every day, and certainly closer with each passing night, was not alive as men understood that word. Oh, he'd seen it often enough – its burning eyes and crumbling features – in various corners of the world, and now here in London finally it had tracked him down, forced him to earth. . .

His eyes had grown accustomed to the tunnel's darkness now, where the nitrous walls with their foxfire luminosity sufficed however faintly to light his way, so that matches were no longer required. A good thing, too, for his box was severely depleted. But he had come perhaps, oh, one hundred and fifty yards along this ancient passage from the river, and knew that it would soon open out into a series of high-vaulted cellars. There would be stone steps leading up, and at their top a dark oak door standing open. Beyond that a high-walled, echoing room – five-sided, containing round its walls five

wooden benches, and at its centre a pedestal bearing a
stone bowl – would wait within a greater hall which, for
all that it remained unseen, the fugitive had always
known must be vast. And here a second oaken door
would be locked, permitting no further exploration. Or
at least, the door had always been locked when he was a
boy.

As to what the place was: he had never known for
sure, but had often guessed. A library, perhaps, long
disused; or some forgotten factory once powered by the
river? And the tunnel would have served as an exit route
for refuse, with the tidal Thames as the agent of dispersal.
Whichever, to him it had always been a refuge, a
sanctuary. And now it must play that role again, at least
until the dawn. His pursuer was least active in daylight,
so that with luck he should make a clean getaway for
parts further afield. Meanwhile —

He was into the vaults now, where ribbed stone
ceilings rose to massy keystone centres; and there,
beyond this junction of bare subterrene rooms, he
recognized at once the old stone steps rising into gloom.
Crossing echoing flags to climb those steps, at last he
arrived at the door and shouldered it open on hinges
which had not known oil for many a year. And as the
squealing reverberations died away, so he gazed again
into that dusty, cobwebbed pentagon of carved stonework, whose walls partitioned it off from the unseen but
definitely *sensed* far greater hall of which it must be the
merest niche.

The light was better here, still faint and confused by
dust and ropes of grey cobwebs, but oh so gradually
gathering strength as night crept toward day. And there
were the benches where often the fugitive had lain
through long, lonely nights; and there, too, central in the

room, the pedestal and its bowl, but draped now with a white cloth; and over there, set in the farthest of the five walls, the second oaken door . . . *ajar!*

Hands shaking so badly he could scarce control them, the fugitive struck another match and held it high, driving back the shadows. And there on the stone flags of the floor – footprints other than his own! Fresh prints in the dust of – how many years? The clean sheet, too, draped across the stone basin . . . what did these things mean?

The fugitive crossed to the basin, turned back a corner of the sheet. Fresh water in the bowl, its surface softly gleaming. He scooped up a little in his hand, sniffed at it, finally drank and slaked his burning thirst.

And as he turned from the pedestal, so he almost collided with a slender, polished wooden pole set in a circular base, whose top branched over the basin. Shaped like a narrow gallows, still the thing was in no way sinister; depending from its bar on a chain of bronze, a burnished hook hung overhead.

The fugitive began to understand where he was, and knew now how to prove his location beyond any further doubt. Quickly he went to the door where it stood ajar, eased it open and stepped through. And then he knew that he was right, knew what this place was and wondered if he really had any right being here. Probably not.

But in any case he could not stay; the dawn would soon be breaking, when once more he would be safe; he had far, far to go before night fell again. He re-entered the five-sided room, crossed its floor, paused at the pedestal and bowl to adjust the sheet where he'd disturbed it. And that was when the idea came to him and fixed itself in his mind.

He took out the vial and held it up in the gloom, and feeble though the light was, still the Elixir gathered to itself a faintly roseate glow. Was this really what the follower sought? Was this truly the purpose of the pursuit? Yes, it must be so. And *which* was that worm-ravaged ghoul compelled to track: flesh and blood thief, or the object of his thievery? Could the creature be thrown off the trail? And in any case, what good to anyone was the Elixir now?

A good many questions, and the fugitive knew the answers to none of them, not for certain. But there might be a way to find out.

Again, quickly, he turned back the corner of the sheet, unstoppered the tiny bottle, held his face well away and poured the contents out into the stone bowl. Glancing from the corner of his eye, he saw a faint glimmer of gold passing like a stray beam of sunlight over the surface of the water, watched it fade as those smallest of ripples grew still.

There, it was done. He sighed, stoppered the vial, replaced it in his pocket and moved on.

Back through the door at the top of the steps he went, and down those steps to the vault, and so once more to the claustrophobic passage under the earth. Dawn must be mere minutes away; surely by now the pursuer had given up the chase, hidden himself away for the day to come? With his footsteps ringing in his ears, so the fugitive retraced his steps, clambered over the fallen debris close to the entrance, finally stuck his head out of the embrasure in the wall and gazed out over the river.

Not quite dawn yet, no, but there on a distant horizon, on grey roofs a pinkish stain which heralded the rising sun; and already the mist settling back to the river, where it curled like a thick topping of ethereal cream. There was a riming of frost on the stonework now, perhaps the first of winter, but the fugitive ignored the cold as he put up a groping hand to blindly discover and clutch an iron paling. Then, without pause, he swung himself out of the embrasure and began to climb –

– *Only to freeze in that position as irresistible fingers grasped his wrists and drew him effortlessly up!*

The pursuer! There beyond the palings, clinging like a great black leech to the wall! And when their faces were level, when only the iron palings separated them – how the fugitive would have screamed then. But he could not; for transferring both of his trapped wrists to one black and leathery and impossibly powerful claw, the pursuer had shoved his free hand between the bars and *into* his forehead!

The fugitive knew what was happening. He could feel this monstrous undead creature's fingers groping in his brain, fumbling among all his secrets. Also, he knew he was a dead man. The black zombie's fingers had gone into his head effortlessly, flowing into flesh and bone and painlessly mingling – but they need not necessarily come out the same way. And it could be just as slow as the monster wished it. What was that for a way to die?

Hope does not always spring eternal – not when you gaze into eyes like coals under a bellows, worn by a creature spawned in hell.

The fugitive filled his mouth and spat straight into those blazing eyes.

The fingers at once shifted their position in his head, solidified, were withdrawn through his eyes, taking the eyeballs with them. Blood and brains spouted in twin jets. Still clinging to the palings like a leech, the thing jerked the fugitive's head up and quickly back down, impaling it on one of the spikes. His arms and legs flew outwards, jerked spastically, fell back loosely. And he twitched. Not life but death.

The cursed thing sniffed his corpse with tattered nostrils, found nothing. It plucked him from the palings and tossed him down. The mist parted for a moment as he struck the water, then rolled back and eddied as before . . .

Dawn was only a minute or two away and the dead thing knew it. He also knew where the fugitive had been, or at least where he had come from. Like treacle his body dissolved and flowed through the bars on top of the wall, and down into the embrasure where he quickly reassembled. And following the fugitive's old route, the monster flowed forward in darkness, along the passage to the vaults, through them to the upward-leading steps.

Here the thing paused as it felt the first waves of some unknown force, the presence of a Power. But dawn was coming, and the Elixir remained to be found. It flowed forward up the steps, flowed like smoke through the open door and into the five-sided room – and paused again.

Yes, the Elixir was here. Somewhere. *Here*! But something else was here too. The Power was stronger, unbearably strong . . .

Moora Dunda Sanusi crossed the floor to the second door, leaving no footprints. But at the door he paused a third time before something which angered him to a frenzy of hate, something he could not see, something in the air and in the stone and filling the very ether. And in that same instant the sun's first rays struck on high, dusty windows and penetrated them, falling in splintered beams within – beams with all the colours of the rainbow!

Dawn and the light it brought increased the unseen Power tenfold. Moora Dunda Sanusi's magic began to fail him. Unwanted solidarity returned and gave him weight, and faint prints began to show in the dust where he staggered backwards, driven back into the five-sided room and across its stone paving. He reeled against the pedestal and displaced the bowl's sheet, and a flailing hand fell for a moment into the gleaming water.

Agony! Impossible agony! The thing which Dunda was should feel no pain for it had no life as such – and yet there was pain. And Moora Dunda Sanusi knew that pain at once, and knew its source – the Elixir. The Elixir, yes, but no longer contained, no longer safe.

The thing snatched its mummied claw from the water, reeled toward the steps which led down into darkness and safety. But the place was sanctuary no longer. Not for such as Moora Dunda Sanusi, dead for more than two hundred and seventy years. Striking from above through many high-arched, stained-glass windows, the sun's rays formed a fiery lattice of lances, stabbing down into the five-sided room and converging on the undead thing, consuming it even as the Elixir consumed its arm.

Clutching that melting member to him, the zombie crumpled in reeking silence to the flags, foul smoke billowing outwards and bearing his substance away. In a moment the fires in his eyes flickered low, and in the next blinked out, extinguished. The final, solitary sound he made was a sigh of great peace long overdue, and then he was gone.

A breeze, blowing in under the doors of the ancient church, scattered what was left and blended it with the dust of decades.

\* \* \*

The sun came up and London's mists dispersed. Dawn grew into a bright December day.

A local vicar, hurrying along the riverside streets, paused to glance at his watch. 10:00 a.m. – they would be waiting. He made his legs go faster, clucked his tongue against his teeth in annoyance. It was all so irregular. *Very* irregular, but hardly improper. And of course the family were well-known church bene-factors. And maybe it wasn't so irregular after all; for all of the line's children *had* been christened in the old church for several centuries now. A matter of tradition, really . . .

Turning a corner away from the river, the vicar came in view of the church, saw its steeple rising against the sky, where many slates were loose or missing altogether; its beautiful windows, some broken, but all doomed now to demolition, along with the rest of the fine old structure. And they called this progress! But it was still consecrated, still holy, still a proper house of God. For a few weeks more, anyway.

He saw, too, his verger, sneaking along the street with his collar up, coming away from the church – and the vicar nodded grimly to himself. Oh, yes? But he'd told him to see to the old place a full week ago, and not leave it until the last minute.

Approaching, finally the verger saw him, saw too that he was identified. His frown turned to a smile in a moment; he came directly forward, beaming at the vicar. 'Ah, vicar! All's prepared; I've spent the better part of two whole hours in there! But the dust and cobwebs – incredible! I *did* come round earlier in the week, but such a lot to do that—'

'All is understood,' the vicar nodded, holding up his hand. And: 'Are they waiting?'

'Indeed they are – just arrived. I told them you'd be along directly.'

'I'm sure you did,' the vicar nodded again. 'Well, I'd best be seeing to it then.'

A moment later the churchyard was in view, and there up the path between old headstones, just inside the arched, impressive entrance, where the massive doors stood open, the couple themselves and a handful of friends. They saw the vicar hurrying, came to greet him; the normal pleasantries were exchanged; the party entered the towering old building. The vicar had brought the books with him and all preliminaries and signatures and counter-signatures were quickly completed; the little ceremony commenced without a hitch.

Finally the vicar took the crucifix from around his neck and hung it from the hook over the font, held out his arms for the child. He'd done it all a thousand times before, so that it was difficult these days to get any real meaning into the words; but of course they had meaning anyway, and in any case he tried.

And at last all was done. The vicar dipped his hand into the water, sprinkled droplets, made the sign – and the church seemed to hold its breath . . .

But only for an instant.

Then the five-sided room came alive in a glow like burnished gold (the sun, of course, moving out from behind a cloud, burning on the old windows), and smiling, the vicar passed the child in his christening-gown to his father.

'So there we have you,' said the proud, handsome man, his voice deep and strong; and he showed the child to his mother.

A rose of a woman, she gazed with love on the infant, kissed his brow. 'Those eyes,' she said, 'with so much still to see. And that little mind, with so much still to fill it. Look at his face – see how it glows!'

'It's the light in here,' said the vicar. 'It turns the skin to roses! Ah, but indeed a beautiful child.'

'Oh, he *is*!' said the mother, taking him and holding him up. 'He is! So pure, so innocent. Our little Titus. Our little Titus Crow...'

# LORD OF THE WORMS

IF I HAD to choose the definitive Titus Crow story, it would have to be **Lord of the Worms**. It had been 'writing itself' for something like a year, between other stories and novels, when I first mentioned it to Paul Ganley. The way I remember it, he wanted to see it at once. Which meant I had to finish it at once. I think it took me about three weeks to get all the bits together and type it up, following which it was too long and too fresh in my mind for me to read objectively. So I simply sent it to Paul. He found one basic error and corrected it, and the story appeared in the next **Weirdbook**. And I breathed a sigh of relief when finally I read it.

I think this novelette says a lot about the difference between H. P. Lovecraft's 'heroes' and mine. Crow doesn't faint and he doesn't run away. In fact, I didn't even allow him a single gibber in his unrelenting battle with the monstrous

**Lord of the Worms.**

*Twenty-two is the Number of the **Master**! A 22
may only be described in glowing terms, for he is
the Great Man. Respected, admired by all who
know him, he has the Intellect and the Power and
he has the Magic! Aye, he is the Master Magician.
But a word of warning: just as there are Day and
Night, so are there two sorts of Magic – White,
and Black!*

*Grossmann's **Numerology**,
Vienna, 1776.*

# I

The war was well over, Christmas 1945 had gone by and
the New Year festivities were still simmering, and Titus
Crow was out of a job. A young man whose bent for the
dark and mysterious side of life had early steeped him
in obscure occult and esoteric matters, his work for the
War Department had moved in two seemingly uncon-
nected, highly secretive directions. On the one hand he
had advised the Ministry in respect of certain of *Der
Führer*'s supernatural interests, and on the other he had
used the skills of the numerologist and cryptographer to

crack the codes of his goose-stepping war machine. In both endeavours there had been a deal of success, but now the thing was finished and Titus Crow's talents were superfluous.

Now he was at a loss how best to employ himself. Not yet known as one of the world's foremost occultists, nor even suspecting the brilliance he was yet to achieve in many diverse fields of study and learning – and yet fully conscious of the fact that there was much to be done and a course to be run – for the moment he felt without a purpose, a feeling not much to his liking. And this after living and working in bomb-ravaged London through the war years, with the fever and stress of that conflict still bottled inside him.

For these reasons he was delighted when Julian Carstairs – the so-called 'Modern Magus', or 'Lord of the Worms', an eccentric cult- or coven-leader – accepted his agreeable response to an advertisement for a young man to undertake a course of secretarial duties at Carstairs' country home, the tenure of the position not to exceed three months. The money seemed good (though that was not of prime importance), and part of the work would consist of cataloguing Carstairs' enviable occult library. Other than this the advertisement had not been very specific; but Titus Crow had little doubt but that he would find much of interest in the work and eagerly awaited the day of his first meeting with Carstairs, a man he assumed to be more eccentric than necromantic.

Wednesday 9th January, 1946, was that day, and Crow found the address, 'The Barrows,' – a name which immediately conjured mental pictures of tumuli and cromlechs – at the end of a wooded, winding private road not far from the quaint and picturesque town of

Haslemere in Surrey. A large, two-storey house surrounded by a high stone wall and expansive gardens of
dark shrubbery, overgrown paths and gaunt-limbed oaks
weighed down with festoons of unchecked ivy, the place
stood quite apart from any comparable habitation.

That the house had at one time been a residence of
great beauty seemed indisputable; but equally obvious
was the fact that recently, possibly due to the hostilities,
it had been greatly neglected. And quite apart from this
air of neglect and the generally drear appearance of any
country property in England during the first few weeks
of the year, there was also a gloominess about The
Barrows. Something inherent in its grimy upper windows, in the oak-shaded brickwork and shrouding
shrubbery; so that Crow's pace grew measured and just
a trifle hesitant as he entered the grounds through a
creaking iron gate and followed first the drive, then a
briar-tangled path to the front door.

And then, seeming to come too close on the heels of
Crow's ringing of the bell, there was the sudden opening
of the great door and the almost spectral face and figure
of Julian Carstairs himself, whose appearance the young
applicant saw from the start was not in accordance with
his preconceptions. Indeed, such were Carstairs' looks
that what little remained of Crow's restrained but ever-
present exuberance was immediately extinguished. The
man's aspect was positively dismal.

Without introduction, without even offering his hand,
Carstairs led him through the gloomy interior to the
living-room – a room sombre with shadows which
seemed almost painted into the dark oak panelling.
There, switching on lighting so subdued that it did
absolutely nothing to dispel the drabness of the place or
its fungus taint of dryrot, finally Carstairs introduced

himself and bade his visitor be seated. But still he did not offer his hand.

Now, despite the poor light, Crow was able to take in something of the aspect of this man who was to be, however temporarily, his employer; and what he saw was not especially reassuring. Extremely tall and thin almost to the point of emaciation, with a broad forehead, thick dark hair and bushy eyebrows, Carstairs' pallor was one with the house. With sunken cheeks and slightly stooped shoulders, he could have been any age between seventy and eighty-five, perhaps even older. Indeed there was that aura about him, hinting of a delayed or altered process of aging, which one usually associates with mummies in their museum alcoves.

Looking yet more closely at his face (but guardedly and as unobtrusively as possible), Crow discovered the pocks, cracks and wrinkles of years without number; as if Carstairs had either lived well beyond his time, or had packed far too much into a single lifespan. And again the younger man found himself comparing his host to a sere and dusty mummy.

And yet there was also a wisdom in those dark eyes, which at least redeemed for the moment an otherwise chill and almost alien visage. While Crow could in no wise appreciate the outer shell of the man, he believed that he might yet find virtue in his knowledge, the occult erudition with which it was alleged Carstairs had become endowed through a life of remote travels and obscure delvings. And certainly there was that of the scholar about him, or at least of the passionate devotee.

There was a hidden strength there, too, which seemed to belie the supposed age-lines graven in his face and bony hands; and as soon as he commenced to speak, in a voice at once liquid and sonorous, Crow was aware that he was up against a man of great power. At length, after a brief period of apparently haphazard questioning and trivial discourse, Carstairs abruptly asked him the date of his birth. Having spoken he grew silent, his eyes sharp as he watched Crow's reaction and waited for his answer.

Caught off guard for a moment, Crow felt a chill strike him from nowhere, as if a door had suddenly opened on a cold and hostile place; and some sixth sense warned him against all logic that Carstairs' question was fraught with danger, like the muzzle of a loaded pistol placed to his temple. And again illogically, almost without thinking, he supplied a fictitious answer which added four whole years to his actual age:

'Why, 2nd December, 1912,' he answered with a half-nervous smile. 'Why do you ask?'

For a moment Carstairs' eyes were hooded, but then they opened in a beaming if cadaverous smile. He issued a sigh, almost of relief, saying: 'I was merely confirming my suspicion, astrologically speaking, that perhaps you were a Saggitarian – which of course you are. You see, the sidereal science is a consuming hobby of mine, as are a great many of the so-called "abstruse arts". I take it you are aware of my reputation? That my name is linked with all manner of unspeakable rites and dark practices? That according to at least one daily newspaper I am, or believe myself to be, the very antichrist?' And he nodded and mockingly smiled. 'Of course you are. Well, the truth is far less damning, I assure you. I dabble a little, certainly – mainly to entertain my friends with certain trivial talents, one of which happens to be astrology – but as for necromancy and the like . . . I ask you, Mr Crow – in this day and age?' And again he offered his skull-like smile.

Before the younger man could make any sort of

comment to fill the silence fallen over the room, his host spoke again, asking, 'And what are your interests, Mr Crow?'

'My interests? Why, I—' But at the last moment, even as Crow teetered on the point of revealing that he, too, was a student of the esoteric and occult – though a white as opposed to a black magician – so he once more felt that chill as of outer immensities and, shaking himself from a curious lethargy, noticed how large and bright the other's eyes had grown. And at that moment Crow knew how close he had come to falling under Carstairs' spell, which must be a sort of hypnosis. He quickly gathered his wits and feigned a yawn.

'You really must excuse me, sir,' he said then, 'for my unpardonable boorishness. I don't know what's come over me that I should feel so tired. I fear I was almost asleep just then.'

Then, fearing that Carstairs' smile had grown more than a little forced – thwarted, almost – and that his nod was just a fraction too curt, he quickly continued: 'My interests are common enough. A little archaeology, paleontology . . .'

'Common, indeed!' answered Carstairs with a snort. 'Not so, for such interests show an enquiring nature, albeit for things long passed away. No, no, those are admirable pastimes for such a young man.' And he pursed his thin lips and fingered his chin a little before asking:

'But surely, what with the war and all, archaeological work has suffered greatly. Not much of recent interest there?'

'On the contrary,' Crow answered at once. '1939 was an exceptional year. The rock-art of Hoggar and the excavations at Brek in Syria; the Nigerian Ife bronzes;

Bleger's discoveries at Pylos and Wace's at Mycenae; Sir Leonard Woolley and the Hittites ... Myself, I was greatly interested in the Oriental Institute's work at Megiddo in Palestine. That was in '37. Only a bout of ill health held me back from accompanying my father out to the site.'

'Ah! – your interest is inherited then? Well, do not concern yourself that you missed the trip. Megiddo was not especially productive. Our inscrutable oriental friends might have found more success to the north-east, a mere twenty-five or thirty miles.'

'On the shores of Galilee?' Crow was mildly amused at the other's assumed knowledge of one of his pet subjects.

'Indeed,' answered Carstairs, his tone bone dry. 'The sands of time have buried many interesting towns and cities on the shores of Galilee. But tell me: what are your thoughts on the Lascaux cave-paintings, discovered in, er, '38?'

'No, in 1940,' Crow's smile disappeared as he suddenly realised he was being tested, that Carstairs' knowledge of archaeology – certainly recent digs and discoveries – was at least the equal of his own. 'September, 1940. They are without question the work of Cro-Magnon man, some 20 – 25,000 years old.'

'Good!' Carstairs beamed again, and Crow suspected that he had passed the test.

Now his gaunt host stood up to tower abnormally tall even over his tall visitor. 'Very well, I think you will do nicely, Mr Crow. Come then, and I'll show you my library. It's there you will spend most of your time, after all, and you'll doubtless be pleased to note that the room has a deal more natural light than the rest of the house. Plenty of windows. Barred windows, for of course many of my books are quite priceless.'

Leading the way through gloomy and mazy corridors, he mused: 'Of course, the absence of light suits me admirably. I am hemeralopic. You may have noticed how large and dark my eyes are in the gloom? Yes, and that is why there are so few strong electric lights in the house. I hope that does not bother you?'

'Not at all,' Crow answered, while in reality he felt utterly hemmed in, taken prisoner by the mustiness of dryrot and endless, stifling corridors.

'And you're a rock-hound, too, are you?' Carstairs continued. 'That is interesting. Did you know that fossil lampshells, of the sort common here in the south, were once believed to be the devil's cast-off toenails?' He laughed a mirthless, baying laugh. 'Ah, what it is to live in an age enlightened by science, eh?'

## II

Using a key to unlock the library door, he ushered Crow into a large room, then stooped slightly to enter beneath a lintel uncomfortably shallow for a man of his height. 'And here we are,' he unnecessarily stated, staggering slightly and holding up a hand to ward off the weak light from barred windows. 'My eyes,' he offered by way of an explanation. 'I'm sure you will understand . . .'

Quickly crossing the carpeted floor, he drew shades until the room stood in sombre shadows. 'The lights are here,' he said, pointing to switches on the wall. 'You are welcome to use them when I am not present. Very well, Mr Crow, this is where you are to work. Oh, and by the way: I agree to your request as stated in your letter of introduction, that you be allowed your freedom at weekends. That suits me perfectly well, since weekends are really the only suitable time for our get-togethers – that is to say, when I entertain a few friends.

'During the week, however, you would oblige me by staying here. Behind the curtains in the far wall is a lighted alcove, which I have made comfortable with a bed, a small table and a chair. I assure you that you will not be disturbed. I will respect your privacy – on the understanding, of course, that you will respect mine; with regard to which there are certain house rules, as it were. You are not to have guests or visitors up to the house under any circumstances – The Barrows is forbidden to all outsiders. And the cellar is quite out of bounds. As for the rest of the house: with the sole exception of my study, it is yours to wander or explore as you will – though I suspect you'll have little enough time for that. In any case, the place is quite empty. And that is how I like it.

'You do understand that I can only employ you for three months? Good. You shall be paid monthly, in advance, and to ensure fair play and good will on both sides I shall require you to sign a legally binding contract. I do not want you walking out on me with the job only half completed.

'As for the work: that should be simple enough for anyone with the patience of the archaeologist, and I will leave the system entirely up to you. Basically, I require that all my books should be put in order, first by category, then by author, and alphabetically in the various categories. Again, the breakdown will be entirely your concern. All of the work must, however, be cross-referenced; and finally I shall require a complete listing of books by title, and once again alphabetically. Now, are you up to it?'

Crow glanced around the room, at its high shelves and dusty, book-littered tables. Books seemed to be piled everywhere. There must be close on seven or eight thousand volumes here! Three months no longer seemed such a great length of time. On the other hand, from what little he had seen of the titles of some of these tomes . . .

'I am sure,' he finally answered, 'that my work will be to your complete satisfaction.'

'Good!' Carstairs nodded. 'Then today being three-quarters done, I suggest we now retire to the dining-room for our evening meal, following which you may return here if you so desire and begin to acquaint yourself with my books. Tomorrow, Thursday, you begin your work proper, and I shall only disturb you on those rare occasions when I myself visit the library, or perhaps periodically to see how well or ill you are progressing. Agreed?'

'Agreed,' answered Crow, and he once more followed his host and employer out into the house's airless passages. On their way Carstairs handed him the key to the library door, saying:

'You shall need this, I think.' And seeing Crow's frown he explained, 'The house has attracted several burglars in recent years, hence the bars at most of the windows. If such a thief did get in, you would be perfectly safe locked in the library.'

'I can well look after myself, Mr Carstairs,' said Crow.

'I do not doubt it,' answered the other, 'but my concern is not entirely altruistic. If you remain safe, Mr Crow, then so do my books.' And once again his face cracked open in that hideous smile . . .

\* \* \*

They ate at opposite ends of a long table in a dimly lighted dining-room whose gloom was one with the rest of the house. Titus Crow's meal consisted of cold cuts of meat and red wine, and it was very much to his liking; but he did note that Carstairs' plate held different fare, reddish and of a less solid consistency, though the distance between forbade any closer inspection. They ate in silence and when finished Carstairs led the way to the kitchen, a well-equipped if dingy room with a large, well-stocked larder.

'From now on,' Carstairs explained in his sepulchral voice, 'You are to prepare your own meals. Eat what you will, everything here is for you. My own needs are slight and I usually eat alone; and of course there are no servants here. I did note, however, that you enjoy wine. Good, so do I. Drink what you will, for there is more than sufficient and my cellar is amply stocked.'

'Thank you,' Crow answered. 'And now, if I may, there are one or two points. . .'

'By all means.'

'I came by car, and—'

'Ah! Your motorcar, yes. Turn left on the drive as you enter through the gate. There you will find a small garage. Its door is open. Better that you leave your car there during the week, or else as winter lengthens the battery is sure to suffer. Now then, is there anything else?'

'Will I need a key?' Crow asked after a moment's thought. 'A key to the house, I mean, for use when I go away at weekends?'

'No requirement,' Carstairs shook his head. 'I shall be here to see you off on Fridays, and to welcome you when you return on Monday mornings.'

'Then all would appear to be very satisfactory. I do like fresh air, however, and would appreciate the occasional opportunity to walk in your gardens.'

'In my wilderness, do you mean?' and Carstairs gave a throaty chuckle. 'The place is so overgrown I should fear to lose you. But have no fear – the door of the house will not be locked during the day. All I would ask is that when I am not here you are careful not to lock yourself out.'

'Then that appears to be that,' said Crow. 'It only remains for me to thank you for the meal – and of course to offer to wash the dishes.'

'Not necessary.' Again Carstairs shook his head. 'On this occasion I shall do it; in future we shall do our own. Now I suggest you garage your car.'

He led Crow from the kitchen, through gloomy passages to the outer door, and as they went the younger man remembered a sign he had seen affixed to the ivy-grown garden wall. When he mentioned it, Carstairs once more gave his throaty chuckle. 'Ah, yes –"Beware of the Dog!" There is no dog, Mr Crow. The sign is merely to ensure that my privacy is not disturbed. In fact I hate dogs, and dogs hate me!'

On that note Crow left the house, parked his car in the garage provided, and finally returned to Carstairs' library. By this time his host had gone back to the study or elsewhere and Crow was left quite alone. Entering the library he could not help but lick his lips in anticipation. If only one or two of the titles he had seen were the actual books they purported to be . . . then Carstairs' library was a veritable goldmine of occult lore! He went directly to the nearest bookshelves and almost immediately spotted half-a-dozen titles so rare as to make them half-fabulous. Here was an amazingly pristine copy of du Nord's *Liber Ivonie*, and another of Prinn's *De Vermis Mysteriis*. And these marvellous finds were simply inserted willy-nilly in the shelves, between such mundane or common treatises as Miss Margaret Murray's *Witch-Cult* and the much more doubtful works of such as Mme Blavatsky and Scott-Elliot.

A second shelf supported d'Erlette's *Cultes des Goules*, Gauthier de Metz' *Image du Mond*, and Artephous' *The Key of Wisdom*. A third was filled with an incredible set of volumes concerning the theme of oceanic mysteries and horrors, with such sinister-sounding titles as Gantley's *Hydrophinnae*, the *Cthaat Aquadingen*, the German *Unter Zee Kulten*, le Fe's *Dwellers in the Depths*, and Konrad von Gerner's *Fischbuch*, circa 1598.

Moving along the shelved wall, Crow felt his body break out in a sort of cold sweat at the mere thought of the *value* of these books, let alone their contents, and such was the list of recognizably 'priceless' volumes that he soon began to lose all track of the titles. Here were the *Pnakotic Manuscripts*, and here *The Seven Cryptical Books of Hsan;* until finally, on coming across the *R'lyeh Text* and, at the very last, an ancient, ebony-bound, gold-and-silver arabesqued tome which purported to be none other than the *Al Azif* itself! . . . he was obliged to sit down at one of the dusty tables and take stock of his senses.

It was only then, as he unsteadily seated himself and put a hand up to his fevered brow, that he realized all was not well with him. He felt clammy from the sweat which had broken out on him while looking at the titles of the books, and his mouth and throat had been strangely dry ever since he sampled (too liberally, perhaps?) Carstairs' wine. But this dizziness clinched it. He did not think that he had taken overmuch wine, but then again he had not recognized the stuff and so had not realized its potency. Very well, in future he would

41

take only a single glass. He did not give thought, not at this point, to the possibility that the wine might have been drugged.

Without more ado, still very unsteady on his feet, he got up, put on the light in the alcove where his bed lay freshly made, turned off the library lights proper, and stumblingly retired. Almost before his head hit the pillow he was fast asleep.

*He dreamed.*

The alcove was in darkness but dim moonlight entered the library through the barred windows in beams which moved with the stirring of trees in the garden. The curtains were open and four dark-robed, hooded strangers stood about his bed, their half-luminous eyes fixed upon him. Then one of them bent forward and Crow sensed that it was Carstairs.

'Is he sleeping, Master?' an unknown voice asked in a reedy whisper.

'Yes, like a baby,' Carstairs answered. 'The open, staring eyes are a sure sign of the drug's efficacy. What do you think of him?'

A third voice, deep and gruff, chuckled obscenely. 'Oh, he'll do well enough, Master. Another forty or fifty years for you here.'

'Be quiet!' Carstairs immediately hissed, his dark eyes bulging in anger. 'You are never to mention that again, neither here nor anywhere else!'

'Master,' the man's voice was now a gasp. 'I'm sorry! I didn't realize—'

Carstairs snorted his contempt. 'None of you ever realize,' he said.

'What of his sign, Master?' asked the fourth and final figure, in a voice as thickly glutinous as mud. 'Is it auspicious?'

'Indeed it is. He is a Saggitarian, as am I. And his numbers are ... most propitious.' Carstairs' voice was now a purr. 'Not only does his name have nine letters, but in the orthodox system his birth-number is twenty-seven – a triple nine. Totalled individually, however, his date gives an even better result, for the sum is eighteen!'

'The triple six!' the other's gasp was involuntary.

'Indeed,' said Carstairs.

'Well, he seems tall and strong enough, Master,' said the voice of the one already chastised. 'A fitting receptacle, it would seem.'

'Damn you!' Carstairs rounded on him at once. 'Fool! How many times must I repeat—' and for a moment, consumed with rage, his hissing voice broke. Then, 'Out! Out! There's work for you fools, and for the others. But hear me now: he is The One, I assure you – and he came of his own free will, which is as it must always be.'

Three of the figures melted away into darkness but Carstairs stayed. He looked down at Crow one last time, and in a low, even whisper said, 'It was a dream. Anything you may remember of this was only a dream. It is not worth remembering, Mr Crow. Not worth it at all. Only a dream ... a dream ... a dream ...' Then he stepped back and closed the curtains, shutting out the moonbeams and leaving the alcove in darkness. But for a long time it seemed to the sleeping man in the bed that Carstairs' eyes hung over him in the night like the smile of the Cheshire cat in Alice.

Except that they were malign beyond mortal measure ...

## III

In the morning, with weak, grime-filtered January sunlight giving the library a dull, time-worn appearance more in keeping with late afternoon than morning, Crow awakened, stretched and yawned. He had not slept well and had a splitting headache; which itself caused him to remember his vow of the previous night, to treat his employer's wine with more respect in future. He remembered, too, something of his dream – something vaguely frightening – but it had been only a dream and not worth remembering. Not worth it at all ...

Nevertheless, still lying abed, he struggled for a little while to force memories to the surface of his mind. They were there, he was sure, deep down in his subconscious. But they would not come. That the dream had concerned Carstairs and a number of other, unknown men, he was sure, but its details ... (he shrugged the thing from his mind) were not worth remembering.

Yet still he could not rid himself of the feeling that he should remember, if only for his own peace of mind. There was that frustrating feeling of having a word on the tip of one's tongue, only to find it slipping away before it can be voiced. After the dream there had been something else – a continuation, perhaps – but this was far less vague and shadowy. It had seemed to Crow that he had heard droning chants or liturgies of some sort or other echoing up from the very bowels of the house. From the cellars? Well, possibly that had been a mental hangover from Carstairs' statement that the cellars were out of bounds. Perhaps, subconsciously, he had read something overly sinister into the man's warning in that respect.

But talking – or rather thinking – of hangovers, the one he had was developing into something of a beauty! Carstairs' wine? Potent? . . . Indeed!

He got up, put on his dressing-gown, went in search of the bathroom and from there, ten minutes later and greatly refreshed, to the dining-room. There he found a brief note, signed by Carstairs, telling him that his employer would be away all day and urging an early start on his work. Crow shrugged, breakfasted, cleared up after himself and prepared to return to the library. But as he was putting away his dishes he came upon a packet of Aspros, placed conspicuously to hand. And now he had to smile at Carstairs' perception. Why, the man had known he would suffer from last night's over-indulgence, and these pills were to ensure Crow's clear-headedness as he commenced his work!

His amusement quickly evaporated, however, as he moved from kitchen to library and paused to ponder the best way to set about the job. For the more he looked at and handled these old books, the more the feeling grew within him that Carstairs' passion lay not in the ownership of such volumes but in their use. And if that were the case, then yesterday's caution – however instinctive, involuntary – might yet prove to have stood him in good stead. He thought back to Carstairs' question about his date of birth, and of the man's alleged interest — his 'consuming' interest – in astrology. Strange, then, that there was hardly a single volume on that subject to be found amongst all of these books.

Not so strange, though, that in answer to Carstairs'
question he had lied. For as a numerologist Crow had
learned something of the importance of names, numbers
and dates – especially to an occultist! No magician in all
the long, macabre history of mankind would ever have
let the date of his birth be known to an enemy, nor even
his name, if that were at all avoidable. For who could tell
what use the other might make of such knowledge, these
principal factors affecting a man's destiny?

In just such recesses of the strange and mystical mind
were born such phrases of common, everyday modern
usage as: 'That bullet had his number on it,' and, 'His
number is up!' And where names were concerned: from
Man's primal beginnings the name was the identity, the
very spirit, and any wizard who knew a man's name
might use it against him. The Holy Bible was full of
references to the secrecy and sanctity of names, such as
the third and 'secret' name of the rider of the Horse of
Revelations, or that of the angel visiting Samson's
father, who asked: 'Why asketh thou then after my
name, seeing it is secret?' And the Bible was modern
fare compared with certain Egyptian legends concerning the use of names in inimical magic. Well, too
late to worry about that now; but in any case, while
Carstairs had Crow's name, at least he did not have his
number.

And what had been that feeling, Crow wondered,
come over him when the occultist had asked about his
interests, his hobbies? At that moment he would have
been willing to swear that the man had almost succeeded
in hypnotizing him. And again, for some reason he had
been prompted to lie; or if not to lie, to tell only half the
truth. Had that, too, been some mainly subconscious
desire to protect his identity? If so, why? What possible

harm could Carstairs wish to work upon him? The idea was quite preposterous.

As for archaeology and paleontology: Crow's interest was quite genuine and his knowledge extensive, but so too (apparently) was Carstairs'. What had the man meant by suggesting that the Oriental Institute's expedition might have had more success digging in Galilee?

On impulse Crow took down a huge, dusty atlas of the world – by no means a recent edition – and turned its thick, well-thumbed pages to the Middle-East, Palestine and the Sea of Galilee. Here, in the margin, someone had long ago written in reddish, faded ink the date 1602; and on the map itself, in the same sepia, three tiny crosses had been marked along the north shore of Galilee. Beside the centre cross was the word 'Chorazin'.

Now this was a name Crow recognized at once. He went back to the shelves and after some searching found a good copy of John Kitto's *Illustrated Family Bible* in two volumes, carrying the bulky second volume back to his table. In Matthew and in Luke he quickly located the verses he sought, going from them to the notes at the end of Chapter 10 of Luke. There, in respect of Verse 13, he found the following note:

'Chorazin' – This place is nowhere mentioned but in this and the parallel texts, and in these only by way of reference. It would seem to have been a town of some note, on the shores of the Lake of Galilee, and near Capernaum, along with which and Bethsaide its name occurs. The answer of the natives to Dr Richardson, when he enquired concerning Capernaum (see the note on iv, 31),

connected Chorazin in the same manner with that
city . . .

Crow checked the specified note and found a further
reference to Chorazin, called by present-day natives
'Chorasi' and lying in extensive and ancient ruins.
Pursing his lips, Crow now returned to the atlas and
frowned again at the map of Galilee with its three crosses.
If the central one was Chorazin, or the place now
occupied by its ruins, then the other two probably
identified Bethsaide and Capernaum, all cursed and their
destruction foretold by Jesus. As Carstairs had observed:
the sands of time had indeed buried many interesting
towns and cities on the shores of Galilee.

And so much for John Kitto, D.D., F.S.A. A massive
and scholarly work to be sure, his great Bible – but he
might have looked a little deeper into the question of
Chorazin. For to Crow's knowledge this was one of the
birthplaces of 'the antichrist' – which birth, in its most
recent manifestation, had supposedly taken place about
the year 1602 . . .

Titus Crow would have dearly loved to research
Carstairs' background, discover his origins and fathom
the man's nature and occult directions; so much so that
he had to forcefully remind himself that he was not here
as a spy but an employee, and that as such he had work
to do. Nor was he loath to employ himself on Carstairs'
books, for the occultist's collection was in a word
marvellous.

With all of his own esoteric interest, Crow had never
come across so fantastic an assemblage of books in
his life, not even in the less-public archives of such

authoritative establishments as the British Museum and the Bibliothèque Nationale. In fact, had anyone previously suggested that such a private collection existed, Crow might well have laughed. Quite apart from the expense necessarily incurred in building such a collection, where could a man possibly find the time required and the dedication in a single lifetime? But it was another, and to Crow far more astonishing, aspect of the library which gave him his greatest cause to ponder: namely the incredible carelessness or sheer ignorance of anyone who could allow such a collection to fall into such disorder, disuse and decay.

For certainly decay was beginning to show; there were signs of it all about, some of them of the worst sort. Even as midday arrived and he put aside his first rough notes and left the library for the kitchen, just such a sign made itself apparent. It was a worm – a bookworm, Crow supposed, though he had no previous experience of them – which he spotted crawling on the carpeted floor just within the library door. Picking the thing up, he discovered it to be fat, pinkish, vaguely morbid in its smell and cold to the touch. He would have expected a bookworm to be smaller, drier, more insectlike. This thing was more like a maggot! Quickly he turned back into the room, crossed the floor, opened a small window through the vertical bars and dropped the offensive creature into the dark shrubbery. And before making himself a light lunch he very scrupulously washed and dried his hands.

The rest of the day passed quickly and without incident, and Crow forswore dinner until around 9 p.m. when he began to feel hungry and not a little weary. In the interim he had made his preliminary notes, decided upon categories, and toward the last he had begun to move books around and clear a shelf upon which to commence the massive job of work before him.

For a meal this time he heated the contents of a small flat tin of excellent sliced beef, boiled a few potatoes and brewed up a jug of coffee; and last but not least, he placed upon the great and otherwise empty table a single glass and one of Carstairs' obscure but potent bottles. On this occasion, however, he drank only one glass, and then not filled to the brim. And later, retiring to his alcove with a book – E. L. de Marigny's entertaining *The Tarot: a Treatise* – he congratulated himself upon his restraint. He felt warm and pleasantly drowsy, but in no way intoxicated as he had felt on the previous night. About 10:30, when he caught himself nodding, he went to bed and slept soundly and dreamlessly all through the night.

Friday went by very quietly, without Crow once meeting, seeing or hearing Carstairs, so that he could not even be sure that the man was at home. This suited him perfectly well, for he still entertained certain misgivings with regard to the occultist's motives. As Carstairs had promised, however, he was there to see Crow off that evening, standing thin and gaunt on the drive, with a wraith of ground-mist about his ankles as the younger man drove away.

At his flat in London Crow quickly became bored. He did not sleep well that Friday night, nor on Saturday night, and Sunday was one long misery of boredom and depression, sensations he was seldom if ever given to experience. On two occasions he found himself feeling unaccountably dry and licking his lips, and more than once he wished he had brought a bottle of Carstairs' wine home with him. Almost without conscious volition, about 7:30 on Sunday evening, he began to pack a few things ready for the return journey. It had completely escaped his usually pin-point but now strangely confused memory that he was not supposed to return until Monday morning.

About 10 p.m. he parked his car in the small garage in the grounds of The Barrows, and walked with his suitcase past three other cars parked on the drive. Now, approaching the house, he began to feel a little foolish; for Carstairs was obviously entertaining friends, and of course he would not be expecting him. If the door should prove to be unlocked, however, he might just be able to enter without being heard and without disturbing his employer.

The door was unlocked; Crow entered and went quietly to the library; and there, on a table beside his open notebook, he discovered a bottle of wine and this note:

Dear Mr Crow –

I have perused your notes and they seem very thorough. I am well pleased with your work so far. I shall be away most of Monday, but expect to see you before I depart. In the event that you should return early, I leave you a small welcome.
Sleep well –

J. C

All of which was very curious. The note almost made it seem that Carstairs had *known* he would return early!

But at any rate, the man seemed in a good humour; and it would be boorish of Crow not to thank him for the gift of the bottle. He could at least try, and then perhaps he would not feel so bad about sneaking into the house like a common criminal. The hour was not, after all, unreasonable.

So thinking, Crow took a small glass of wine to fortify himself, then went quietly into the gloomy passages and corridors and made his unlighted way to Carstairs' study. Seeing a crack of feeble electric light from beneath the occultist's door and hearing voices, he paused, reconsidered his action and was on the point of retracing his steps when he heard his name mentioned. Now he froze and all his attention concentrated itself upon the conversation being carried on in Carstairs' study. He could not catch every word, but–

'The date ordained . . . Candlemas Eve,' Carstairs was saying. 'Meanwhile, I . . . my will on him. He *works* for me – do you understand? – and so was partly . . . power from the start. My will, aided . . . wine, will do the rest. Now, I . . . decided upon it, and will . . . no argument. I have said it before and now . . . again: he *is* the one. Garbett, what has he in the way of vices?'

A thick, guttural voice answered – a voice which Crow was almost certain he knew from somewhere – saying: 'None at all, that I . . . discover. Neither women – not as a vice – nor drugs, though . . . very occasionally likes a cigarette. He . . . not gamble . . . no spendthrift, he—'

'Is pure!' Carstairs' voice again. 'But you . . . worked for the War Department? In . . . capacity?'

'That is a stone wall, Master . . . as well try . . . into . . . Bank of England! And it . . . dangerous to press too far.'

'Agreed,' answered Carstairs. 'I want as little as possible to link him with us and this place. Afterwards, he will seem to return . . . old haunts, friends, interests. Then the gradual breaking away – and nothing . . . connect he and I. Except . . . shall be one!'

'And yet, Master,' said another voice, which again Crow thought he knew, a voice like a wind-blown reed, 'you seem less . . . completely satisfied . . .'

After a pause Carstairs' voice came yet again. 'He is not, as yet, a subject . . . hypnotism. On our first . . . resisted strongly. But that is not necessarily a bad sign. There is one . . . need to check. I shall attend to that tomorrow, by letter. It is possible, just possible . . . lied . . . birthdate. In which case . . . time to find another.'

'But . . . *little* time!' a fourth voice said. 'They mass within you, Master, ravenous and eager to migrate – and Candlemas. . . so close.' This voice was thickly glutinous, as Crow had somehow suspected it would be; but Carstairs' voice when it came again had risen a note or two. While it still had that sonorous quality, it also seemed to ring – as in a sort of triumph?

'Aye, they mass, the Charnel Horde – for they know it nears their time! Then – that which remains shall be theirs, and they shall have a new host!' His voice came down a fraction, but still rang clear. 'If Crow has lied, I shall deal with him. Then–' and his tone took on a sudden, demonic bite, a sort of crazed amusement, 'perhaps *you* would volunteer, Durrell, for the feasting of the worm? Here, *see how taken they are with you!*'

At that there came a scuffle of feet and the scraping sound of table and chairs sharply moved. A gurgling, glutinous cry rang out, and Crow had barely sufficient time to draw back into a shallow, arched alcove before the study door flew open and a frantic figure staggered out into the corridor, almost toppling a small occasional table which stood there. White-faced, with bulging eyes, a man of medium build hurried past Crow and toward the main door of the house. He stumbled as he went and uttered a low moan, then threw something down which plopped on the fretted carpet.

When the house door slammed after him, Crow made his way breathlessly and on tiptoe back to the library. He noted, in passing, that something small and pink crawled on the floor where Durrell had thrown it. And all the while the house rang with Carstairs' baying laughter . . .

## IV

It might now reasonably be assumed that Titus Crow, without more ado, would swiftly take his leave of The Barrows and Carstairs forever; that he would go home to London or even farther afield, return the month's wages that Carstairs had paid him in advance, revoke the contract he had signed and so put an end to the . . . whatever it was that his employer planned for him. And perhaps he would have done just that; but already the wine was working in him, that terribly potent and rapidly addictive wine which, along with Carstairs' sorcerous will, was binding him to this house of nameless evil.

And even sensing his growing dependence on the stuff, having heard it with his own ears from Carstairs' own lips, still he found himself reaching with trembling hand for that terrible bottle, and pouring another glass for himself in the suddenly morbid and prisonlike library. All sorts of nightmare visions now raced through Crow's mind as he sat there a-tremble – chaotic visions of immemorial madness, damnable conclusions totalled from a mass of vague and fragmentary evidences and suspicions – but even as his thoughts whirled, so he sipped, until his senses became totally confounded and he slipped into sleep slumped at the table, his head cushioned upon his arm.

And once more he seemed to dream . . .

*This time there were only three of them.* They had come silently, creeping in the night, and as they entered so one of them, probably Carstairs, had switched off the library lights. Now, in wan moonlight, they stood about him and the hour was midnight.

'See,' said Carstairs, 'my will and the wine combined have sufficed to call him back, as I said they would. He is now bound to The Barrows as by chains. In a way I am disappointed. His will is not what I thought it. Or perhaps I have made the wine too potent.'

'Master,' said the one called Garbett, his voice thickly glutinous as ever. 'It may be my eyes in this poor light, but—'

'Yes?'

'I think he is trembling! And why is he not in his bed?'

Crow felt Garbett's hand, cold and clammy, upon his fevered brow. 'See, he trembles!' said the man. 'As if in fear of something . . .'

'Ah!' came the occultist's voice. 'Yes, your powers of observation do you credit, friend Garbett, and you are a worthy member of the coven. Yes, even though the wine holds him fast in its grip, still he trembles. Perhaps he has heard something of which it were better he remained in ignorance. Well, that can be arranged. Now help me with him. To leave him here like this would not be a kindness – and prone upon his bed he will offer less resistance.'

Crow felt himself lifted up by three pairs of hands, steadied and guided across the floor, undressed, put to bed. He could see dimly, could feel faintly, could hear quite sharply. The last thing he heard was Carstairs' hypnotic voice, telling him to forget . . . forget. Forget anything he might have overheard this night. For it was all a dream and unimportant, utterly unimportant . . .

On Monday morning Crow was awakened by Carstairs' voice. The weak January sun was up and the hands on his wrist watch stood at 9:00 a.m. 'You have slept late, Mr Crow. Still, no matter . . . Doubtless you need the rest after a hectic weekend, eh? I am going out and shall not be back before nightfall. Is there anything you wish me to bring back for you? Something to assist you in your work, perhaps?'

'No,' Crow answered, 'nothing that I can think of. But thanks anyway.' He blinked sleep from his eyes and felt the first throb of a dull ache developing in the front of his skull. 'This is unpardonable – my sleeping to this hour. Not that I slept very well . . .'

'Ah?' Carstairs tut-tutted. 'Well, do not concern yourself – nothing is amiss. I am sure that after breakfast you will feel much better. Now you must excuse me. Until tonight, then.' And he turned and strode from the room.

Crow watched him go and lay for a moment thinking,

trying to ignore the fuzziness inside his head. There had been another dream, he was sure, but very little of it was clear and fine details utterly escaped him. He remembered coming back to The Barrows early... after that nothing. Finally he got up, and as soon as he saw the half-empty bottle on the table he understood – or believed he understood – what had happened. That damned wine!

Angry with himself, at his own stupidity, he went through the morning's routine and returned to his work on Carstairs' books. But now, despite the fact that the sun was up and shining with a wintry brightness, it seemed to Crow that the shadows were that much darker in the house and the gloom that much deeper.

The following day, with Carstairs again absent, he explored The Barrows from attic to cellar, but not the cellar itself. He did try the door beneath the stairs, however, but found it locked. Upstairs the house had many rooms, all thick with dust and sparsely furnished, with spots of mould on some of the walls and woodworm in much of the furniture. The place seemed as disused and decayed above as it was below, and Crow's inspection was mainly perfunctory. Outside Carstairs' study he paused, however, as a strange and shuddersome feeling took momentary possession of him.

Suddenly he found himself trembling and breaking out in a cold sweat; and it seemed to him that half-remembered voices echoed sepulchrally and ominously in his mind. The feeling lasted for a moment only, but it left Crow weak and full of a vague nausea. Again angry with himself and not a little worried, he tried the study door and found it to be open. Inside the place was different again from the rest of the house.

Here there was no dust or disorder but a comparatively well-kept room of fair size, where table and chairs stood upon an eastern-styled carpet, with a great desk square and squat beneath a wall hung with six oil paintings in matching gilt frames. These paintings attracted Crow's eyes and he moved forward the better to see them. Proceeding from right to left, the pictures bore small metallic plaques which gave dates but no names.

The first was of a dark, hawk-faced, turbaned man in desert garb, an Arab by his looks. The dates were 1602–68. The second was also of a Middle-Eastern type, this time in the rich dress of a sheik or prince, and his dates were 1668–1734. The third was dated 1734–90 and was the picture of a statuesque, high-browed negro of forceful features and probably Ethiopian descent; while the fourth was of a stern-faced young man in periwig and smallclothes, dated 1790–1839. The fifth was of a bearded, dark-eyed man in a waistcoat and wearing a monocle – a man of unnatural pallor – dated 1839–88; and the sixth –

The sixth was a picture of Carstairs himself, looking almost exactly as he looked now, dated 1888–1946!

Crow stared at the dates again, wondering what they meant and why they were so perfectly consecutive. Could these men have been the previous leaders of Carstairs' esoteric cult, each with dates which corresponded to the length of his reign? But 1888 . . . yes, it made sense; for that could certainly *not* be Carstairs' birth date. Why, he would be only fifty-seven years of age! He looked at least fifteen or twenty years older than that; certainly he gave the impression of advanced age, despite his peculiar vitality. And what of that final date, 1946?

Was the man projecting his own death? – or was this to be the year of the next investiture?

Then, sweeping his eyes back across the wall to the first picture, that of the hawk-faced Arab, something suddenly clicked into place in Crow's mind. It had to do with the date 1602 ... and in another moment he remembered that this was the date scrawled in reddish ink in the margin of the old atlas. 1602, the date of birth of the supposed antichrist, in a place once known as Chorazin the Damned!

Still, it made very little sense – or did it? There was a vague fuzziness in Crow's mind, a void desperately trying to fill itself, like a mental jigsaw puzzle with so many missing pieces that the picture could not come together. Crow knew that somewhere deep inside he had the answers – and yet they refused to surface.

As he left Carstairs' study he cast one more half-fearful glance at the man's sardonic picture. A pink crawling thing, previously unnoticed, dropped from the ledge of the frame and fell with a plop to the floor's boukhara rug ...

Left almost entirely on his own now, Crow worked steadily through the rest of Tuesday, through Wednesday and Thursday morning; but after a light lunch on Thursday he decided he needed some fresh air. This coincided with his discovering another worm or maggot in the library, and he made a mental note that sooner or later he must speak to Carstairs about the possibility of a health hazard.

Since the day outside was bright, he let himself out of the house and into the gardens, choosing one of the many overgrown paths rather than the wide, gravelly drive. In a very little while all dullness of the mind was dissipated and he found himself drinking gladly and deeply of the cold air. This was something he must do more often, for all work and no play was beginning to make Titus Crow a very dull boy indeed.

He was not sure whether his employer was at home or away; but upon reaching the main gate by a circuitous route he decided that the latter case must apply. Either that or the man had not yet been down to collect the mail. There were several letters in the box, two of which were holding the metal flap partly open. Beginning to feel the chill, Crow carried the letters with him on a winding route back to the house. Out of sheer curiosity he scanned them as he went, noting that the address on one of them was all wrong. It was addressed to a 'Mr Castaigne, Solicitor,' at 'The Burrows'. Alongside the postage stamps the envelope had been faintly franked with the name and crest of Somerset House in London.

Somerset House, the central registry for births and deaths? Now what business could Carstairs have with –

And again there swept over Titus Crow that feeling of nausea and faintness. All the cheeriness went out of him in a moment and his hand trembled where it held the suspect envelope. Suddenly his mind was in motion, desperately fighting to remember something, battling with itself against an invisible inner voice which insisted that it did not matter. But he now knew that it did.

Hidden by a clump of bushes which stood between himself and the house, Crow removed the crested envelope from the bundle of letters and slipped it into his inside jacket pocket. Then, sweating profusely if coldly, he delivered the bulk of the letters to the occasional table outside the door of Carstairs' study. On his way back to the library he saw that the cellar door stood open under the stairs, and he heard someone moving about down below. Pausing, he called down:

'Mr Carstairs, there's mail for you. I've left the letters outside your study.' The sounds of activity ceased and finally Carstairs' voice replied:

'Thank you, Mr Crow. I shall be up immediately.'

Not waiting, Crow hurried to the library and sat for a while at the table where he worked, wondering what to do and half-astonished at the impulse which had prompted him to steal the other's mail; or rather, to take this one letter. He had early installed an electric kettle in the library with which to make himself coffee, and as his eyes alighted upon the kettle an idea dawned. For it was far too late now for anything else but to let his persuasions carry him all the way. He must now follow his instincts.

Against the possibility of Carstairs' sudden, unannounced entry, he prepared the makings of a jug of 'instant' coffee, an invention of the war years which found a certain favour with him; but having filled the jug to its brim with boiling water, he used the kettle's surplus steam to saturate the envelope's gummed flap until it came cleanly open. With trembling fingers he extracted the letter and placed the envelope carefully back in his pocket. Now he opened the letter in the pages of his notebook, so that to all intents and purposes he would seem to be working as he read it.

The device was unnecessary, since he was not disturbed; but this, written in a neat hand upon the headed stationery of Somerset House, was what he read:

Dear Mr Castaigne –

In respect of your inquiry on behalf of your client, we never answer such by telephone. Nor do we normally divulge information of this nature except to proven relatives or, occasionally, the police. We expect that now that hostilities are at an end, these restrictions may soon be lifted. However, since you have stressed that this is a matter of some urgency, and since, as you say, the person you seek could prove to be beneficiary of a large sum of money, we have made the necessary inquiries.

There were several Thomas Crows born in London in 1912 and one Trevor Crow; but there was no Titus. A Timeus Crow was born in Edinburgh, and a Titus Crew in Devon.

The name Titus Crow is, in fact, quite rare, and the closest we can come to your specifications is the date 1916, when a Titus Crow was indeed born in the city on the 2nd December. We are sorry if this seems inconclusive . . .

If you wish any further investigations made, however, we will require some form of evidence, such as testimonials, of the validity of your credentials and motive.

Until then, we remain –

etc . . .

Feeling a sort of numbness spreading through all his limbs, his entire body and mind, Crow read the letter again and yet again. Evidence of Carstairs' credentials and motive, indeed!

Very well, whatever it was that was going on, Titus Crow had now received all the warnings he needed. Forewarned is forearmed, they say, and Crow must now properly arm himself – or at least protect himself – as best he could. One thing he would not do was run, not from an as yet undefined fear, an unidentified threat. His interest in the esoteric, the occult, had brought him to The Barrows, and those same interests must now sustain him.

And so, in his way, he declared war. But what were the enemy's weapons, and what was his objective? For the rest of the afternoon Crow did very little of work but sat in thoughtful silence and made his plans . . .

## V

At 4:45 p.m. he went and knocked on Carstairs' door. Carstairs answered but did not invite him in. Instead he came out into the corridor. There, towering cadaverously over Crow and blocking out even more of the gloomy light of the place, he said, 'Yes, Mr Crow? What can I do for you?'

'Sir,' Crow answered, 'I'm well up to schedule on my work and see little problem finishing it in the time allowed. Which prompts me to ask a favour of you. Certain friends of mine are in London tonight, and so—'

'You would like a long weekend, is that it? Well, I see no real problem, Mr Crow . . .' But while Carstairs' attitude seemed genuine enough, Crow suspected that he had in fact presented the man with a problem. His request had caught the occultist off guard – surprised and puzzled him – as if Carstairs had never for a moment considered the possibility of Crow's wishing to take extra time off. He tried his best not to show it, however, as he said: 'By all means, yes, do go off and see your friends. And perhaps you would do me the honour of accepting a little gift to take with you? A bottle of my wine, perhaps? Good! When will you be going?'

'As soon as possible,' Crow answered at once. 'If I leave now I'll have all of tomorrow and Saturday to spend with my friends. I may even be able to return early on Sunday, and so make up for lost time.'

'No, I wouldn't hear of it,' Carstairs held up long, tapering hands. 'Besides, I have friends of my own coming to stay this weekend – and this time I really do not wish to be disturbed.' And he looked at Crow pointedly. 'Very well, I shall expect to see you Monday morning. Do enjoy your weekend and I do urge you to take a bottle of my wine with you.' He smiled his ghastly smile.

Crow said, 'Thank you,' and automatically stuck out his hand – which Carstairs ignored or pretended not to see as he turned and passed back into his study . . .

At 5:20 Crow pulled up at a large hotel on the approaches to Guildford and found a telephone booth. On his first day at The Barrows Carstairs had given him his ex-directory number, in case he should ever need to contact him at short notice. Now he took out the letter from Somerset House, draped his handkerchief over the mouthpiece of the telephone and called Carstairs' number.

The unmistakable voice of his employer answered almost at once. 'Carstairs here. Who is speaking?'

'Ah, Mr Castaigne,' Crow intoned. 'Er – you did say Castaigne, didn't you?'

There was a moment's silence, then: 'Yes, Mr Castaigne, that's correct. Is that Somerset House?'

'Indeed, sir, I am calling in respect of your inquiry about a Mr Crow?'

'Of course, yes. Titus Crow,' Carstairs answered. 'I was expecting a communication of one sort or another.'

'Quite,' said Crow. 'Well, the name Titus Crow is in fact quite rare, and so was not difficult to trace. We do indeed have one such birth on record, dated 2nd December 1912.'

'Excellent!' said Carstairs, his delight clearly in evidence.

'However,' Crow hastened on, 'I must point out that we do not normally react to unsolicited inquiries of this nature and advise you that in future—'

'I quite understand,' Carstairs cut him off. 'Do not concern yourself, sir, for I doubt that I shall ever trouble you again.' And he replaced his telephone, breaking the connection.

And that, thought Crow as he breathed a sigh of relief and put down his own handset, is that. His credentials were now authenticated, his first line of defence properly deployed.

Now there were other things to do. . .

Back in London, Crow's first thought was to visit a chemist friend he had known and studied with in Edinburgh. Taylor Ainsworth was the man, whose interests in the more obscure aspects of chemistry had alienated him from both tutors and students alike. Even now, famous and a power in his field, still there were those who considered him more alchemist than chemist proper. Recently returned to London, Ainsworth was delighted to renew an old acquaintance and accepted Crow's invitation to drinks at his flat that night, with one reservation: he must be away early on a matter of business.

Next Crow telephoned Harry Townley, his family doctor. Townley was older than Crow by at least twenty years and was on the point of giving up his practice to take the cloth, but he had always been a friend and confidant; and he, too, in his way was considered unorthodox in his chosen field. Often referred to as a charlatan, Townley held steadfastly to his belief in hypnotism, homeopathy, acupuncture and such as tremendous aids to more orthodox treatments. Later it would be seen that there was merit in much of this, but for now he was considered a crank.

The talents of these two men, as opposed to those of more mundane practitioners, were precisely what Crow needed. They arrived at his flat within minutes of each other, were introduced and then invited to sample – in very small doses – Carstairs' wine. Crow, too, partook, but only the same minute amount as his friends, sufficient to wet the palate but no more. Oh, he felt the need to fill his glass, certainly, but he now had more than enough of incentives to make him refrain.

'Excellent!' was Harry Townley's view.

'Fine stuff,' commented Taylor Ainsworth. 'Where on earth did you find it, Titus?' He picked up the bottle and peered closely at the label. 'Arabic, isn't it?'

'The label is, yes,' Crow answered. 'It says simply, "table wine", that much at least I know. So you both believe it to be of good quality, eh?'

They nodded in unison and Townley admitted, 'I wouldn't mind a bottle or two in my cellar, young Crow. Can you get any more?'

Crow shook his head. 'I really don't think I want to,' he said. 'It seems I'm already partly addicted to the stuff – and it leaves me with a filthy headache! Oh, and you certainly shouldn't take it if you're driving. No, Harry, I've other stuff here you can drink while we talk. Less potent by far. This bottle is for Taylor.'

'For me?' Ainsworth seemed pleasantly surprised. 'A

gift, do you mean? That's very decent of you . . .' Then he
saw Crow's cocked eyebrow. 'Or is there a catch in it?'

Crow grinned. 'There's a catch in it, yes. I want an
analysis. I want to know if there's anything in it. Any
drugs or such like.'

'I should be able to arrange that OK,' said the other.
'But I'll need a sample.'

'Take the bottle,' said Crow at once, 'and do what you
like with it afterwards – only get me that analysis. I'll be
in touch next weekend, if that's all right with you?'

Now Crow pulled the cork from a commoner brand
and topped up their glasses. To Townley he said, 'Harry,
I think I'm in need of a checkup. That's why I asked you
to bring your tools.'

'What, you?' The doctor looked surprised. 'Why,
you're fit as a fiddle – you always have been.'

'Yes,' said Crow. 'Well, to my knowledge the best
fiddles are two hundred years old and stringy! And that's
just how I feel,' and he went on to describe in full his
symptoms of sudden nausea, headaches, bouts of
dizziness and apparent loss of memory. 'Oh, yes,' he
finished, 'and it might just have been something to do
with that wine which both of you find so excellent!'

While Townley prepared to examine him, Ainsworth
excused himself and went off to keep his business
appointment. Crow let him go but made him promise
not to breathe a word of the wine or his request for an
analysis to another soul. When he left, Carstairs' bottle
was safely hidden from view in a large inside pocket of
his overcoat.

Townley now sounded Crow's chest and checked his
heart, then examined his eyes – the latter at some length
– following which he frowned and put down his
instruments. Then he seated himself facing Crow and

tapped with his fingers on the arms of his chair. The frown stayed on his face as he sipped his wine.

'Well?' Crow finally asked.

'You may well say "well", young Crow,' Townley answered. 'Come on now, what have you been up to?'

Crow arched his eyebrows. 'Up to? Is something wrong with me, then?'

Townley sighed and looked a little annoyed. 'Have it your own way, then,' he said. 'Yes, there is something wrong with you. Not a great deal, but enough to cause me some concern. One: there is some sort of drug in your system. Your pulse is far too slow, your blood pressure too high – oh, and there are other symptoms I recognize, including those you told me about. Two: your eyes. Now eyes are rather a specialty of mine, and yours tell me a great deal. At a guess – I would say you've been playing around with hypnosis.'

'I most certainly have not!' Crow denied, but his voice faltered on the last word. Suddenly he remembered thinking that Carstairs had a hypnotic personality.

'Then perhaps you've been hypnotized,' Townley suggested, 'without your knowing it?'

'Is that possible?'

'Certainly.' Again the doctor frowned. 'What sort of company have you been keeping just lately, Titus?'

'Fishy company indeed, Harry,' the other answered. 'But you've interested me. Hypnosis and loss of memory, eh? Well, now,' and he rubbed his chin thoughtfully. 'Listen, could you possibly de-hypnotize me? Trace the trouble back to its source, as it were?'

'I can try. If you've been under once – well, it's usually far easier the second time. Are you game?'

'Just try me,' Crow grimly answered. 'There's something I have to get to the bottom of, and if hypnosis is the way – why, I'll try anything once!'

An hour later, having had Crow in and out of trance half-a-dozen times, the good doctor finally shook his head and admitted defeat. 'You *have* been hypnotized, I'm sure of it,' he said. 'But by someone who knows his business far better than I. Do you remember any of the questions I asked you when you were under?'

Crow shook his head.

'That's normal enough,' the other told him. 'What's extraordinary is the fact that I can get nothing out of you concerning the events of the last couple of weeks!'

'Oh?' Crow was surprised. 'But I'll gladly tell you all about the last few weeks if you like – without hypnosis.'

'*All* about them?'

'Of course.'

'I doubt it,' Townley smiled, 'for that's the seat of the trouble. You don't *know* all about them. What you remember isn't the whole story.'

'I see,' Crow slowly answered, and his thoughts went back again to those dim, shadowy dreams of his and to his strange pseudo-memories of vague snatches of echoing conversation. 'Well, thank you, Harry,' he finally said. 'You're a good friend and I appreciate your help greatly.'

'Now listen, Titus.' The other's concern was un-feigned. 'If there's anything else I can do – anything at all – just let me know, and—'

'No, no, there's nothing.' Crow forced himself to smile into the doctor's anxious face. 'It's just that I'm into something beyond the normal scope of things, something I have to see through to the end.'

'Oh? Well, it must be a damned funny business that you can't tell me about. Anyway, I'm not the prying type – but I do urge you to be careful.'

'It *is* a funny business, Harry,' Crow nodded, 'and I'm only just beginning to see a glimmer of light at the end of the tunnel. As for my being careful – you may rely upon that!'

Seeing Townley to the door, he had second thoughts. 'Harry, do I remember your having a gun, a six-shooter?'

'A .45 revolver, yes. It was my father's. I have ammunition, too.'

'Would you mind if I borrowed it for a few weeks?'

Townley looked at him very hard, but finally gave a broad grin. 'Of course you can,' he said. 'I'll drop it round tomorrow. But there is such a thing as being too careful, you know!'

# VI

Following a very poor night's sleep, the morning of Friday 18th January found Titus Crow coming awake with a start, his throat dry and rough and his eyes gritty and bloodshot. His first thought as he got out of bed was of Carstairs' wine – and his second was to remember that he had given it to Taylor Ainsworth for analysis. Stumbling into his bathroom and taking a shower, he cursed himself roundly. He should have let the man take only a sample. But then, as sleep receded and reason took over, he finished showering in a more thoughtful if still sullen mood.

No amount of coffee seemed able to improve the inflamed condition of Crow's throat, and though it was ridiculously early he got out the remainder of last night's bottle of his own wine. A glass or two eased the problem a little, but within the hour it was back, raw and painful as ever. That was when Harry Townley turned up with his revolver, and seeing Crow's distress he examined him and immediately declared the trouble to be psychosomatic.

'What?' said Crow hoarsely, 'you mean I'm imagining it? Well, that would take a pretty vivid imagination!'

'No,' said Townley, 'I didn't say you were imagining it. I said it isn't a physical thing. And therefore there's no physical cure.'

'Oh, I think there is,' Crow answered. 'But last night I gave the bottle away!'

'Indeed?' And Townley's eyebrows went up. 'Withdrawal symptoms, eh?'

'Not of the usual sort, no,' answered Crow. 'Harry, have you the time to put me into trance just once more? There's a certain precaution I'd like to take before I resume the funny business we were talking about last night.'

'Not a bad idea,' said the doctor, 'at least where this supposed sore throat of yours is concerned. If it is psychosomatic, I might be able to do something about it. I've had a measure of success with cigarette smokers.'

'Fine,' said Crow, 'but I want you to do more than just that. If I give you a man's name, can you order me never to allow myself to fall under his influence – never to be hypnotized by him – again?'

'Well, it's a tall order,' the good doctor admitted, 'but I can try.'

Half an hour later when Townley snapped his fingers and Crow came out of trance, his throat was already feeling much better, and by the time he and Townley left his flat the trouble had disappeared altogether. Nor was he ever bothered with it again. He dined with the doctor in the city, then caught a taxi and went on alone to the British Museum.

Through his many previous visits to that august building and establishment he was well acquainted with the Curator of the Rare Books Department, a lean, learned gentleman thirty-five years his senior, sharp-eyed and with a dry and wicked wit. Sedgewick was the man's name, but Crow invariably called him 'sir'.

'What, you again?' Sedgewick greeted him when Crow sought him out. 'Did no one tell you the war was over? And what code-cracking business are you on this time, eh?'

Crow was surprised. 'I hadn't suspected you knew about that,' he said.

'Ah, but I did! Your superiors saw to it that I received orders to assist you in every possible way. You didn't suppose I just went running all over the place for any old body, did you?'

'This time,' Crow admitted, 'I'm here on my own behalf. Does that change things, sir?'

The other smiled. 'Not a bit, old chap. Just tell me what you're after and I'll see what I can do for you. Are we back to cyphers, codes and cryptograms again?'

'Nothing so common, I'm afraid,' Crow answered. 'Look, this might seem a bit queer, but I'm looking for something on worm worship.'

The other frowned. 'Worm worship? Man or beast?'

'I'm sorry?' Crow looked puzzled.

'Worship of the annelid – family, *Lumbricidae* – or of the man, Worm?'

'The man-worm?'

'Worm with a capital "W," ' Sedgewick grinned. 'He was a Danish physician, an anatomist. Olaus Worm. Around the turn of the 16th Century, I believe. Had a number of followers. Hence the word "Wormian," relating to his discoveries.'

'You get more like a dictionary every day!' Crow jokingly complained. But his smile quickly turned to a frown. 'Olaus Worm, eh? Could a Latinized version of that be Olaus Wormius, I wonder?'

'What, old Wormius who translated the Greek *Necronomicon*? No, not possible, for he was 13th Century.'

Crow sighed and rubbed his brow. 'Sir,' he said, 'you've thrown me right off the rails. No, I meant worship of the beast – the annelid, if you like – worship of the maggot.'

Now it was Sedgewick's turn to frown. 'The maggot!' he repeated. 'Ah, but now you're talking about a different kettle of worms entirely. A maggot is a grave-worm. Now if that's the sort of worm you mean . . . have you tried *The Mysteries of the Worm*?'

Crow gasped. *The Mysteries of the Worm*! He had seen a copy in Carstairs' library, had even handled it. Old Ludwig Prinn's *De Vermis Mysteriis*!

Seeing his look, Sedgewick said: 'Oh? Have I said something right?'

'Prinn,' Crow's agitation was obvious. 'He was Flemish, wasn't he?'

'Correct! A sorcerer, alchemist and necromancer. He was burned in Brussels. He wrote his book in prison shortly before his execution, and the manuscript found its way to Cologne where it was posthumously published.'

'Do you have a copy in English?'

Sedgewick smiled and shook his head. 'I believe there is such a copy – circa 1820, the work of one Charles Leggett, who translated it from the German black-letter – but we don't have it. I can let you see a black-letter, if you like?'

Crow shook his head. 'No, it gives me a headache just thinking of it. My knowledge of antique German simply wouldn't run to it. What about the Latin?'

'We have half of it. Very fragile. You can see but you can't touch.'

'Can't touch? Sir – I want to borrow it!'

'Out of the question, old chap. Worth my job.'

'The black-letter, then,' Crow was desperate. 'Can I have a good long look at it? Here? Privately?'

The other pursed his lips and thought it over for a moment or two, and finally smiled. 'Oh, I dare say so. And I suppose you'd like some paper and a pen, too, eh? Come on, then.'

A few minutes later, seated at a table in a tiny private room, Crow opened the black-letter – and from the start he knew he was in for a bad time, that the task was near hopeless. Nonetheless he struggled on, and two hours later Sedgewick looked in to find him deep in concentration, poring over the decorative but difficult pages. Hearing the master librarian enter, Crow looked up.

'This could be exactly what I'm looking for,' he said. 'I think it's here – in the chapter called *Saracenic Rituals*.'

'Ah, the Dark Rites of the Saracens, eh?' said Sedgewick. 'Well, why didn't you say so? We have the *Rituals* in a translation!'

'In English?' Crow jumped to his feet.

Sedgewick nodded. 'The work is anonymous, I'm afraid – by Clergyman X, or some such, and of course I can't guarantee its reliability – but if you want it—'

'I do!' said Crow.

Sedgewick's face grew serious. 'Listen, we're closing up shop soon. If I get it for you – that is if I let you take it with you – I must have your word that you'll take infinite care of it. I mean, my heart will quite literally be in my mouth until it's returned.'

'You know you have my word,' Crow answered at once.

Ten minutes later Sedgewick saw him out of the building. Along the way Crow asked him, 'Now how do you suppose Prinn, a native of Brussels, knew so much about the practice of black magic among the Syria-Arabian nomads?'

Sedgewick opened his encyclopedic mind. 'I've read something about that somewhere,' he said. 'He was a much-travelled man, Prinn, and lived for many years among an order of Syrian wizards in the Jebel el Ansariye. That's where he would have learned his stuff. Disguised as beggars or holy men, he and others of the order would make pilgrimages to the world's most evil places, which were said to be conducive to the study of demonology. I remember one such focal point of evil struck me as singularly unusual, being as it was situated on the shore of Galilee! Old Prinn lived in the ruins there for some time. Indeed, he names it somewhere in his book.' Sedgewick frowned. 'Now what was the place called . . . ?'

'Chorazin!' said Crow flatly, cold fingers clutching at his heart.

'Yes, that's right,' answered the other, favouring Crow with an appraising glance. 'You know, sometimes I think you're after my job! Now do look after that pamphlet, won't you?'

That night, through Saturday and all of Sunday, Crow spent his time engrossed in the *Saracenic Rituals* reduced to the early 19th Century English of 'Clergyman X', and though he studied the pamphlet minutely still it remained a disappointment. Indeed, it seemed that he might learn more from the lengthy preface than from the text itself. 'Clergyman X' (whoever he had been) had obviously spent a good deal of time researching Ludwig Prinn, but not so very much on the actual translation.

In the preface the author went into various dissertations on Prinn's origins, his lifestyle, travels, sources and sorceries – referring often and tantalizingly to other chapters in *De Vermis Mysteriis*, such as those on familiars, on the demons of the Cthulhu Myth Cycle, on divination, necromancy, elementals and vampires – but when it came to actually getting a few of Prinn's blasphemies down on paper, here he seemed at a loss. Or perhaps his religious background had deterred him.

Again and again Crow would find himself led on by the writer, on the verge of some horrific revelation, only to be let down by the reluctance of 'X' to divulge Prinn's actual words. As an example, there was the following passage with its interesting extract from Alhazred's *Al Azif*, which in turn gave credit to an even older work by Ibn Schacabao:

And great Wisdom was in Alhazred, who had seen the Work of the Worm and knew it well. His Words were ever cryptic, but never less than here, where he discusses the Crypts of the Worm-Wizards of olden Irem, and something of their Sorceries:

'The nethermost Caverns,' (said he) 'are not for the fathoming of Eyes that see; for their Marvels are strange and terrific. Cursed the Ground where dead Thoughts live new and oddly bodied, and evil the Mind that is held by no Head. Wisely did Ibn Schacabao say, that happy is the Town whose

Wizards are all Ashes. For it is of old Rumour that
the Soul of the Devil-bought hastes not from his
charnel Clay, but fats and instructs *the very Worm
that gnaws*, till out of corruption horrid Life springs,
and the dull Scavengers of Earth wax crafty to vex
it and swell monstrous to plague it. Great Holes
secretly are digged where Earth's Pores ought to
suffice, and Things have learnt to walk that ought
to crawl . . .'

In Syria, with my own Eyes, I Ludwig Prinn saw
one Wizard of Years without Number transfer
himself to the Person of a younger man, whose
Number he had divined; when at the appointed
Hour he spoke the Words of the Worm. And this is
what I saw . . .' [Editor's note: Prinn's description
of the dissolution of the wizard and the investment
of himself into his host is considered too horrific
and monstrous to permit of any merely casual or
unacquainted perusal – 'X']

Crow's frustration upon reading such as this was
enormous; but in the end it was this very passage which
lent him his first real clue to the mystery, and to
Carstairs' motive; though at the time, even had he
guessed the whole truth, still he could not have believed
it. The clue lay in the references to the wizard knowing
the younger man's number – and on rereading that
particular line Crow's mind went back to his first
meeting with Carstairs, when the man had so abruptly
enquired about his date of birth. Crow had lied, adding
four whole years to his span and setting the date at 2nd
December, 1912. Now, for the first time, he considered
that date from the numerologists' point of view, in
which he was expert.

According to the orthodox system, the date 2nd
December 1912 would add up thus:

$$2$$
$$12$$
$$1$$
$$9$$
$$1$$
$$\underline{2}$$
$$= 27 \quad \text{and } 2 + 7 = \text{Nine}$$
$$\text{Or: } 27 = \text{Triple Nine.}$$

Nine could be considered as being either the Death
Number or the number of great spiritual and mental
achievement. And of course the finding would be
reinforced by the fact that there were nine letters in
Crow's name – *if* that was the true date of his birth, which
it was not.

To use a different system, the fictional date's numbers
would add up thus:

$$2$$
$$1$$
$$2$$
$$1$$
$$9$$
$$1$$
$$\underline{2}$$
$$= 18 \quad \text{and } 1 + 8 = \text{Nine,}$$
$$\text{Or: } 18 = \text{Triple Six.}$$

Triple six! The number of the Beast in Revelations!
Crow's head suddenly reeled. Dimly, out of some forgotten corner of his mind, he heard an echoing voice

say, '*His numbers are most propitious ... propitious ... propitious ...*' And when he tried to tie that voice down it wriggled free, saying, '*Not worth it ... just a dream ... unimportant ... utterly unimportant ...*'

He shook himself, threw down his pen – then snatched it back up. Now Crow glared at the familiar room about him as a man suddenly roused from nightmare. 'It *is* important!' he cried. 'Damned important!'

But of course there was no one to hear him.

Later, fortified with coffee and determined to carry on, he used the Hebrew system to discover his number, in which the letters of the alphabet stand for numbers and a name's total equals the total of the man. Since this system made no use of the 9, he might reasonably expect a different sort of answer. But this was his result:

| 1 | 2 | 3 | 4 | 5 | 6 | 7 | 8 |
|---|---|---|---|---|---|---|---|
| A | B | C | D | E | U | O | F |
| I | K | G | M | H | V | Z | P |
| Q | R | L | T | N | W |   |   |
| J |   | S |   |   | X |   |   |
| Y |   |   |   |   |   |   |   |

Titus Crow equals T,4 I,1 T,4 U,6 S,3 C,3 R,2 O,7 W,6. Which is 4+1+4+6+3+3+2+7+6 = 36. And 3+6 = Nine. Or 36, a double 18. The Beast redoubled!

Propitious? In what way? For whom? Certainly not for himself!

For Carstairs?

Slowly, carefully, Titus Crow put down his pen ...

# VII

To Carstairs, waiting in the shadow of his doorway, it seemed that Crow took an inordinately long time to park his car in the garage, and when he came into view there were several things about him which in other circumstances might cause concern. A semi-dishevelled look to his clothes; a general tiredness in his bearing; an unaccustomed hang to his leonine head and a gritty redness of eye. Carstairs, however, was not at all concerned; on the contrary, he had expected no less.

As for Crow: despite his outward appearance, he was all awareness! The inflammation of his eyes had been induced by a hard rubbing with a mildly irritating but harmless ointment; the tardy condition of his dress and apparent lack of will were deliberately affected. In short, he was acting, and he was a good actor.

'Mr Crow,' said Carstairs as Crow entered the house. 'Delighted to have you back.' And the other sensed a genuine relief in the occultist's greeting. Yes, he *was* glad to have him back. 'Have you breakfasted?'

'Thank you, yes – on my way here.' Crow's voice was strained, hoarse, but this too was affected.

Carstairs smiled, leading the way to the library. At the door he said, 'Ah, these long weekends! How they take it out of one, eh? Well, no doubt you enjoyed the break.'

As Crow passed into the library, Carstairs remained in the corridor. 'I shall look in later,' he said, 'when perhaps you'll tell me something of the system you've devised for your work – and something of the progress you are making. Until then . . .' And he quietly closed the door on Crow.

Now the younger man straightened up. He went

directly to his work table and smiled sardonically at the bottle of wine, its cork half-pulled, which stood there waiting for him. He pulled the cork, poured a glass, took the bottle to the barred windows and opened one a crack – then stuck the neck of the bottle through the bars and poured the filthy stuff away into the garden. The empty bottle he placed in his alcove bedroom, out of sight.

Then, seating himself and beginning to work, he forced himself to concentrate on the task in hand – the cataloguing of Carstairs' books, as if that were the real reason he was here – and so without a break worked steadily through the morning. About midday, when he was sure that he had done enough to satisfy his employer's supposed curiosity, should that really be necessary, he made himself coffee. Later he would eat, but not for an hour or so yet.

The morning had not been easy. His eyes had kept straying to the library shelf where he knew an edition of Prinn's book stood waiting for his eager attention. But he dared not open the thing while there was a chance that Carstairs might find him with it. He must be careful not to arouse the occultist's suspicions. Also, there was the glass of red wine close to hand, and Crow had found himself tempted. But in removing the symptoms of his supposed 'addiction', Harry Townley had also gone a good deal of the way toward curbing the need itself; so that Crow half-suspected it was his own perverse nature that tempted him once more to taste the stuff, as if in contempt of Carstairs' attempted seduction of his senses.

And the glass was still there, untouched, when half-an-hour later Carstairs quietly knocked and strode into the room. His first act on entering was to go directly to the windows and draw the shades, before moving to the table and picking up Crow's notes. Saying nothing, he studied them for a moment, and Crow could see that he was mildly surprised. He had not expected Crow to get on quite so well, that much was obvious. Very well, in future he would do less. It made little difference, really, for by now he was certain that the 'work' was very much secondary to Carstairs' real purpose in having him here. If only he could discover what that purpose really was . . .

'I am very pleased, Mr Crow,' said Carstairs presently. 'Extremely so. Even in adverse conditions you appear to function remarkably well.'

'Adverse conditions?'

'Come now! It is dim here – drab, lonely and less than comfortable. Surely these are adverse conditions?'

'I work better when left alone,' Crow answered. 'And my eyes seem to have grown accustomed to meagre light.'

Carstairs had meanwhile spotted the glass of wine, and turning his head to scan the room he casually searched for the bottle. He did not seem displeased by Crow's apparent capacity for the stuff.

'Ah . . .' Crow mumbled. 'Your wine. I'm afraid I—'

'Now no apologies, young man,' Carstairs held up a hand. 'I have more than plenty of wine. Indeed, it gives me pleasure that you seem to enjoy it so. And perhaps it makes up for the otherwise inhospitable conditions, which I am sure are not in accordance with your usual mode of existence. Very well, I leave you to it. I shall be here for the rest of today – I have work in my study – but tomorrow I expect to be away. I shall perhaps see you on Wednesday morning?' And with that he left the library.

Satisfied that he was not going to be disturbed any further, without bothering to open the window shades, Crow took down *De Vermis Mysteriis* from its shelf and was at once dismayed to discover the dark, cracked leather bindings of the German black-letter, almost the duplicate of the book he had looked into in the British Museum. His dismay turned to delight, however, on turning back the heavy cover and finding, pasted into the old, outer shell, a comparatively recent work whose title page declared it to be:

THE MYSTERIES OF THE WORM
being
THE COMPLETE BOOK
in sixteen chapters
With many dozens wood engravings;
representing
THE ORIGINAL WORK
of
LUDWIG PRINN,
after translation
By Charles Leggett,
and including his notes;
this being Number Seven of
a very Limited Edition,
LONDON
1821

Crow immediately took the book through into his alcove room and placed it under his pillow. It would keep until tonight. Then he unpacked a few things, hiding Townley's gun under his mattress near the foot of the bed. Finally, surprised to find he had developed something of an appetite, he decided upon lunch.

But then, as he drew the curtains on the alcove and crossed the room toward the library door, something caught his eye. It was an obscene, pink wriggling shape on the faded carpet where Carstairs had stood. He took it to the window but there, even as he made to toss it into the garden, discovered a second worm crawling on the wainscotting. Now he was filled with revulsion. These were two worms too many!

He disposed of the things, poured the still untouched glass of wine after them and went straight to Carstairs' study. Knocking, he heard dull movements within, and finally the occultist's voice:

'Come in, Mr Crow.'

This surprised him, for until now the room had supposedly been forbidden to him. Nevertheless he opened the door and went in. The gloom inside made shadows of everything, particularly the dark figure seated at the great desk. A thick curtain had been drawn across the single window and only the dim light of a desk-lamp, making a pool of feeble yellow atop the desk, gave any illumination at all. And now, here in these close quarters, the musty smell of the old house had taken to itself an almost charnel taint which was so heavy as to be over-powering.

'I was resting my eyes, Mr Crow,' came Carstairs' sepulchral rumble. 'Resting this weary old body of mine. Ah, what it must be to be young! Is there something?'

'Yes,' said Crow firmly. 'A peculiar and very morbid thing. I just thought I should report it.'

'A peculiar thing? Morbid? To what do you refer?' Carstairs sat up straighter behind his desk.

Crow could not see the man's face, which was in shadow, but he saw him start as he answered, 'Worms! A good many of them. I've been finding them all over the house.'

The figure in the chair trembled, half-stood, sat down again. 'Worms?' There was a badly-feigned tone of surprise in his voice, followed by a short silence in which Crow guessed the other sought for an answer to this riddle. He decided to prompt him:

'I really think you should have it seen to. They must be eating out the very heart of the house.'

Now Carstairs sat back and appeared to relax. His chuckle was throaty when he answered. 'Ah, no, Mr Crow – for they are not of the house-eating species. I rather fancy they prefer richer fare. Yes, I too have seen them. They are maggots!'

'Maggots?' Crow could not keep the disgusted note out of his voice, even though he had half-suspected it. 'But . . . is there something dead here?'

'There was,' Carstairs answered. 'Shortly after you arrived here I found a decomposing rabbit in the cellar. The poor creature had been injured on the road or in a trap and had found a way into my cellar to die. Its remains were full of maggots. I got rid of the carcass and put down chemicals to destroy the maggots. That is why you were forbidden to go into the cellar; the fumes are harmful.'

'I see . . .'

'As for those few maggots you have seen: doubtless some escaped and have found their way through the cracks and crevices of this old house. There is nothing for them here, however, and so they will soon cease to be a problem.'

Crow nodded.

'So do not concern yourself.'

'No, indeed.' And that was that.

Crow did not eat after all. Instead, feeling queasy, he went out into the garden for fresh air. But even out there the atmosphere now seemed tainted. It was as if a pall of gloom hovered over the house and grounds, and that with every passing minute the shadows deepened and the air grew heavy with sinister presences.

Some sixth, psychic sense informed Crow that he walked the strands of an incredibly evil web, and that a great bloated spider waited, half-hidden from view, until the time was just right – or until he took just one wrong step. Now a longing sprang up in him to be out of here and gone from the place, but there was that obstinate streak in his nature which would not permit flight. It was a strange hand that Fate had dealt, where at the moment Carstairs seemed to hold more than his fair share of the aces and Titus Crow held only one trump card.

Even now he did not realize how much depended upon that card, but he felt sure that he would very soon find out.

# VIII

Crow did little or no work that afternoon but, affected by a growing feeling of menace – of hidden eyes watching him – searched the library wall to wall and over every square inch of carpeting, wainscotting, curtains and alcove, particularly his bed, for maggots. He did not for one moment believe Carstairs' explanation for the presence of the things, even though logic told him it was a perfectly plausible one. But for all that his search was very thorough and time-consuming, he found nothing.

That night, seated uneasily in the alcove behind drawn curtains, he took out *De Vermis Mysteriis* and opened it to the *Saracenic Rituals* – only to discover that the greater part of that chapter was missing, the pages cleanly removed with a razor-sharp knife. The opening to the chapter was there, however, and something of its middle. Reading what little remained, Crow picked out three items which he found particularly interesting. One of these fragments concerned that numerology in which he was expert, and here was an item of occult knowledge written down in terms no one could fail to understand:

> The Names of a Man, along with his Number, are all-important. Knowing the First, a Magician knows something of the Man; knowing the Second, he knows his Past, Present, and Future; and he may control the Latter by means of his Sorceries, even unto the Grave and beyond!

Another offered a warning against wizardly generosity:

> Never accept a Gift from a Necromancer, or any Wizard or Familiar. Steal which may be stolen, buy which may be bought, earn it if that be at all possible and if it must be had – but do *not* accept it, neither as a Gift nor as a Legacy . . .

Both of these seemed to Crow to have a bearing on his relationship with Carstairs; but the last of the three interested and troubled him the most, for he could read in it an even stronger and far more sinister parallel:

> A Wizard will not offer the Hand of Friendship to one he would seduce. When a Worm-Wizard refuses his Hand, that is an especially bad Omen.

And having once refused his Hand, if he then offers
it – that is even worse!

Finally, weary and worried but determined in the end to
get to the root of the thing, Crow went to bed. He lay in
darkness and tossed and turned for a long time before
sleep finally found him; and this was the first time, before
sleeping, that he had ever felt the need to turn his key in
the lock of the library door.

On Tuesday morning Crow was awakened by the sound
of a motorcar's engine. Peeping through half-closed
window shades he saw Carstairs leave the house and
get into a car which waited on the winding drive. As
soon as the car turned about and bore the occultist away,
Crow quickly dressed and went to the cellar door under
the stairs in the gloomy hall. The door was locked, as he
had expected.

Very well, perhaps there was another way in. Carstairs
had said that a rabbit had found its way in; and even if
that were untrue, still it suggested that there *might* be
such an entry from the grounds of the house. Going into
the garden, Crow first of all ensured that he was quite
alone, then followed the wall of the house until, at the
back, he found overgrown steps leading down to a
basement landing. At the bottom a door had been heavily
boarded over, and Crow could see at a glance that it
would take a great deal of work to get into the cellar by
that route. Nor would it be possible to disguise such a
forced entry. To one side of the door, completely opaque
with grime, a casement window next offered itself for
inspection. This had not been boarded up, but many
successive layers of old paint had firmly welded frame
and sashes into one. Using a penknife, Crow worked for

a little while to gouge the paint free from the joint; but then, thinking to hear an unaccustomed sound, he stopped and hastily returned to the garden. No one was there, but his nerves had suffered and he did not return to his task. That would have to wait upon another day.

Instead he went back indoors, washed, shaved and breakfasted (though really he did not have much of an appetite) and finally climbed the stairs to scan the countryside all around through bleary windows. Seeing nothing out of the ordinary, he returned to the ground floor and once more ventured along the corridor to Carstairs' study. That door, too, was locked; and now Crow's frustration and jumpiness began to tell on him. Also he suspected that he was missing the bolstering – or deadening – effect of the occultist's wine. And Carstairs had not been remiss in leaving him a fresh bottle of the stuff upon the breakfast table.

Now, fearing that he might weaken, he rushed back to the kitchen and picked up the bottle on the way. Only when he had poured it down the sink, every last drop, did he begin to relax; and only then did he realize how tired he was. He had not slept well; his nerves seemed frayed; at this rate he would never have the strength to solve the mystery, let alone see it through to the end.

At noon, on the point of preparing himself a light meal, he found yet another maggot – this time in the kitchen itself. That was enough. He could not eat here. Not now.

He left the house, drove into Haslemere and dined at an hotel, consumed far too many brandies and returned to The Barrows cheerfully drunk. All the rest of the day he spent sleeping it off – for which sheer waste of time he later cursed himself – and awakened late in the evening with a nagging hangover.

Determined now to get as much rest as possible, he

made himself a jug of coffee and finally retired for the night. The coffee did not keep him awake; and once again he had locked the library door.

Wednesday passed quickly and Crow saw Carstairs only twice. He did a minimum of 'work' but searched the library shelves for other titles which might hint at his awful employer's purpose. He found nothing, but such was his fascination with these old books – the pleasure of reading and handling them – that his spirits soon rose to something approaching their previous vitality. And throughout the day he kept up the pretence of increasing dependence on Carstairs' wine, and he continued to effect a hoarse voice and to redden his eyes by use of the irritating ointment.

On Thursday Carstairs once again left the house, but this time he forgot to lock his study door. By now Crow felt almost entirely returned to his old self, and his nerves were steady as he entered that normally forbidden room. And seeing Carstairs' almost antique telephone standing on an occasional table close to the desk, he decided upon a little contact with the outside world.

He quickly rang Taylor Ainsworth's number in London. Ainsworth answered, and Crow said: 'Taylor, Titus here. Any luck yet with that wine?'

'Ah!' said the other, his voice scratchy with distance. 'So you couldn't wait until the weekend, eh? Well, funny stuff, that wine, with a couple of really weird ingredients. I don't know what they are or how they work, but they do. They work on human beings like aniseed works on dogs! Damned addictive!'

'Poisonous?'

'Eh? Dear me, no! I shouldn't think so, not in small amounts. You wouldn't be talking to me now if they were! Listen, Titus, I'd be willing to pay a decent price if you could—'

'Forget it!' Crow snapped. Then he softened. 'Listen, Taylor, you're damned *lucky* there's no more of that stuff, believe me. I think it's a recipe that goes back to the very blackest days of Man's history – and I'm pretty sure that if you knew those secret ingredients you'd find them pretty ghastly! Thanks anyway, for what you've done.' And despite the other's distant protests he put down the telephone.

Now, gazing once more about that dim and malodorous room, Crow's eyes fell upon a desk calendar. Each day, including today, had been scored through with a thick black line. The 1st February, however, Candlemas Eve, had been ringed with a double circle.

Candlemas Eve, still eight days away . . .

Crow frowned. There was something he should remember about that date, something quite apart from its religious connections. Dim memories stirred sluggishly. Candlemas Eve, the date ordained.

Crow started violently. The date ordained? Ordained for what? Where had that idea come from? But the thought had fled, had sunk itself down again into his subconscious mind.

Now he tried the desk drawers. All were locked and there was no sign of a key. Suddenly, coming from nowhere, Crow had the feeling that there were eyes upon him! He whirled, heart beating faster – and came face to face with Carstairs' picture where it hung with the others on the wall. In the dimness of that oppressive room, the eyes in the picture seemed to glare at him piercingly . . .

After that the day passed uneventfully and fairly quickly. Crow visited the sunken casement window again at the rear of the house and did a little more work on it, scraping away at the old, thick layers of paint, seeming to make very little impression. As for the rest of the time: he rested a good deal and spent an hour or so on Carstairs' books – busying himself with the 'task' he had been set – but no more than that.

About 4:30 p.m. Crow heard a car pull up outside and going to the half-shaded windows he saw Carstairs walking up the drive as the car pulled away. Then, giving his eyes a quick rub and settling himself at his work table, he assumed a harassed pose. Carstairs came immediately to the library, knocked and walked in.

'Ah, Mr Crow. Hard at it as usual, I see?'

'Not really,' Crow hoarsely answered, glancing up from his notebook. 'I can't seem to find the energy for it. Or maybe I've gone a bit stale. It will pass.'

Carstairs seemed jovial. 'Oh, I'm sure it will. Come, Mr Crow, let's eat. I have an appetite. Will you join me?' Seeing no way to excuse himself, Crow followed Carstairs to the dining-room. Once there, however, he remembered the maggot he had found in the kitchen and could no longer contemplate food under any circumstances.

'I'm really not very hungry,' he mumbled.

'Oh?' Carstairs raised an eyebrow. 'Then I shall eat later. But I'm sure you wouldn't refuse a glass or two of wine, eh?'

Crow was on the point of doing just that – until he remembered that he could not refuse. He was not supposed to be able to refuse! Carstairs fetched a bottle from the larder, pulled its cork and poured two liberal glasses. 'Here's to you, Mr Crow,' he said. 'No – to us!'

And seeing no way out, Crow was obliged to lift his glass and drink . . .

## IX

Nor had Carstairs been satisfied to leave it at that. After the first glass there had been a second, and a third, until Titus Crow's head was very quickly spinning. Only then was he able to excuse himself, and then not before Carstairs had pressed the remainder of the bottle into his hand, softly telling him to take it with him, to enjoy it before he retired for the night.

He did no such thing but poured it into the garden; and then, reeling as he went, made his way to the bathroom where he drank water in such amounts and so quickly as to make himself violently ill. Then, keeping everything as quiet as possible, he staggered back to the library and locked himself in.

He did not think that a great deal of wine remained in his stomach – precious little of anything else, either – but his personal remedy for any sort of excess had always been coffee. He made and drank an entire jug of it, black, then returned to the bathroom and bathed, afterward thoroughly dousing himself with cold water. Only then did he feel satisfied that he had done all he could to counteract the effects of Carstairs' wine.

All of this had taken it out of him, however, so that by 8 p.m. he was once again listless and tired. He decided to make an early night of it, retiring to his alcove with *De Vermis Mysteriis*. Within twenty minutes he was nodding over the book and feeling numb and confused in his mind. The unvomited wine was working on him, however gradually, and his only hope now was that he might sleep it out of his system.

Dazedly returning the heavy book to its shelf, he stumbled back to his bed and collapsed onto it. In that same position, spread-eagled and face down, he fell asleep; and that was how he stayed for the next four hours.

Crow came awake slowly, gradually growing aware that he was being addressed, aware too of an unaccustomed feeling of cold. Then he remembered what had gone before and his mind began to work a little faster. In the darkness of the alcove he opened his eyes a fraction, peered into the gloom and made out two dim figures standing to one side of his bed. Some instinct told him that there would be more of them on the other side, and only by the greatest effort of will was he able to restrain himself from leaping to his feet.

Now the voice came again, Carstairs' voice, not talking to him this time but to those who stood around his bed. 'I was afraid that the wine's effect was weakening – but apparently I was wrong. Well, my friends, you are here tonight to witness an example of my will over the mind and body of Titus Crow. He cannot be allowed to go away this weekend, of course, for the time is too near. I would hate anything to happen to him.'

'So would we all, Master,' came a voice Crow recognized. 'For—'

'For then I would need to make a second choice, eh, Durrell? Indeed, I *know* why you wish nothing to go amiss. But you *presume*, Durrell! You are no fit habitation.'

'Master, I merely—' the other began to protest.

'Be quiet!' Carstairs hissed. 'And watch.' Now his words were once more directed at Crow, and his voice grew deep and sonorous.

'Titus Crow, you are dreaming, only dreaming. There is nothing to fear, nothing at all. It is only a dream. Turn over onto your back, Titus Crow.'

Crow, wide awake now – his mind suddenly clear and realizing that Harry Townley's counter-hypnotic device was working perfectly – forced himself to slow, languid movement. With eyes half-shuttered, he turned over, relaxed and rested his head on his pillow.

'Good!' Carstairs breathed. 'That was good. Now sleep, Titus Crow, sleep and dream.'

Now Garbett's voice said: 'Apparently all is well, Master.'

'Yes, all is well. His Number is confirmed, and he comes more fully under my spell as the time approaches. Now we shall see if we can do a little more than merely command dumb movement. Let us see if we can make him talk. Mr Crow, can you hear me?'

Crow, mind racing, opened parched lips and gurgled, 'Yes, I hear you.'

'Good! Now, I want you to remember something. Tomorrow you will come to me and tell me that you have decided to stay here at The Barrows over the weekend. Is that clear?'

Crow nodded.

'You do want to stay, don't you?'

Again he nodded.

'Tell me you wish it.'

'I want to stay here,' Crow mumbled, 'over the weekend.'

'Excellent!' said Carstairs. 'There'll be plenty of wine for you here, Titus Crow, to ease your throat and draw the sting from your eyes.'

Crow lay still, forcing himself to breathe deeply.

'Now I want you to get up, turn back your covers and get into bed,' said Carstairs. 'The night air is cold and we do not wish you to catch a chill, do we?'

Crow shook his head, shakily stood up, turned back

his blankets and sheets and lay down again, covering himself.

'Completely under your control!' Garbett chuckled, rubbing his hands together. 'Master, you are amazing!'

'I have been amazing, as you say, for almost three and a half centuries,' Carstairs replied with some pride. 'Study my works well, friend Garbett, and one day you too may aspire to the Priesthood of the Worm!'

On hearing these words so abruptly spoken, Crow could not help but give a start – but so too did the man Durrell, a fraction of a second earlier, so that Crow's movement went unnoticed. And even as the man on the bed sensed Durrell's frantic leaping, so he heard him cry out: '*Ugh!* On the floor! I trod on one! The maggots!'

'Fool!' Carstairs hissed. 'Idiot!' And to the others, 'Get him out of here. Then come back and help me collect them up.'

After that there was a lot of hurried movement and some scrambling about on the floor, but finally Crow was left alone with Carstairs; and then the man administered that curious droning caution which Crow was certain he had heard before.

'It was all a dream, Mr Crow. Only a dream. There is nothing really you should remember about it, nothing of any importance whatever. But you will come to me tomorrow, won't you, and tell me that you plan to spend the weekend here? Of course you will!'

And with that Carstairs left, silently striding from the alcove like some animated corpse into the dark old house. But this time he left Crow wide awake, drenched in a cold sweat of terror and with little doubt in his mind but that this had been another attempt of Carstairs' to subvert him to his will – at which he had obviously had no little success in the recent past!

Eyes staring in the darkness, Crow waited until he heard engines start up and motorcars draw away from the house – waited again until the old place settled down – and when far away a church clock struck one, only then did he get out of bed, putting on lights and slippers, trembling in a chill which had nothing at all in common with that of the house. Then he set about to check the floor of the alcove, the library, to strip and check and reassemble his bed blanket by blanket and sheet by sheet; until at last he was perfectly satisfied that there was no crawling thing in this area he had falsely come to think of as his own place, safe and secure. For the library door was still locked, which meant either that Carstairs had a second key, or –

Now, with Harry Townley's .45 tucked in his dressing-gown pocket, he examined the library again, and this time noticed that which very nearly stood his hair on end. It had to do with a central section of heavy shelving set against an internal wall. For in merely looking at this mighty bookcase, no one would ever suspect that it had a hidden pivot – and yet such must be the case. Certain lesser books where he had left them stacked on the carpet along the frontage of the bookshelves had been moved, swept aside in an arc; and now indeed he could see that a small gap existed between the bottom of this central part and the carpeted floor proper.

Not without a good deal of effort, finally Crow found the trick of it and caused the bookcase to move, revealing a blackness and descending steps which spiralled steeply down into the bowels of the house. At last he had discovered a way into the cellar; but for now he was satisfied simply to close that secret door and make for himself a large jug of coffee, which he drank to its last drop before making another.

And so he sat through the remaining hours of the night, sipping coffee, occasionally trembling in a preternatural chill, and promising himself that above all else, come what may, he would somehow sabotage whatever black plans Carstairs had drawn up for his future . . .

The weekend was nightmarish.

Crow reported to Carstairs Saturday morning and begged to be allowed to stay at The Barrows over the weekend (which, it later occurred to him in the fullness of his senses, whether *he himself* willed it or not, was exactly what he had been instructed to do!) to which suggestion, of course, the master of the house readily agreed. And after that things rapidly degenerated.

Carstairs was there for every meal, and whether Crow ate or not his host invariably plied him with wine; and invariably, following a routine which now became a hideous and debilitating ritual, he would hurry from dining-room to bathroom there to empty his stomach disgustingly of its stultifying contents. And all of this time he must keep up the pretence of falling more and more willingly under Carstairs' spell, though in all truth this was the least of it. For by Sunday night his eyes were inflamed through no device of his own, his throat sore with the wine and bathroom ritual, and his voice correspondingly hoarse.

He did none of Carstairs' 'work' during those hellish days, but at every opportunity pored over the man's books in the frustrated hope that he might yet find something to throw more light on the occultist's current activities. And all through the nights he lay abed, desperately fighting the drugs which dulled his mind and movements, listening to cellar-spawned chantings and howlings until with everything else he could very easily imagine himself the inhabitant of bedlam.

Monday, Tuesday and Wednesday passed in like fashion – though he did manage to get some food into his system, and to avoid excessive contact with Carstairs' wine – until, on Wednesday evening over dinner, the occultist offered him the break he so desperately longed for. Mercifully, on this occasion, the customary bottle of wine had been more than half-empty at the beginning of the meal; and Crow, seizing the opportunity to pour, had given Carstairs the lion's share, leaving very little for himself; and this without attracting the attention of the gaunt master of the house, whose thoughts seemed elsewhere. So that Crow felt relieved in the knowledge that he would not have to concern himself yet again with the morbid bathroom ritual.

At length, gathering his thoughts, Carstairs said: 'Mr Crow, I shall be away tomorrow morning, probably before you are up and about. I will return about mid-afternoon. I hesitate to leave you alone here, however, for to be perfectly frank you do not seem at all well.'

'Oh?' Crow hoarsely mumbled. 'I feel well enough.'

'You do not look it. Perhaps you are tasking yourself too hard.' His eyes bored into Crow's along the length of the great table, and his voice assumed its resonant, hypnotic timbre. 'I think you should rest tomorrow, Mr Crow. Rest and recuperate. Lie late abed. Sleep and grow strong.'

At this Crow deliberately affected a fluttering of his eyelids, nodding and starting where he sat, like an old man who has difficulty staying awake. Carstairs laughed.

'Why!' he exclaimed, his voice assuming a more casual tone. 'Do you see how right I am? You were almost asleep at the table! Yes, that's what you require, young man: a little holiday from work tomorrow. And Friday should see you back to normal, eh?'

Crow dully nodded, affecting disinterest – but his mind raced. Whatever was coming was close now. He could feel it like a hot wind blowing from hell, could almost smell the sulphur from the fires that burned behind Carstairs' eyes. . .

Amazingly, Crow slept well and was awake early. He remained in bed until he heard a car pull up to the house, but even then some instinct kept him under his covers. Seconds later Carstairs parted the alcove's curtains and silently entered; and at the last moment hearing his tread, with no second to spare, Crow fell back upon his pillow and feigned sleep.

'That's right, Titus Crow, sleep,' Carstairs softly intoned. 'Sleep deep and dreamlessly – for soon your head shall know no dreams, no thoughts but mine! Sleep, Titus Crow, sleep . . .' A moment later and the rustling of the curtains signalled his leaving; but still Crow waited until he heard the receding crunch of the car's tyres on the gravel of the drive.

After that he was up in a moment and quickly dressed. Then: out of the house and around the grounds, and upstairs to spy out the land all around. Finally, satisfied that he was truly alone, he returned to the library, opened the secret bookcase door and descended to the Stygian cellar. The narrow stone steps turned one full circle to leave him on a landing set into an arched alcove in the cellar wall, from which two more paces sufficed to carry him into the cellar proper. Finding a switch, he put on subdued lighting – and at last saw what sort of wizard's lair the place really was!

Now something of Crow's own extensive occult

knowledge came to the fore as he moved carefully about the cellar and examined its contents; something of that, and of his more recent readings in Carstairs' library. There were devices here from the very blackest days of Man's mystical origins, and Titus Crow shuddered as he read meaning into many of the things he saw.

The floor of the cellar had been cleared toward its centre, and there he found the double, interlocking circles of the Persian Mages, freshly daubed in red paint. In one circle he saw a white-painted ascending node, while in the other a black node descended. A cryptographic script, immediately known to him as the blasphemous *Nyhargo Code*, patterned the brick wall in green and blue chalks, its huge Arabic symbols seeming to leer where they writhed in obscene dedication. The three remaining walls were draped with tapestries so worn as to be threadbare, which could only be centuries old, depicting the rites of immemorial necromancers and wizards long passed into the dark pages of history; wizards robed, Crow noted, in the forbidden pagan cassocks of ancient *deserta Arabia*, lending them an almost holy aspect.

In a cobwebbed corner he found scrawled pentacles and zodiacal signs; and hanging upon hooks robes similar to those in the tapestries, embroidered with symbols from the *Lemegeton*, such as the Double Seal of Solomon. Small jars contained hemlock, henbane, mandrake, Indian hemp and a substance Crow took to be opium – and again he was given to shudder and to wonder at the constituents of Carstairs' wine . . .

Finally, having seen enough, he retraced his steps to the library and from there went straight to Carstairs' study. Twice before he had found this door unlocked, and now for the third time he discovered his luck to be holding. This was hardly unexpected, however:

knowing Crow would sleep the morning through, the magician had simply omitted to take his customary precautions. And inside the room . . . another piece of luck! The keys to the desk dangled from a drawer keyhole.

With trembling hands Crow opened the drawers, hardly daring to disturb their contents; but in the desk's bottom left-hand drawer, at last he was rewarded to find that which he most desired to see. There could be no mistaking it: the cleanly sliced margins, the woodcut illustrations, the precise early 19th Century prose of one Charles Leggett, translator of Ludwig Prinn. This was the missing section from Leggett's book: these were the *Saracenic Rituals*, the Mysteries of the Worm!

Closing the single window's shades, Crow switched on the desk lamp and proceeded to read, and as he read so time seemed to suspend itself in the terrible lore which was now revealed. Disbelievingly, with eyes that opened wider and wider, Crow read on; and as he turned the pages, so the words seemed to leap from them to his astonished eyes. An hour sped by, two, and Crow would periodically come out of his trance long enough to glance at his watch, or perhaps pass tongue over parched lips, before continuing. For it was all here, all of it – and finally everything began to click into place.

Then . . . it was as if a floodgate had opened, releasing pent-up, forbidden memories to swirl in the maelstrom of Crow's mind. He suddenly *remembered* those hypnotically-erased night visits of Carstairs', the conversations he had been willed to forget; and rapidly these pieces of the puzzle slotted themselves together, forming a picture of centuries-old nightmare and horror out of time. He *understood* the mystery of the paintings with their consecutive dates, and he *knew* Carstairs' meaning when the man had hinted at a longevity dating back almost three and a half centuries. And at last, in blinding clarity, he could see the part that the wizard had planned for him in his lust for sorcerous survival.

For Crow was to be the receptacle, the host body, youthful haven of flesh for an ancient black phoenix risen again from necromantic ashes! As for Crow himself, the *Identity*, Titus Crow: that was to be cast out – exorcised and sent to hell – *replaced by the mind and will of Carstairs, a monster born of the blackest magicks in midnight ruins by the shore of Galilee in the year 1602 . . . !*

Moreover, he knew when the deed was to be done. It was there, staring at him, ringed in ink on Carstairs' desk calendar: the 1st day of February, 1946.

Candlemas Eve, 'the day ordained'.

*Tomorrow night!*

## X

That night, though he had never been much of a believer, Titus Crow said his prayers. He did manage to sleep – however fitfully and with countless startings awake, at every tiniest groan and creak of the old place – and in the morning looked just as haggard as this last week had determined he should look. Which was just as well, for as the time approached Carstairs would hardly let him out of his sight.

On four separate occasions that morning, the man came to visit him in the library, eyeing him avidly, like a great and grotesque praying-mantis. And even knowing Carstairs' purpose with him – *because* he knew that purpose – Crow must keep up his pretence of going to the slaughter like a lamb, and not the young lion his looks normally suggested.

Lunch came and went, when Crow – mainly by deft sleight of hand – once more cut his wine intake to a minimum; and at 6:00 p.m. he negotiated the evening repast with similar skill and success. And through all of this it was plain to him that a morbid excitement was building in Carstairs, an agitation of spirit the man could barely contain.

At 7:30 – not long after Crow had finished off an entire jug of coffee and as he sat in silence by the light of one dim lamp, memorizing tonight's monstrous rite from what he had read of it in the *Saracenic Rituals* – Carstairs came and knocked upon the library door, walking in as usual before Crow could issue the customary invitation. No need now for Crow to feign haggardness or the weary slump of his shoulders, for the agonizingly slow buildup to the night's play had itself taken care of these particulars.

'Mr Crow,' said Carstairs in unusually unctuous tones, 'I may require a little assistance tonight . . .'

'Assistance?' Crow peered at the other through red-rimmed eyes. 'My assistance?'

'If you have no objection. I have some work to do in the cellar, which may well keep me until the middle of the night. I do not like to keep you from your bed, of course, but in the event I should call for you–' his voice stepped slyly down the register, 'you will answer, won't you?'

'Of course,' Crow hoarsely answered, his eyes now fixed on the burning orbs of the occultist.

'You will come, when I call?' Carstairs now droned, driving the message home. 'No matter how late the hour? You will awaken and follow me? You will come to me in the night, when I call?'

'Yes,' Crow mumbled.

'Say it, Titus Crow. Tell me what you will do, when I call.'

'I shall come to you,' Crow obediently answered. 'I will come to you when you call me.'

'Good!' said Carstairs, his face ghastly as a skull. 'Now rest, Titus Crow. Sit here and rest – and wait for my call. Wait for my call . . .' Silently he turned and strode from the room, quietly closing the door behind him.

Crow got up, waited a moment, switched off the one bulb he had allowed to burn. In his alcove bedroom he drew the curtains and put on the light, then quickly changed into his dressing-gown. He took Harry Townley's .45 revolver out from under his mattress, loaded it and tucked it out of sight in the large pocket of his robe. Now he opened the curtains some twelve inches and brushed through them into the library proper, pacing the floor along the pale path of light from the alcove.

To and fro he paced, tension mounting, and more than once he considered flight; even now, close as he was to those dark mysteries which at once attracted and repelled him. The very grit of his makeup would not permit it, however, for his emotions now were running more to anger than the terror he had expected. He was to be, to *have been*, this monster Carstairs' victim! How now, knowing what the outcome would be – praying that it *would be* as he foresaw it – could he possibly turn away? No, flight was out of the question; Carstairs would find a substitute: the terror would continue. Even if Crow were to go, who could say what revenge might or might not fly hot on his heels?

At 9:30 cars pulled up at the house, quiet as hearses and more of them than at any other time, and through a crack in his shades Crow watched shadowy figures enter the house. For a little while then there were faint, subdued murmurings and creakings; all of which Crow heard with ears which strained in the library's darkness, fine-tuned to catch the merest whisper. A little later, when it seemed to him that the noises had descended beneath the house, he put out the alcove light and sat in unmitigated darkness in the chair where Carstairs had left him. And all about him the night grew heavy, until it weighed like lead upon his head and shoulders.

As the minutes passed he found his hand returning again and again to the pocket where Townley's revolver lay comfortably heavy upon his thigh, and every so often he would be obliged to still the nervous trembling of his limbs. Somewhere in the distance a great clock chimed the hour of eleven, and as at a signal Crow heard the first sussurations of a low chanting from beneath his feet. A cold sweat immediately stood out upon his brow, which he dabbed away with a trembling handkerchief.

The Ritual of the Worm had commenced!

Angrily Crow fought for control of himself . . . for he knew what was coming. He cursed himself for a fool – for several fools – as the minutes ticked by and the unholy chanting took on rhythm and volume. He stood up, sat down, dabbed at his chill brow, fingered his revolver . . . and started at the sudden chiming of the half hour.

Now, in an instant, the house seemed full of icy air, the temperature fell to zero! Crow breathed the black, frigid atmosphere of the place and felt the tiny hairs crackling in his nostrils. He smelled sharp fumes – the unmistakable reek of burning henbane and opium – and sat rigid in his chair as the chanting from the cellar rose yet again, in a sort of frenzy now, throbbing and echoing as with the acoustics of some great cathedral.

The time must surely approach midnight, but Crow no longer dared glance at his watch.

Whatever it had been, in another moment his terror passed; he was his own man once more. He sighed raggedly and forced himself to relax, knowing that if he did not, then the emotional exhaustion must soon sap his strength. Surely the time –

– Had come!

The chanting told him: the way it swelled, receded and took on a new metre. For now it was his own name he heard called in the night, just as he had been told he would hear it.

Seated bolt upright in his chair, Crow saw the bookshelf door swing open, saw Carstairs framed in the faintly luminous portal, a loose-fitting cassock belted about his narrow middle. Tall and gaunt, more cadaverous than ever, the occultist beckoned.

'Come, Titus Crow, for the hour is at hand. Rise up and come with me, and learn the great and terrible mysteries of the worm!'

Crow rose and followed him, down the winding steps, through reek of henbane and opium and into the now luridly illumined cellar. Braziers stood at the four corners, glowing red where heated metal trays sent aloft spirals of burned incense, herbs and opiates; and round the central space a dozen robed and hooded acolytes stood, their heads bowed and facing inwards, toward the painted, interlocking circles. Twelve of them, thirteen including Carstairs, a full coven.

Carstairs led Crow through the coven's ring and pointed to the circle with the white-painted ascending node. 'Stand there, Titus Crow,' he commanded. 'And have no fear.'

Doing as he was instructed, Crow was glad for the cellar's flickering lighting and its fume-heavy atmosphere, which made faces ruddy and mobile and his trembling barely noticeable. And now he stood there, his feet in the mouth of the ascending node, as Carstairs took up his own position in the adjoining circle. Between them, in the 'eye' where the circles interlocked, a large hourglass trickled black sand from one almost empty globe into another which was very nearly full.

Watching the hourglass and seeing that the sands had nearly run out, now Carstairs threw back his cowl and commanded: 'Look at me, Titus Crow, and heed the Wisdom of the Worm!' Crow stared at the man's eyes, at his face and cassocked body.

The chanting of the acolytes grew loud once more, but their massed voice no longer formed Crow's name. Now they called on the Eater of Men himself, the loathsome master of this loathsome ritual:

'Wamas, Wormius, Vermi, WORM!'

'Wamas, Wormius, Vermi, WORM!'

'Wamas, Wormius, Vermi—'

And the sand in the hourglass ran out!

'*Worm!*' Carstairs cried as the others fell silent. '*Worm, I command thee – come out!*'

Unable, not daring to turn his eyes away from the man, Crow's lips drew back in a snarl of sheer horror at the transition which now began to take place. For as Carstairs convulsed in a dreadful agony, and while his eyes stood out in his head as if he were splashed with molten metal, still the man's mouth fell open to issue a great baying laugh.

And out of that mouth – out from his ears, his nostrils, even the hair of his head – there now appeared a writhing pink flood of maggots, grave-worms erupting from his

every orifice as he writhed and jerked in his hellish
ecstasy!

'Now, Titus Crow, now!' cried Carstairs, his voice a
glutinous gabble as he continued to spew maggots. 'Take
my hand!' And he held out a trembling, quaking mass of
crawling horror.

'No!' said Titus Crow. 'No, I will not!'

Carstairs gurgled, gasped, cried, '*What*?' His cassock
billowed with hideous movement. 'Give me your hand –
*I command it!*'

'Do your worst, wizard,' Crow yelled back through
gritted teeth.

'But . . . I have your Number! You *must* obey!'

'Not my Number, wizard,' said Crow, shaking his
head and at once the acolyte circle began to cower back,
their sudden gasps of terror filling the cellar.

'You lied!' Carstairs gurgled, seeming to shrink into
himself. 'You . . . *cheated*! No matter – a small thing.' In
the air he shaped a figure with a forefinger. 'Worm, he is
yours. I command you – *take him!*'

Now he pointed at Crow, and now the tomb-horde at
his feet rolled like a flood across the floor – and drew back
from Crow's circle as from a ring of fire. 'Go on!' Carstairs
shrieked, crumbling into himself, his head wobbling
madly, his cheeks in tatters from internal fretting. 'Who is
*he*? What does he know? I command you!'

'I know many things,' said Crow. 'They do not want
me – they dare not touch me. And I will tell you why: I
was born not in 1912 but in 1916 – on 2nd December of
that year. Your ritual was based on the wrong date, Mr
Carstairs!'

The 2nd December 1916! A concerted gasp went up
from the wavering acolytes. '*A Master!*' Crow heard the
whisper. '*A twenty-two!*'

'No!' Carstairs fell to his knees. *'No!'*

He crumpled, crawled to the rim of his circle, beckoned with a half-skeletal hand. 'Durrell, to me!' His voice was the rasp and rustle of blown leaves.

'Not me!' shrieked Durrell, flinging off his cassock and rushing for the cellar steps. 'Not me!' Wildly he clambered from sight – and eleven like him hot on his heels.

*'No!'* Carstairs gurgled once more.

Crow stared at him, still unable to avert his eyes. He saw his features melt and flow, changing through a series of identities and firming in the final – the first! – dark Arab visage of his origin. Then he fell on his side, turned that ravaged, sorcerer's face up to Crow. His eyes fell in and maggots seethed in the red orbits. The horde turned back, washed over him. In a moment nothing remained but bone and shreds of gristle, tossed and eddied on a ravenous tide.

Crow reeled from the cellar, his flesh crawling, his mind tottering on the brink. Only his Number saved him, the 22 of the Master Magician. And as he fumbled up the stone steps and through that empty, gibbering house, so he whispered words half-forgotten, which seemed to come to him from nowhere:

'For it is of old renown that the soul of the devil-bought hastes not from his charnel clay, but fats and instructs *the very worm that gnaws*; till out of corruption horrid life springs . . .'

Later, in his right mind but changed forever, Titus Crow drove away from The Barrows into the frosty night. No longer purposeless, he knew the course his life must now take. Along the gravel drive to the gates, a pinkish horde lay rimed in white death, frozen where they crawled. Crow barely noticed them.

The tyres of his car paid them no heed whatever.

# THE CALLER OF THE BLACK

*THIS NEXT STORY was the first ever Titus Crow tale. It was the first time I used the character in a story; in fact I believe it was among the first half-dozen stories I submitted for professional consideration. And looking at it now, well, I realize what a beginner I was at that time. But it must have had something. August Derleth used it for the title of my first book.*

*On monoliths did ancients carve their warning*
*To those who use night's forces lest they bring*
*A doom upon themselves that when, in mourning,*
*They be the mourned . . .*

                                        – Justin Geoffrey

One night, not so long ago, I was disturbed, during the study of some of the ancient books it is my pleasure to own, by a knock at the solid doors of my abode, Blowne House. Perhaps it would convey a more correct impression to say that the assault upon my door was more a frenzied hammering than a knock. I knew instinctively from that moment that something out of the ordinary was to come – nor did this premonition let me down.

It was blowing strongly that night and when I opened the door to admit the gaunt stranger on my threshold the night wind gusted in with him a handful of autumn leaves which, with quick, jerky motions, he nervously brushed from his coat and combed from his hair. There was a perceptible aura of fear about this man and I wondered what it could be that inspired such fear. I was soon to learn. Somewhat shakily he introduced himself as being Cabot Chambers.

Calmed a little, under the influence of a good brandy,

Chambers sat himself down in front of my blazing fire and told a story which even I, and I have heard many strange things, found barely credible. I knew of certain legends which tell that such things once were, long ago in Earth's pre-dawn youth, but was of the belief that most of this Dark Wisdom had died at the onset of the *present* reign of civilized man – or, at the very latest, with the Biblical *Burning of the Books*. My own ample library of occult and forbidden things contains such works as Feery's *Original Notes on The Necronomicon*, the abhorrent *Cthaat Aquadingen*, Sir Amery Wendy-Smith's translation of the *G'harne Fragments* (incomplete and much abridged) – a tattered and torn copy of the *Pnakotic Manuscripts* (possibly faked) – a literally priceless *Cultes des Goules* and many others, including such anthropological source books as the *Golden Bough* and Miss Murray's *Witch Cult*, yet my knowledge of the thing of which Chambers spoke was only very vague and fragmentary.

But I digress. Chambers, as I have said, was a badly frightened man and this is the story he told me:

'Mr Titus Crow,' he said, when he was sufficiently induced and when the night chill had left his bones, 'I honestly don't know why I've come to you for try as I might I can't see what you can do for me. I'm doomed. Doomed by Black Magic, and though I've brought it on myself and though I know I haven't led what could be called a very *refined* life, I certainly don't want things to end for me the way they did for poor Symonds.' Hearing that name, I was startled, for Symonds was a name which had featured very recently in the press and which had certain unpleasant connections. His alleged heart failure or brain seizure had been as unexpected as it was unexplained but now, to some extent, Chambers was able to explain it for me.

'It was that fiend Gedney,' Chambers said. 'He destroyed Symonds and now he's after me. Symonds and I, both quite well-to-do men you could say, joined Gedney's Devil-Cult. We did it out of boredom. We were both single and our lives had become an endless parade of night-clubs, sporting-clubs, men's-clubs and yet more clubs. Not a very boring life, you may think, but believe me, after a while even the greatest luxuries and the most splendid pleasures lose their flavours and the palate becomes insensitive to all but the most delicious – or perverse – sensations. So it was with Symonds and I when we were introduced to Gedney at a club, and when he offered to supply those sensations, we were eager to become initiates of his cult.

'Oh, it's laughable! D'you know he's thought of by many as just another crank? We never guessed what would be expected of us and having gone through with the first of the initiation processes at Gedney's country house, not far out of London, processes which covered the better part of two weeks, we suddenly found ourselves face to face with the truth. Gedney is a devil – and of the very worst sort. The *things* that man does would make the Marquis de Sade in his prime appear an anaemic cretin. By God, if you've read Commodus you have a basic idea of Gedney but you must look to the works of Caracalla to really appreciate the depths of his blasphemous soul. Man, *look at the Missing Persons columns sometime!*

'Of course we tried to back out of it all and would have managed it too if Symonds, the poor fool, hadn't gone and blabbed about it. The trouble with Symonds was drink. He took a few too many one night and openly down-graded Gedney and his whole box of tricks. He wasn't to know it but the people we were with at the time were Gedney's crew – and fully-fledged members at that! Possibly the fiend had put them on to us just to check us out. Anyway, that started it. Next thing we knew Gedney sent us an invitation to dinner at a club he uses, and out of curiosity we went. I don't suppose it would have made much difference if we hadn't gone. Things would have happened a bit sooner, that's all. Naturally Gedney had already hit us for quite a bit of money and we thought he was probably after more. We were wrong! Over drinks, in his best "rest assured" manner, he threatened us with the foulest imaginable things if we ever dared to "slander" him again. Well, at that, true to his nature, Symonds got his back up and mentioned the police. If looks could kill Gedney would have had us there and then. Instead, he just upped and left but before he went he said something about a "visit from The Black". I still don't know what he meant.'

During the telling of his tale, Chambers' voice had hysterically gathered volume and impetus but then, as I filled his glass, he seemed to take a firmer grip on himself and continued in a more normal crone.

'Three nights ago I received a telephone-call from Symonds – yes, on the very night of his death. Since then I've been at the end of my rope. Then I remembered hearing about you and how you know a lot about this sort of thing, so I came round. When Symonds called me that night, he said he had found a blank envelope in his letter-box and that he didn't like the design on the card inside it. He said the thing reminded him of something indescribably evil and he was sure Gedney had sent it. He asked me to go round to his place. I had driven to within half a mile of his flat in town when my damned car broke down. Looking back, it's probably just as well that it did. I set out on foot and I only had another block to walk when I saw Gedney. He's an evil-looking type and once you see him you can never forget how he looks. His hair is black as night and swept back from a point low in the centre of his forehead. His eyebrows are bushy above hypnotic eyes of the type you often find in people with very strong characters. If you've ever seen any of those Bela Lugosi horror films you'll know what I mean. He's exactly like that, though thinner in the face, cadaverous in fact.

'There he was, in a telephone kiosk, and he hadn't seen me. I ducked back quickly and got out of sight in a recessed doorway from where I could watch him. I was lucky he hadn't seen me, but he seemed solely interested in what he was doing. He was using the telephone, crouched over the thing like a human vulture astride a corpse. God! But the *look* on his face when he came out of the kiosk! It's a miracle he didn't see me for he walked right past my doorway. I had got myself as far back into a shadowy corner as I could – and while, as I say, he failed to see me, I could see him all right. And he was *laughing*; that is, if I dare use that word to describe what he was doing with his face. Evil? I tell you I've never seen anyone looking so hideous. And, do you know, in answer to his awful laugh there came a distant scream?

'It was barely audible at first but as I listened it suddenly rose in pitch until, at its peak, it was cut off short and only a far-off echo remained. It came from the direction of Symonds' flat.

'By the time I got there someone had already called the police. I was one of the first to see him. It was horrible. He was in his dressing-gown, stretched out on the floor, dead as a doornail. And the *expression* on his face! I tell you, Crow, something monstrous happened that night.

'But – taking into account what I had seen before, what Gedney had been up to in the telephone kiosk – the thing that really caught my eye in that terrible flat, the thing that scared me worst, *was the telephone*. Whatever had happened must have taken place while Symonds was answering the 'phone – *for it was off the hook, dangling at the end of the flex . . .*'

Well, that was just about all there was to Chambers' story. I passed him the bottle and a new glass, and while he was thus engaged I took the opportunity to get down from my shelves an old book I once had the good fortune to pick up in Cairo. Its title would convey little to you, learned though I know you to be, and it is sufficient to say that its contents consist of numerous notes purporting to relate to certain supernatural invocations. Its wording, in parts, puts the volume in that category 'not for the squeamish'. In it, I knew, was a reference to *The Black*, the thing Gedney had mentioned to Chambers and Symonds, and I quickly looked it up. Unfortunately the book is in a very poor condition, even though I have taken steps to stop further disintegration, and the only reference I could find was in these words:

> *Thief of Light, Thief of Air . . .*
> *Thou The Black – drown me mine enemies . . .*

One very salient fact stood out. Regardless of what actually caused Symonds' death, the newspapers recorded the fact *that his body showed all the symptoms of suffocation . . .*

I was profoundly interested. Obviously Chambers could not tell his story to the police, for what action could they take? Even if they were to find something inexplicably unpleasant about the tale, and perhaps would like to carry out investigations, Chambers himself was witness to the fact that Gedney was in a telephone kiosk at least a hundred yards away from the deceased at the time of his death. No, he could hardly go to the police. To speak to the Law of Gedney's *other* activities would be to involve himself – in respect of his 'initiation' – and he did not want that known. Yet he felt he must do something. He feared that a similar fate to that which had claimed Symonds had been ordained for him – nor was he mistaken.

Before Chambers left me to my ponderings that night, I gave him the following instructions. I told him that if, in some manner, he received a card or paper like the one Symonds had mentioned, with a peculiar design upon it, he was to contact me immediately. Then, until he had seen me, he was to lock himself in his house admitting no one. Also, after calling me, he was to disconnect his telephone.

After he had gone, checking back on his story, I got out my file of unusual newspaper cuttings and looked up Symonds' case. The case being recent, I did not have far to search. I had kept the Symonds cuttings because I had been unhappy about the coroner's verdict. I had had a suspicion about the case, a sort of sixth sense, telling me it was unusual. My memory had served me well. I reread that which had made me uneasy in the first place. The police had discovered, clenched in one of Symonds' fists, the crushed fragments of what was thought to have been some type of card of very brittle paper. Upon it were strange, inked characters, but the pieces had proved impossible to reconstruct. The fragments had been passed over as being irrelevant.

I knew that certain witch-doctors of some of this world's less civilized peoples are known for their habit of serving an intended victim with a warning of his impending doom. The trick is usually accomplished by handing the unfortunate one an evil symbol and – having let him worry himself half to death – the sorcerer then invokes, in the victim's presence or *within his hearing*, whichever devil is to do the dirty work. Whether or not any devil actually appears is a different kettle of fish. But one thing is sure – *the victim nearly always dies . . .* Naturally, being superstitious and a savage to boot, he dies of fright . . . Or does he?

At first I believed something of the sort was the case with Symonds and Chambers. One of them, perhaps helped along in some manner, had already worried himself to death and the other was going the same way. Certainly Chambers had been in a bad way regards his nerves when I had seen him. However, my theory was wrong and I soon had to radically revise it. Within a few hours of leaving Blowne House Chambers 'phoned me and he was hysterical.

'I've got one, by God! The devil's sent me one. Listen, Crow. You must come at once. I went for a drink from your place and I've just got in. Guess what I found in the hall? An envelope, that's what, *and there's a damned funny looking card inside it!* It's frightening the daylights out of me. He's after me! The swine's after me! Crow, I've sent my man home and locked the doors like you said. I can open the front door electronically from my room to let you in when you arrive. You drive a Merc', don't you? Yes, thought so. As soon as you say you'll come I'll put down the 'phone and disconnect it. Now, will you come?'

I told him I would only be a few minutes and hung up. I dressed quickly and drove straight round to his house. The drive took about fifteen minutes for his place lay on the outskirts of town, near the old Purdy Watermill. The house is completely detached and as I pulled into the driveway I was surprised to note that every light in the house was on – *and the main door was swinging open*! Then as I slowed to a halt, I was partly blinded by the lights of a second Mercedes which revved up and roared past me out onto the road. I leapt out of my car to try to get the other vehicle's number but was distracted from this task by the screams which were just starting.

Within seconds, screams of utter horror were pouring from upstairs and, looking up, I saw a dark shadow cast upon a latticed window. The shadow must have been strangely distorted for it had the general outline of a man, yet it was *bulky* beyond human dimensions – more like the shadow of a gorilla. I watched, hypnotized, as this black caricature clawed frantically at itself – *in a manner which I suddenly recognized!* The shadow was using the same brushing motions which I had seen Chambers use earlier to brush those leaves from himself in my hallway.

But surely this could not be Chambers? This shadow was that of a far heavier person, someone obese, even allowing for inexplicable distortion! Horrified, I watched, incapable of movement, as the screams rose to an unbearable pitch and the tottering, clawing shadow grew yet larger. Then, abruptly, the screams gurgled into silence, the shadow's diseased scrabbling at itself became a convulsive *heaving* and the bloated arms lifted jerkily, as if in supplication. Larger still the monstrous silhouette grew as its owner stumbled, seemingly unseeing, towards the window. And then, briefly as it fell against the thinly-latticed panes, I saw it. A great, black imitation of a human, it crashed through the window, shattering the very frame outwards in a tinkling of broken glass and a snapping of fractured lats. Tumbling into the night it came, to fall with a sickening, bone-breaking crunch at my feet.

*The broken thing which lay before me on the gravel of the drive was the quite ordinary, quite lifeless body of Cabot Chambers!*

When I was able to bring my shrieking nerves under a semblance of control, I dared to prise open the tightly clenched right hand of the corpse and found that which I had guessed would be there. Those stiffening fingers held crushed, brittle shards which I knew had once had the outlines of a card of some sort. On some of the larger pieces I could make out characters which, so far as I know, can only be likened to certain cuneiform inscriptions on the Broken Columns of Geph.

I 'phoned the police anonymously and quickly left the place, for the smell of weird, unnatural death now hung heavily over the entire house. Poor Chambers, I thought as I drove away – seeing that second Mercedes he must have thought his other visitor was I. I tried not to think about the shadow or what it meant.

I did not sleep too well that night. The first thing I did when I awoke the next morning was to discreetly check up on the activities of a certain Mr James D. Gedney. I have many friends in positions which, to say the least, make them extremely useful to me when a bit of detective work is necessary. These friends helped me now and through their exertions my task was made considerably easier. I checked Gedney's telephone number, which was not in the book, and made notes of his personal likes and dislikes. I memorized the names of his friends and the clubs and places he frequented and generally built up my picture of the man. What I discovered only confirmed Chambers' opinion. Gedney's *contacts* were the worst sort of people and his favourite haunts were, in the main, very doubtful establishments. He had no visible means of support yet appeared to be most affluent – owning, among his many effects, a large country house and, most interesting yet, a brand-new Mercedes. All the other things I discovered about Gedney paled beside that one fact.

My next logical step, having completed my 'file' on Gedney, was to find out as much as I could about that mystical identity 'The Black,' and towards this end I spent almost a week in the pursuit of certain singular volumes in dim and equally singular archives at the British Museum and in the perusal of my own unusual books. At the museum, with the permission of the Curator of the Special Books Department, another friend, I was allowed to study at my leisure all but the most secret and hideous of volumes. I was out of luck. The only reference I found – a thing which, in the light of what I later learned, I find of special significance – was, as was that other reference I have mentioned, in one of my own books. Justin Geoffrey supplied this second fragment in his raving *People of the Monolith*; but apart from these four inexplicable lines of poetry I found nothing more:

> *On monoliths did ancients carve their warning*
> *To those who use night's forces lest they bring*
> *A doom upon themselves that when, in mourning,*
> *They be the mourned . . .*

Then I remembered an American friend of mine; a man wonderfully erudite in his knowledge of folklore and things of dread and darkness. He had studied in bygone years under that acknowledged genius of Earth's elder-lore, Wilmarth of Miskatonic University. We exchanged one or two interesting telegrams and it was this New Englander who first told me of the Ptetholites – a prehistoric, sub-human race who allegedly were in the habit of calling up devils to send against their enemies. At the very beginning of recorded time, if one can believe the legends of Hyperborea, the Ptetholites sent such devils against Edril Ghambiz and his Hell-Hordes, ensconced on the pre-neolithic isle of Esipish in what was then the North Sea. Unfortunately for the Ptetholites they had seemingly forgotten their own warnings, for it had been elders of their own tribe, in even older days, who had inscribed on the Broken Columns of Geph:

*Let him who calls The Black*
*Be aware of the danger*
*His victim may be protected*
*By the spell of running water*
*And turn the called up darkness*
*Against the very caller . . .*

Hence, I believe, Geoffrey's remarkable lines. Exactly what happened to the Ptetholites has gone unrecorded, or such records have been destroyed, except for the vaguest of hints in the most obscure tomes. There are, I now know, certain monks of a peculiar order in Tibet who know and understand many of these things. If history *did* pass down anything but the most sketchy details of the destruction of the Ptetholites such records were probably burned in the time of the witch hunts of the 16th and 17th centuries; certainly, except in those few cases I have mentioned, such knowledge is non-existent today.

Apart from this information from Arkham the remaining results of my research were disappointing.

One thing was positive though; I had now definitely given up my theory of self-induced death through fear. Both Symonds and Chambers had been far too intelligent ever to have succumbed to the suggestions of any witch-doctor and besides – there was that disturbing thing about Chambers' shadow. Moreover, Gedney was certainly no quack witch-doctor and somehow I felt sure that he had access to a very real and destructive magical device. The final telegram I received from America convinced me.

I have great faith in Abdul Alhazred, whom many have called the 'mad' Arab, and while my copy of *Feery's Notes on the Necronomicon* is hardly what one could call a reliable guide, Alhazred's actual book, or a translation of it, at Miskatonic University, is something else again. My learned friend had found a dream-reference in the *Necronomicon* in which *The Black* was mentioned. The said reference read thus:

> . . . from the space which is not space, into any time when the Words are spoken, can the holder of the Knowledge summon The Black, blood of Yibb-Tstll, that which liveth apart from *him* and eateth souls, that which smothers and is called Drowner. Only in water can one escape the drowning; that which is in water drowneth not . . .

This was the foundation I needed upon which to build my plan. A hazardous plan, but – taking into account how touchy Gedney appeared to be about people threatening him – one which was sure to produce results.

Soon I began to put my plan into operation. First, in the guise of a drunk, I frequented the places Gedney used when pursuing his jaded pleasures. Eventually, in a dingy night-club, I had him pointed out to me for future reference. This was hardly necessary, for Chambers' description fitted him perfectly and from it alone I would have recognized the man had the place not been so crowded and dimly lighted.

Next I made it known, in conversation with people I knew to be directly connected with Gedney, that I was a former friend of both the dead men and that from what they had told me of Gedney he was an abominable creature whom, if the opportunity presented itself, I would gladly expose. I put it about, drunkenly, that I was collecting a dossier on him which I intended eventually to present to the appropriate authorities. But though I play-acted the part of a regular inebriate the truth is that I have never been more sober in my entire life. Dealing such antagonistic cards to Gedney, I was sure, would produce results which only a very sober person could hope to turn to his advantage.

Yet it was over a week before my assault took effect. I was in the dimly lit Demon Club, slumped in a typically alcoholic attitude against the bar. Perhaps I was over-acting, for before I realized Gedney was even in the place I found him at my elbow. I had been forewarned of his overpowering character but even so I was unprepared for the meeting. The man radiated power. He was so tall that I, myself six feet tall, had to look up at him. Typically dressed in a cloak with a flaring collar and with his dark, hypnotic eyes, he gave an impression of amused tolerance – which I knew was forced.

'Mr Titus Crow, I believe? Need I introduce myself? No, I thought not; you already know me, or *think* you do. Let me tell you something, Mr Crow. You are following a very dangerous trail. I am sure you get my meaning. Take my advice, Mr Crow, and let sleeping dogs lie. I've heard of you. An occultist of sorts; a mere dabbler, one I would not normally bother with. Unfortunately you're blessed with an unpleasant turn of mind and a slanderous tongue. My advice is this; stop poking your nose into matters which do not concern you before I am forced to take reprisals. How about it, Mr Crow?'

'Gedney,' I said, 'if I am correct you are the very foulest kind of evil and you have access to knowledge the like of which, in *your* hands, is an abomination and a threat to the sanity of the entire world. But you don't frighten me. I shall do my level best to prove you are responsible for the deaths of at least two men and will play whatever part I can in bringing you to justice.'

It was important to let Gedney know I was onto something without making him feel that I had any tricks up my sleeve. Having said my piece and without waiting for an answer, I brushed past the man and staggered out into the late evening. Quickly I lost myself amidst the pleasure seekers and made my way to my car. Then I drove to Blowne House and set up my defences.

I live alone and the next night, as I was making the rounds of Blowne House before retiring, I found that a blank envelope had been dropped through my letter-box. I had expected it. I knew exactly what I would find inside the thing; not that I intended to open it. I was not *entirely* convinced that Gedney's powers were magical and there was always the chance that the card within the envelope was heavily impregnated with some deadly and obscure poison; a poison which, of necessity, would have to have the power of almost instant dispersal.

I fully anticipated the next occurrence, but even so I still froze solid for an instant when my telephone rang. I lifted the receiver an inch from the cradle and let it fall, breaking the connection. I was obliged to repeat this action three times in the course of the next half-hour; for while I have been guilty of *certain* follies in the past, one of them was never indiscretion – or lunacy, as it would have been to answer that 'phone.

Symonds had *died* answering his 'phone, and whether it was a case of hearing a trigger-word in connection with some post-hypnotic suggestion or other which Gedney had previously supplied – or the more fanciful one of hearing an invocation – I was not sure; and I was certainly not eager to learn.

Then, though I waited a further twenty minutes, the telephone remained silent. It was time for the action to begin.

Gedney, I reasoned, must now have a damned good idea that I knew just a bit too much for his good. The fact that I would not answer my 'phone showed that I obviously knew *something*. If I had merely disconnected the 'phone on receipt of the envelope there was the possiblity that Gedney, on getting no dialling-tone, might have thought I was not at home. But he had heard the receiver lifted and dropped. He *knew* I was at home and if he had taken the trouble to check up on me he must know I lived alone. I hoped my refusal to answer his call had not frightened him off.

I did something then which I know must seem the ultimate madness. I unlocked the main door of Blowne House! I was satisfied Gedney would come.

After about thirty minutes I heard the sound of a car driving by outside. By this time I was in my bedroom, seated in an easy-chair with my back to the wall, facing the door to the hall. Close to my right hand was that abhorrent envelope. I was wearing my dressing-gown and at my immediate left hung ceiling to floor plastic curtains. Directly in front of me stood a small table on which lay the envelope and a book of poems. It was my intention, on Gedney's arrival, to *appear* to be reading.

Now, Blowne House is a sprawling bungalow, and one particularly suited to my own singular tastes. I had utilized the unique design of the place in my plan and was satisfied that my present position offered the maximum of safety from the assault which I was reasonably sure was about to commence.

Presently I heard the car again and this time it stopped right outside the house. Before the sound of the motor died away I heard the distinct crunch of gravel which told me the car had entered my driveway. After a few seconds a knock sounded upon the outside door. Again came the knock, following a short silence, but I remained quiet, not moving a fraction from my chair. As my hair stood slowly on end, a few more seconds crawled by and then I heard the outer door groan open. With a shock I realized that the sudden constriction I felt in my chest was caused by lack of air. Such was my concentration I had momentarily stopped breathing.

My nerves had started to silently scream and though every light in the house was on, the place may as well have been as dark as the pit the way I felt. Slow footsteps sounded in the hall, approached past my study and halted just beyond the door facing me. My nerves stretched to breaking point and then, with startling abruptness, the door flew open to admit Gedney.

As he strode in I rose from my seat and put down the book of poems. I was still acting but this time, though I tried to appear just a trifle drunk, my main role was one of utter astonishment. As I got to my feet I burst out:

'Gedney! What on Earth . . . ?' I leaned forward aggressively over the table. 'What the devil's the meaning of this? Who invited you here?' My heart was in my mouth but I played my part as best I could.

'Good evening, Mr Crow.' Gedney smiled evilly. 'Who invited me? Why! You did; by your refusal to accept my warning and by your unwillingness to use your telephone. Whatever it is you know about me is matterless, Crow, and doomed to die with you tonight. At least you have the satisfaction of knowing that you were correct. I do have access to strange knowledge; knowledge which I intend to use right now. So I repeat: Good evening, Mr Crow – *and goodbye!*'

Gedney was standing between the table and the door, and as he finished speaking he threw up his hands and commenced bellowing, in a cracked, droning tone, an invocation of such evil inference that merely hearing it would have been sufficient to mortify souls only slightly more timid than mine. I had never heard this particular chant before, though I have heard others, but as the crescendo died away, its purpose became immediately apparent. During the invocation I had been frozen, literally *paralyzed* by the sound of the thing, and I could fully understand how it was that Symonds had been forced to listen to it over his 'phone. From the first word Symonds would have stood like a statue with the receiver pressed to his ear, unable to move as his death-certificate was signed over the wire.

As the echoes of that hideous droning died away Gedney lowered his hands and smiled. He had seen the envelope at my fingertips – and as his awful laugh began to fill the room I discovered the meaning of 'The Black' . . .

No witch-doctor's curse this but an aeon-old fragment of sorcery handed down through nameless centuries. *This* came from a time in Earth's abysmal past when unthinkable creatures from an alien and unknown universe spawned weird things in the primeval slime. The horror of it . . .

*A black snowflake landed on me!* That is what the thing looked like. A cold, black snowflake which spread like a stain on my left wrist. But before I had time to examine that abnormality another fell onto my forehead. And then, rapidly, from all directions they came, ever faster, settling on me from out of the nether-regions. Horror-flakes that blinded and choked me.

*Blinded? . . . Choked?*

Before my mind's eye, in shrieking letters, flashed those passages from Geoffrey, the *Necronomicon* and the *Ibigib*. 'Thief of Light – Thief of Air . . .' The inscriptions at Geph, ' . . . The spell of running water . . .' Alhazred – 'That which is in water drowneth not . . .'

The bait was taken; all that remained was to spring the trap. And if I were mistaken?

Quickly, while I was still able, I drew the curtains at my left to one side and flicked the still-unopened envelope towards Gedney's feet. Shedding my dressing-gown I stepped naked onto the tiles behind the curtains, tiles which were now partly visible to the fiend before me. Frantic, for a gibbering terror now held me in its icy grip, I clawed at the tap. The second or so the water took to circulate through the plumbing seemed an eternity, in which thousands more of those blasphemous flakes flew at me, forming a dull, black layer on my body.

And then, mercifully, as the water poured over me, 'The Black' was gone! The stuff did not *wash* from me – it simply vanished. No, that is not quite true – *for it instantly reappeared elsewhere!*

Gedney had been laughing, baying like some great hound, but as I stepped into the shower and as the water started to run, he stopped. His mouth fell open and his eyes bugged horribly. He gurgled something unrecognizable and made ghastly, protesting gestures with his hands. He could not take in what had happened, for it had all been too fast for him. His victim was snatched from the snare and he could not believe his eyes. But believe he had to as the first black flakes began to fall upon him! The shadows darkened under his suddenly comprehending eyes and his aspect turned an awful grey as I spoke these words from the safety of the shower:

'Let him who calls The Black,
Be aware of the danger
His victim may be protected
By the spell of running water
And turn the called-up darkness
Against the very caller . . .'

Nor did this alone satisfy me. I wanted Gedney to remember me in whichever hell he was bound for; and so, after repeating that warning of the elder Ptetholites, I said:

'Good evening, Mr Gedney – *and goodbye . . .*'

Cruel? Ah! You may call me cruel – but had not Gedney planned the same fate for me? And how many others, along with Symonds and Chambers, had died from the incredible sorceries of this fiend?

He had started to scream. Taken by surprise, he was almost completely covered by the stuff before he could move but now, as the horrible truth sank in, he tried to make it across the room to the shower. It was his only possible means of salvation and he stumbled clumsily round the table towards me. But if Gedney was a fiend so, in my own right, was I – and I had taken precautions.

In the shower recess I had previously placed a window-pole, and snatching it up I now put it to use fending off the shrilly shrieking object before me.

As more of 'The Black,' the evil blood of Yibb-Tstll, settled on him, Gedney began the frantic brushing motions which I remembered so well, all the while babbling and striving to fight his way past my window-pole. By now the stuff was thick on him, inches deep, a dull, black mantle which covered him from head to toe. Only one eye and his screaming mouth remained visible and his outline was rapidly becoming the bloated duplicate of that hideous shadow I had seen on the night of Chambers' death.

It was now literally *snowing* black death in my room and the end had to follow quickly. Gedney's bulging eye and screaming, frothing mouth seemed to sink into the ever thickening blackness and the *noises* he was making were instantly shut off. For a few seconds he did a monstrous, shuffling dance of agony, and unable to bear the sight any longer I used the pole to push him off his feet. My prayer that this action would put a quick end to it was answered. *He pulsed!* Yes, that is the only way I can describe the motion of his smothered body: he pulsed for a moment on the carpet – and then was still. Briefly then, the lights seemed to dim and a rushing wind filled the house. I must have momentarily fainted for I awoke to find myself stretched out full length on the carpet with the shower still hissing behind me. As mysteriously as it had come, 'The Black' had departed, back to that other-dimensional body which housed it, taking Gedney's soul and leaving his lifeless shell behind . . .

Later, after a stiff drink, I opened the envelope and found the flaking, brittle shards I had expected. Later still, with the rapidly stiffening, lolling corpse beside me,

I drove out towards Gedney's country home. I parked his car in a clump of trees, off the road, and in the small hours made my way back on foot to Blowne House. The brightening air was strangely sweet.

# THE VIKING'S STONE

**THE VIKING'S STONE** is another of those tales which seem to write themselves: it is as if, once you start, the story takes over. And that's something which should happen far more often! It is, of course, a 'ghost story' – but perhaps you should first be reminded that Titus Crow isn't one for meeting up with conventional ghosts. Or very much of conventional anything else, for that matter!

'De Marigny!' Titus Crow's voice sounded tense and urgent over the telephone. 'De Marigny, tell me – did you ever lend that book of yours, Loftsson's *Saga-Englendingabok*, to Benjamin Sorlson?'

'Why, yes, Titus,' I yawningly answered, rubbing the sleep from my eyes, '– but I got it back all right, and Sorlson seems a genuine enough chap. You know him, though, surely?'

'I know him, yes,' Crow's growl came back, strangely tinny over the wire. 'I know him for a damn good archaeologist, a damned argumentative fool . . . and I know him for a friend, of sorts. But that hardly matters now. Henri, I think I might need your help – if only to talk Sorlson out of it.'

'Talk Sorlson out of it?' Dully, apathetically, I repeated him. 'Titus, isn't it a bit early in the morning for cryptic messages? And what on Earth are you doing up at this hour anyway?' I was well aware of Crow's habit of working late and rising even later.

' "This hour," de Marigny, is 9:00 a.m. – and I'm up to check the mail. I've had a letter from Sorlson. He's gone to Skardaborg – and he's found the stone of Ragnar Gory-Axe!'

Gory-Axe? Skardaborg? What in heaven — My foggy, sleep-sodden mind would not bring the man's words into focus. I had attended a meeting – a rather bawdy meeting toward the end, not at all Crow's sort of thing – of the London Mystery Writers' Society the previous evening, and I was now suffering the consequences. I briefly explained this to Crow.

'Coffee, de Marigny,' he barked. 'I'd prescribe three or four mugs at least, and black! Then, if you're interested, bring Loftsson's book with you and meet me at King's Cross for the first afternoon train north. I'll explain it all then.'

Well, a summons from Titus Crow is not something to be lightly put aside – the man has been my friend and mentor ever since my father sent me out of America as a youth – and so I got up and dressed, made a hurried breakfast (including, as my friend had suggested, a great pot of black coffee), placed the book Crow had requested in my briefcase, and then caught a taxi for King's Cross.

In the taxi I took out the *Saga-Englendingabok* and looked up 'Skardaborg'. The book was very rare, I knew that, for it was a manuscript copy in longhand from the original Latin – or so its preface led me to believe. Crow, after borrowing the book one summer some four years earlier, had told me he believed it to be a translation of Jon Loftsson's lost Latin work on the Kings of Norway and the adventures of the Vikings in England; he doubted if any other copy remained extant. He had referred to it as 'Loftsson's book' ever since. Certainly there *was* a lost Latin work, believed to be circa 1115, but I secretly disputed Crow's authority to claim my book as being related to that work.

Skardaborg! Yes, there it was: Scarborough, as I had guessed. So, Benjamin Sorlson, the celebrated if un-orthodox archaeologist and expert in Viking and other

ancient Norwegian matters, was in Scarborough. Now
. . . what of Ragnar Gory-Axe?

Before I could further follow my enquiry the taxi
arrived at King's Cross. I put the book away, paid the
driver, and made my way to the ticket-booth. There, like
a fool, I asked for a return ticket to Skardaborg before
realizing my slip; but eventually I found myself on the
northbound platform searching for my friend, Titus
Crow.

He was impossible to miss. Tall in his dark suit, with
his leonine head and imposing looks, he would have
seemed prominent in any crowd; but when I stood with
him it would be safe to say that few if any of the other
people on the platform recognized us as 'two of London's
foremost occultists'.

Now, I oppose such a description as applied in any
derogative manner to myself (and as in the past certain
members of the press have found occasion so to use it)
but I do not deny my interest in occult matters. How
could I, and own to a father, Etienne-Laurent de Marigny,
who was one of the greatest of modern mystics? It is
merely that I myself am no great adept, and if I were I
should certainly *not* use dark forces to my own ends.

Crow, too, deplores this 'Black Magician' tag, for he is
one to whom, in his unending search for mysteries and
discoveries of marvels, the occult has been simply a
passage down which his wanderings have taken him;
where he has learned, on more than one occasion, *outré*
things unheard of in the more mundane world of
ordinary men. Crow may, in that sense, be called an
occultist – but so is he a most knowledgeable man and
something of an expert in many fields.

We managed to get a compartment to ourselves on
the train, but it was only after the journey commenced

that Titus made any attempt to explain his purpose in following Sorlson to Scarborough, and then not without a little prodding on my part.

'Er, you said Sorlson had "found the stone of Ragnar Gory-Axe" . . . ?'

'So he has,' Crow answered, nodding, 'and damn him for a fool, he intends to bring the thing back to London!'

'Just what is this stone, Titus, and why is it so important to you?'

'The stone? Oh, excuse me, de Marigny, but I thought you were on intimate terms with that book of yours. The stone is a Bauta-stein or *menhir* – though you'd usually only use the latter term in Celtic connections – raised near a tomb for the spirit of the occupant to rest upon at night, like a perch, and by means of which the ghost might find its way back to the tomb at daybreak.'

'How very homely,' I answered, with something of a shudder. 'Then it's an important historical and archaeological find. Surely Sorlson only wants to present the thing to a museum or some such authority?'

'He wants it for himself,' Crow bleakly told me, 'and that's exactly where the trouble lies. That stone *must not* be interfered with! There's a curse on the thing, one that goes back eight hundred years to the Viking wars – and it is still operative!

'You see, de Marigny,' he went on after a brief pause, 'unlike us Sorlson sees little to fear in this sort of thing. He laughed at me when I let it slip about the stone and its curse three months ago. In fact he made it clear that he thought I was pulling his leg about the stone's very existence . . . Or so I thought! But in truth he must have known something of Ragnar Gory-Axe before; and then, when I told him of your book. . . Well, no matter how slim the chance, Sorlson obviously thought my story was at least worth looking into.' He stroked his chin. 'When did he borrow the book, by the way?'

'Just six weeks ago. He only kept it for a week. Then he made me a fantastic offer for it, which I refused. I remembered how rare you believed it to be.'

'Not rare, unique!' he answered. 'Kept it for a week, eh? Yes, that would be ample time to copy the information he needed.'

'Information?'

'Directions from the book,' Crow explained. 'Oh, they're in there, all right! In the prose related to the poems, and—'

'Hang on a minute, Titus,' I rudely cut him off. 'I'm afraid you're moving a bit too fast for me. You mean you've actually known of this – *menhir* – for some time?'

'For four years, yes, since I myself borrowed Loftsson's book from you and tracked the tomb down. Incidentally, did you bring the book with you? Ah, I see you did! Give it to me and I'll show you what I mean. The initial clues are here in the poems. I've always been interested in these battle sagas, and being something of an archaeologist – albeit an amateur – well, I couldn't resist the challenge. I wish I had now. But listen–' He found his page and commenced to read.

> *'In Skardaborg we had no yearn,*
> *To pillage, plunder, sack, and burn;*
> *We'd plow the waves to Whitby where*
> *We knew a war fleet waited there.*
> *But Skardaborg's men laid a trap,*
> *Our great wavebiters to enwrap*
> *In floating nets till, tangle-oared,*
> *We had to stand and fight the horde.*
> *No quarter asked and none proffered,*

*As shields were lifted, spears prepared,*
*Till came the furious battle-clash,*
*And axe and sword were soon awash . . .'*

Crow paused in his reading and looked up: 'So
commenced the battle,' he commented. 'Now, de
Marigny, the poem goes on in pretty much the same
"thud and blunder" fashion for many a couplet, until
King Eystein, ever in the thick of the battle, notices one
of his ships to be doing extremely well. With blood in his
eyes so that he can't see to his best advantage, Eystein
flings yet another spear while enquiring of one of his
men:

' *"The sea-chief, name him, of yon ship,*
*Aye, him who stands with mail adrip,*
*In foemen's guts, in berserk glee;*
*Now tell me, Gudrod, who is he?"*

'He is answered:

' *"Tis Ragnar, son of Hildursleif,*
*Commands the Seasnake like a chief,*
*Aye, Ragnar Gory-Axe his name,*
*And in the stern there, see that Dame?*
*A witch most learned of Lapland's art,*
*'Tis Ragnar's mother, legs athwart,*
*Calling no doubt to Ragnar's side,*
*The Aesir o'er the bloodied tide."*
*"Of wizard or witch-son I've no ken,*
*But say thee, Gudrod, given ten*
*Like him who wields yon axe so red,*
*We'd soon put all these foe to bed!"*

'So you see, Henri, this Ragnar Gory-Axe was only an "up-and-comer", unnoticed of Eystein until this battle at Scarborough. And yet – if we can believe the book, and of course we've proof in the stone that we can – he'd been in many a fray before; and always with his mother, Hildursleif the witch, beside him. The poem goes on to describe Ragnar's death, Eystein's wrath, and Hildursleif's woe. Let's see, now – yes, here:

> *'And then on Seasnake's bloodied flank,*
> *Tossing his helm down to the plank,*
> *Young Ragnar with a berserk shriek,*
> *Turned on the foe his dragon's beak.*
> *But as his golden locks flew free,*
> *An arrow speeding o'er the sea,*
> *Brought forth a scream the world to chill,*
> *And gored his brain with iron bill –*

'Of course,' Crow paused again, 'you'll notice that the poems aren't up to the standard of Skalaglam's or Thjodolf's – but I can't tell if the faults lie in the original work, which I would consider unlikely, or in the translation. The *kenning* is too slight to warrant comment. Anyway, Eystein wins the battle, and the saga goes on like this:

> *'With dragons fore and snekkes behind,*
> *King Eystein in his blood-rage blind,*
> *Slid in the bay and took the town,*
> *And burned Skardaborg to the ground.*
> *Grey Hildursleif, calling the Aesir,*
> *Made heard her voice through all the ether,*
> *And raised a storm and Thor's bright blade,*
> *To guide her to a forest glade.*

*In craggy cleft she made his mound,*
*Where Ragnar's Bauta-stein she found,*
*And writ in ancient, northern rune,*
*A curse upon't before his tomb.*
*The stone was raised in forest bower,*
*Where died the Dame in that same hour,*
*And Seasnake's lads, all sore dismayed,*
*Beside her son the witch-wife laid . . .*

'So there you are, de Marigny... Of course I looked for further references in the prose, and eventually I tracked down the tomb in Allerston Forest.'

'The tomb? Gory-Axe's tomb?' I stupidly queried, still feeling the dull weight of the previous night's party.

'Ragnar's tomb, yes,' Crow sighed at my slowness. 'And his Bauta-stein, with the runes still on it beneath the moss of centuries. Now Sorlson has found it, too – and it's my fault, I fear!'

Here my interest picked up greatly. 'And you say the curse is still active? You think Sorlson's in danger, then?'

'That's exactly it, Henri. He's in desperate trouble if ever he tries to move that stone, or even interfere with it. That part of the forest site is abhorred by locals, has been for hundreds of years. They say the area's haunted – and of course it is – and they won't go near it. The shade of the Viking walks there still, and the runes on the stone make it clear that there's a doom in store for anyone foolish enough to disturb it!'

'And you could read those "ancient northern runes"?' I asked.

'No, not immediately, but I made a copy and later used Walmsley's *Notes on Deciphering Codes, Cryptograms, and Ancient Inscriptions* to translate the thing. More about that later.'

'But didn't Ragnar's, er, shade – didn't his ghost make itself known to you?'

'I copied the runes – that's all. I made no attempt to disturb the stone, none whatever. But I did have a rather peculiar dream, yes!'

'A dream, Titus? What sort of dream?'

'Never mind, de Marigny,' he frowned. 'It was sufficient, though, to warn me off Ragnar's tomb forever – and that's why I blame myself for having let the thing slip to Sorlson in the first place. Why, at times I swear the man's as avaricious as old Bannister Brown-Farley used to be! Not for money, mind you, or even power or acclaim. He simply likes to *own* things.' He passed my book back across to me with a thin smile. 'Here, do yourself a favour and read it. I could never appreciate people who own wonderful things simply for the sake of ownership!'

So there it was; I found myself compared with Bannister Brown-Farley, a rather unscrupulous explorer-adventurer type, infamous for his smuggling of stolen foreign antiques into England! And so I sat abashed, immersed in guts and gore, Loftsson's book on my lap, for the rest of the journey. . .

After changing at York we were in Scarborough by 7:00 p.m., and we took a taxi to the Queen's Hotel where Crow knew Sorlson to be staying. We found him in the bar, well into his fifth or sixth drink, and it was plain that Benjamin Sorlson was not a particularly happy man. He did not see us approach and started inordinately when Crow took him by the arm.

'Titus Crow!' he exclaimed after a moment's hesitation. 'And Henri de Marigny, too. It's good to see you – both of you!'

Sorlson was a small but stocky man, unlike the popular image of his Norwegian ancestors, with grey eyes, sandy hair, and gangling arms. As he welcomed us to the bar and ordered drinks I could see that the hands at the ends of those long arms were visibly trembling. Crow, too, at first sight, had picked up the man's obvious nervousness. My friend became immediately concerned, I could see that, but he hid his worry for the moment in a question:

'The stone, Benjamin – you've really found it?'

'I have,' Sorlson answered. 'Indeed I have! The directions in Henri's book were, as you yourself told me, quite explicit.' He turned to me and grinned, a forced grin I thought, then asked Crow: 'Well, what's your next step, Titus? Are you going to shop me to the Royal Archaeological Society or something like that? It won't make any difference, you know – "finders keepers", and all that.'

'You just don't want to understand, do you, Benjamin? Man, you're *already* shopped – and to a far greater power than any Archaeological Society, believe me!' Crow's eyes narrowed as they studied the other's face. 'But then, perhaps I'm wrong – perhaps you are beginning to understand after all!'

'Eh? What d'you mean, Crow?'

'I mean, Benjamin, that the bar's scarcely open but already you seem well on your way to getting drunk. I don't remember you for a drinking man? Secondly, you should be cock-a-hoop over your coup here – but the fact is you look more than a trifle worried. Been having any dreams during your stay, by any chance?'

'Dreams?' Sorlson visibly flinched at the word. 'Why, yes I have, these last two or three nights – since I found the stone, in fact – but that's hardly surprising, is it? All that rot you fed me about curses and so on . . .'

'But that was three months ago, Benjamin,' Titus quietly reminded him. 'And in any case – you've seen the inscriptions for yourself now. What did you make of them?'

'Plenty of time for translations later, Titus; and anyway, what if the stone does carry a – curse?' He tried to make light of it and reached up to clap Crow on the shoulder. 'I'll never fail to be amazed at how any man as intelligent as you are can believe in such—'

'I've heard all that before, my friend,' Crow harshly cut him off, 'but it doesn't alter the fact that this curse is real and extant! Man, I can sense these things, and so can de Marigny here. For God's sake, why don't you just take our word for it? Leave the stone where it is, Benjamin – leave it completely alone!'

Sorlson turned his eyes away. 'It's a bit late for that, Titus.'

'What's that?' I broke in. 'What's that you say, Benjamin?'

'You mean you've . . . already—?' Crow let the question hang, his voice falling to a whisper on the last word.

'I have, yes – I've had the stone moved!'

'How did you do it?' Crow sounded tired, as if all of his energy had gone out of him in a moment. 'I mean, I remember that the stone stood almost eight feet tall, and there was plenty of it bedded in the ground, too. It must have weighed almost – four tons?'

'Just over three and a half, in fact. I hired three men and an ex-army truck fitted with pulleys and tackle. We dug around the base of the stone and then hoisted it aboard. That was about 5:30 this afternoon. They should be well on their way to London by now.'

Titus Crow's eyes were suddenly bleak, his face drawn and grey as he asked: 'And the tomb? Is that why you yourself stayed back here in Scarborough?' He waited on Sorlson's answer.

'No, no – I found the cleft in the cliff, of course,' Sorlson eventually answered, 'but—'

'But something *stopped* you; is that it, Benjamin?'

'The truth is . . . yes, Crow. And you're right about those dreams I've been having. They've . . . they've worried me. It's not natural for me to dream – not that sort of dream, at any rate . . .'

Sorlson paused, tossed back his drink and turned from the bar. 'I'm simply not willing to take any more chances, that's all. The stuff in the cleft can wait – Gory-Axe's bones, his armour and weapons.' Yet even as he spoke a greedy light glittered in the archaeologist's eyes.

'Benjamin,' Crow quietly said, 'I've only just realized. For a long time now I've called you friend – but it wasn't the man I admired, only the mind. Now I'm not even sure about that. Why, you're nothing but a thief, a ghoul, a looter of tombs. I just—'

'No, Titus, you're wrong about me,' Sorlson broke in. 'And if it means that much to you, why – I'll put the stone back again. They can always build a museum round it, I suppose!'

'Do you mean it, Benjamin?' I asked.

'Yes – yes, I do, Henri. But it's not truly out of "the-goodness-of-my-heart", as it were. Don't get me wrong – I'd have the stone and everything that goes with it, if I dared. But there's been something wrong, out of tune, ever since I found the stone in the forest.' He turned back to Crow: 'What train are you catching tonight?'

'Train?' Crow was taken by surprise. 'Tonight?'

'Yes, certainly. The sooner we get back down to

London, the sooner Gory-Axe gets his stone back. Those men with the truck are staying in London overnight. I'm paying them tomorrow when they deliver it to my place. You know, I rather fancied it in my conservatory, along with—' He paused and shuddered. 'But not now.'

While Sorlson was collecting his notebooks, case, and overcoat, I waited in the bar with Titus Crow.

'De Marigny,' my friend said after a while, 'I hope we're in time. I mean, the inscription on that stone mentions nothing of a stay of execution for good intention!'

We spoke no more and soon Sorlson returned . . .

We were down country almost as far as Peterborough when I was snatched rudely from my nap. Crow, too, nodding quietly in his corner seat, jerked fearfully awake as Sorlson's terror-fraught shriek filled the dimly lighted compartment.

'Wh . . . What in the name of . . . ?' I began.

Sorlson was sitting bolt upright facing Crow, his eyes wide open and full of horror.

'What is it, Benjamin?' Crow shook himself awake and leaned across to take the archaeologist's shoulder.

'Another dream, Titus – a hellish nightmare!' Sorlson gasped. 'Worse than the others. Far worse! It was Ragnar again, but this time he wasn't merely threatening; he was – *after me!* With his great axe smeared in blood. A . . . a Viking, his head a skull, his eye-sockets full of balefire!'

'Do you feel it, de Marigny?' Crow turned abruptly to me, his face strained and chalky grey, his voice hushed. Until then I had 'felt' nothing, but even as Crow spoke an odd sensation began to creep into my bones. A

151

coldness, the chill of ocean spray driven on the north wind.

'I warned you, Sorlson–' Crow's voice was now oddly remote, almost faint. 'And by God, *I was right to do so!*'

The sway and rock of the train and the clatter of its wheels had lessened now, seemed muffled, and a great wall of mist had built up outside to press in on the speeding carriages; particularly on the left, that side of the train facing the fens, The Wash, and the North Sea beyond.

Sorlson was muttering – more to himself than to anyone else – his eyes wide, staring wildly about the compartment and at the swirling greyness beyond the windows: 'It's a trick! Some sort of joke! You're trying to frighten me, Crow – that's it, isn't it?' There was desperation in his strangely muted voice.

'No trick, Benjamin,' Titus answered. 'God! – but I wish it were!'

Sorlson was on his feet now, peering in dreadful premonition out into the mist. I leaned across and gripped Crow's elbow: 'Titus! What in hell's happening?' My voice sounded as if it came from far away.

'I . . . I don't know, de Marigny – I've known nothing like this before.' As Crow answered, I saw Sorlson stiffen where he stood at the window, and I looked up at the side of the man's face. He was opening and closing his mouth soundlessly like a fish, gesticulating weakly at something out beyond the shut window.

'Titus!' I cried, moving over beside Sorlson to press my face to the glass. 'Look!' Frankly, I needed Crow's corroboration of the thing. I could not believe my own eyes!

*For outside, riding the mist in ghostly majesty, a great Viking dragonship lay parallel with our compartment, its sides adorned with moisture-dripping shields. And behind those shields, spears raised in hideous salutation, ranks of armoured skeletons gave their chief the kill!*

Their chief?

In the prow, at the neck of the great, rearing dragon's head, a mist-wreathed figure stood tall and proud ... but naked of flesh as its demon companions! The *Thing* turned its head in horrid and deliberate disdain, and sparse blond locks blew in a ghost-wind about the fleshless skull. Above grinning jaws, red lights burned in black-walled eye-sockets like coals in the bellows' blast; and those eye-sockets were turned with grim intent directly upon the fear-twisted features of Benjamin Sorlson! Then the *Thing* drew back its ivory arm, and a shining axe gleamed wetly in bony claw.

All normal motion of the train seemed to have stopped by then, to be replaced by the slow heave and swell of an ethereal sea, and even with the windows firmly shut I could clearly hear the slap of waves and the creaking of the dragonship's rigging.

Dimly, as if from eight hundred years back in the abysses of time, I heard Crow's voice shouting instructions: 'Down, de Marigny – for your soul's sake *get down!*' He was already on the floor, his hands clawing at the legs of Sorlson who stood spreadeagled against the compartment door and its window. 'Leave the window alone, Sorlson—' he shouted from a million miles away. *'Leave it alone!'*

Even as I threw myself down I saw Ragnar's skeletal arm sweep forward in a powerful arc – saw him release the great axe from his graveyard fist – and as I hit the floor beside Crow I heard the window slam down and open, and Sorlson's death-scream as he hurtled backwards over our huddled forms! The stocky body of the archaeologist crashed into the opposite door of the compartment and slid in a crumpled heap between the seats. One glance in his direction told me all I needed to know; the haft of a Viking axe stuck out from the left side of his chest. And yet, as I gazed hypnotized at that terrible weapon, slowly the steel melted into mist and vanished . . . *and the breast of Sorlson's suit was clean and unmarked!*

In the next second I realized that the normal train sounds and motions had returned, that the slap of waves and the keening of the wind had faded to the dark oblivion of their origin. Moisture-laden fog was pouring into the compartment through the open window, but Crow was already on his feet attending to that. The dragonship, too, was gone – back to whichever hell spawned the thing, or perhaps Valhalla, who can say?

'We're lucky,' Crow panted, strength and sanity surging back into his voice and manner. 'Myself in particular. But then, I did Ragnar's stone no harm – neither his stone nor his tomb.'

'And Sorlson?' I questioned, knowing the answer before it came.

'Oh, yes,' Crow answered with a nod, bending over the crumpled body. 'He's dead. Heart attack – or at least, that's what they'll call it!'

And of course Crow was right.

Two mornings later, at Crow's invitation, I went round to Blowne House, his sprawling bungalow home on the outskirts of the city. When I arrived he had just done with sticking a newspaper clipping in one of his many, voluminous files of weird and unnatural events. I had, however, already taken note of the incident in question;

it had been given space in most of the previous day's newspapers:

### THREE DIE IN MYSTERY CRASH ON M1

At 9:15 last night, northbound travellers on the Ml at Hemel Hempstead were brought to a halt when a crashed ex-army truck blocked all three lanes with blazing debris. Apparently the vehicle had been travelling south at the time of the as yet un-explained accident, but somehow ended up on the northbound lanes! After the fire had been put out local police were baffled by the extent of damage to the truck. No other vehicle seemed to have been involved, and yet the burned-out shell of the truck showed a severely sliced superstructure and chassis. One of the policemen at the scene remarked that 'it looked as though something had tried to cut the truck in half!' Three bodies – identification not yet complete – were found in the wreckage. Police investigations are continuing . . .

Of Ragnar's stone there was no mention; but on that subject there was something I had yet to ask Crow. This is how he answered me:

'The inscription, Henri? Why, yes – I copied down the original runes and translated them later. I even put the thing to rhyme, as I believe it was inscribed, but of course my *kenning* isn't much to mention:

'*Here lies the Axe, of witch-wife's blood,*
*Whose blade was sharp, whose aim was good,*
*Who washed himself in crimson flood,*
    *Each time the war was waged;*

*Would-be defilers of this tomb,*
*Let Seasnake's shadow darkly loom,*
*And Ragnar's spirit seal thy doom –*
*His curse-lust to assuage!'*

Crow also mentioned his intention of returning to Allerston Forest one day – to see if he was correct in his belief that Ragnar had sailed his marker home again. I, for one, shall not be going with him . . .

# THE MIRROR OF NITOCRIS[1]

---

1. The one and only 'solo' appearance of Henri-Laurent de Marigny.

TITUS CROW'S APPRENTICE, Henri-Laurent de Marigny (who as we've seen plays Watson to Crow's Holmes), was sometimes witness and even participant in Crow's strange adventures. Why, at this very moment he's out there somewhere in weird spatial and temporal abysses – in the time-clock, of course – trying to track Crow down and so discover the road into Elysia, the place of the Elder Gods. But that of course is another story, even another novel! Before ever he stepped into the dear old time-clock's cavity – 'a gateway on all space and time' – he very nearly got himself involved in an entirely different dimension, in

*The Mirror of Nitocris.*

*Hail, The Queen!*
*Bricked up alive,*

*Never more to curse her hive;*
*Walled-up 'neath the pyramid,*

*Where the sand*
*Her secret hid.*
*Buried with her glass*
*that she,*

*At the midnight hour might see*
*Shapes from other spheres called;*

*Alone with them,*
*entombed, appalled*
*– to death!*

*– Justin Geoffrey*

Queen Nitocris' Mirror!

I had heard of it, of course – was there ever an occultist who had not? – I had even read of it, in Geoffrey's raving *People of the Monolith*, and knew that it was whispered of in certain dark circles where my presence is abhorred; I

knew Alhazred had hinted of its powers in the forbidden
*Necronomicon*, and that certain desert tribesmen still
make a heathen sign which dates back untold centuries
when questioned too closely regarding the legends of its
origin.

So how was it that some fool auctioneer could stand
up there and declare that this was Nitocris' Mirror? How
*dare* he?

Yet the glass was from the collection of Bannister
Brown-Farley – the explorer-hunter-archaeologist who,
before his recent disappearance, was a recognized
connoisseur of rare and obscure *objets d'art* – and its
appearance was quite as *outré* as the appearance of an
object with its alleged history ought to be. Moreover, was
this not the self-same auctioneer, fool or otherwise, who
had sold me Baron Kant's silver pistol only a year or two
before? Not, mind you, that there was a single shred of
evidence that the pistol, or the singular ammunition that
came with it, had ever really belonged to the witch-
hunting Baron; the ornately inscribed 'K' on the weapon's
butt might stand for anything!

But of course, I made my bid for the mirror, and for
Bannister Brown-Farley's diary, and got them both. 'Sold
to Mr, er, it is Mr de Marigny, isn't it, Sir? Thought so! –
sold to Mr Henri-Laurent de Marigny, for . . .' For an
abominable sum.

As I hurried home to the grey stone house which has
been my home ever since my father sent me out of
America, I could not help but wonder at the romantic
fool in me which prompts me all too often to spend my
pennies on such pretty tomfooleries as these. Obviously
an inherited idiosyncrasy which, along with my love of
dark mysteries and obscure and antique wonders, was
undoubtedly sealed into my personality as a permanent

stamp of my world-famous father, the great New Orleans mystic Etienne-Laurent de Marigny.

Yet if the mirror really *was* once the possession of that awful sovereign – why! What a wonderful addition to my collection. I would hang the thing between my bookshelves, in company with Geoffrey, Poe, d'Erlette, and Prinn. For of course the legends and myths I had heard and read of it were *purely* legends and myths, and nothing more; heaven forbid!

With my ever-increasing knowledge of night's stranger mysteries I should have known better.

At home I sat for a long time, simply admiring the thing where it hung on my wall, studying the polished bronze frame with its beautifully moulded serpents and demons, ghouls and efreets; a page straight out of *The Arabian Nights*. And its surface was so perfect that even the late sunlight, striking through my windows, reflected no glare but a pure beam of light which lit my study in a dream-engendering effulgence.

Nitocris' Mirror!

Nitocris. Now *there* was a woman – or a monster – whichever way one chooses to think of her. A sixth-dynasty Queen who ruled her terror-stricken subjects with a will of supernatural iron from her seat at Gizeh – who once invited all her enemies to a feast in a temple below the Nile, and drowned them by opening the water-gates – whose mirror allowed her glimpses of the nether-pits where puffed Shoggoths and creatures of the Dark-Spheres carouse and sport in murderous lust and depravity.

Just suppose this was the real thing, the abhorred glass which they placed in her tomb before sealing her up alive; where could Brown-Farley have got hold of it?

Before I knew it, it was nine, and the light had grown

so poor that the mirror was no more than a dull golden glow across the room in the shadow of the wall. I put on my study light, in order to read Brown-Farley's diary, and immediately – on picking up that small, flat book, which seemed to fall open automatically at a well-turned page – I became engrossed with the story which began to unfold. It appeared that the writer had been a niggardly man, for the pages were too closely-written, in a crabbed hand, from margin to margin and top to bottom, with barely an eighth of an inch between lines. Or perhaps he had written these pages in haste, begrudging the seconds wasted in turning them and therefore determined to turn as few as possible?

The very first word to catch my eye was – *Nitocris!*

The diary told of how Brown-Farley had heard it put about that a certain old Arab had been caught selling items of fabulous antiquity in the markets of Cairo. The man had been jailed for refusing to tell the authorities whence the treasures had come. Yet every night in his cell he had called such evil things down on the heads of his jailers that eventually, in fear, they let him go. And he had blessed them in the name of Nitocris! Yet Abu Ben Reis was not one of those tribesmen who swore by her name – or against it! He was not a Gizeh man, nor even one of Cairo's swarthy sons. His home tribe was a band of rovers wandering far to the east, beyond the great desert. Where, then, had he come into contact with Nitocris' name? Who had taught him her foul blessing – or where had he read of it? For through some kink of fate and breeding Abu Ben Reis had an un-common knack with tongues and languages other than his own.

Just as thirty-five years earlier the inexplicable *possessions* of one Mohammad Hamad had attracted archaeologists of the calibre of Herbert E. Winlock to the eventual discovery of the tomb of Thutmosis III's wives, so now did Abu Ben Reis's hinted knowledge of ancient burial grounds – and in particular the grave of the Queen of elder horror – suffice to send Brown-Farley to Cairo to seek his fortune.

Apparently he had not gone unadvised; the diary was full of bits and pieces of lore and legend in connection with the ancient Queen. Brown-Farley had faithfully copied from Wardle's *Notes on Nitocris*; and in particular the paragraph on her 'Magical Mirror': ' . . . handed down to their priests by the hideous gods of inner-Earth before the earliest civilizations of the Nile came into existence – a "gateway" to unknown spheres and worlds of hellish horror in the shape of a mirror. Worshipped, it was, by the pre-Imer Nyahites in Ptathlia at the dawn of Man's domination of the Earth, and eventually enshrined by Nephren-Ka in a black, windowless crypt on the banks of the Shibeli. Side-by-side, it lay, with the Shining Trapezohedron, and who can say what things might have been reflected in its depths? Even the Haunter of the Dark may have bubbled and blasphemed before it! Stolen, it remained hidden, unseen for centuries in the bat-shrouded labyrinths of Kith, before finally falling into Nitocris' foul clutches. Numerous the enemies she locked away, the mirror as sole company, full knowing that by the next morning the death-cell would be empty save for the sinister, polished glass on the wall. Numerous the vilely chuckled hints she gave of the *features* of those who leered at midnight from out the bronze-barriered gate. But not even Nitocris herself was safe from the horrors locked in the mirror, and at the midnight hour she was wise enough to gaze but fleetingly upon it . . .'

The midnight hour! Why! It was ten already. Normally I would have been preparing for bed by this time; yet here I was, so involved, now, with the diary that I did not give my bed a second thought. Better, perhaps, if I had . . .

I read on. Brown-Farley had eventually found Abu Ben Reis and had plied him with liquor and opium until finally he managed to do that which the proper authorities had found impossible. The old Arab gave up his secret – though the book hinted that this knowledge had not been all *that* easy to extract – and the next morning Brown-Farley had taken a little-used camel-track into the wastes beyond those pyramids wherein lay Nitocris' *first* burial place.

But from here on there were great gaps in the writing – whole pages having been torn out or obliterated with thick, black strokes, as though the writer had realized that too much was revealed by what he had written – and there were rambling, incoherent paragraphs on the mysteries of death and the lands beyond the grave. Had I not known the explorer to have been such a fanatical antiquarian (his auctioned collection had been unbelievably varied) and were I not aware that he had delved, prior to his search for Nitocris' second tomb, into many eldritch places and *outré* settings, I might have believed the writer mad from the contents of the diary's last pages. Even in this knowledge I half believed him mad anyway.

Obviously he had found the last resting place of Nitocris – the scribbled hints and suggestions were all too plain – but it seemed there had been nothing left worth removing. Abu Ben Reis had long since plundered all but the fabled mirror, and it was after Brown-Farley had taken that last item from the ghoul-haunted tomb that the first of his real troubles began. From what I could make out from the now-garbled narrative, he had begun to develop a morbid fixation about the mirror, so that by night he kept it constantly draped!

But it was no good; before I could continue my perusal of the diary I had to get down my copy of Feery's *Notes on the Necronomicon*. There was something tickling me, there at the back of my mind, a memory, something I should know, something which Alhazred had known and written about. As I took down Feery's book from my shelves I came face to face with the mirror. The light in my study was bright and the night was quite warm – with that oppressive heaviness of air which is ever the prelude to violent thunderstorms – yet I shuddered strangely as I saw my face reflected in that glass. Just for a moment it had seemed to leer at me.

I shrugged off the feeling of dread which immediately sprang up in my inner-self and started to look up the section concerning the mirror. A great clock chimed out the hour of eleven somewhere in the night and distant lightning lit up the sky to the west beyond the windows of my room. One hour to midnight.

Still, my study *is* the most disconcerting place. What with those eldritch books on my shelves, their aged leather and ivory spines dully agleam with the reflection of my study light; and the *thing* I use as a paper-weight, which has no parallel in any sane or ordered universe; and now with the mirror and diary, I was rapidly developing an attack of the fidgets unlike any I had ever known before. It was a shock for me to realize that I was just a little uneasy!

I thumbed through Feery's often fanciful recon-struction of the *Necronomicon* until I found the relevant passage. The odds were that Feery had not altered this section at all; except, perhaps, to somewhat modernize the 'mad' Arab's old-world phraseology. Certainly it read like genuine Alhazred. Yes, there it was. And there, yet again, was that recurring hint of happenings at midnight:

> ' . . . for while the Surface of the Glass is still – even as the Crystal Pool of Yith-Shesh, even as the Lake of Hali when the Swimmers are not at the Frothing – and while its Gates are locked in all the Hours of Day; yet, at the Witching Hour, One who knows – even One who guesses – may see in it all the Shades and Shapes of Night and the Pit, wearing the Visage of Those who saw before. And though the Glass may lie forgotten forever its Power may not die, and it should be known:
>
> **That is not dead which can forever lie,**
> **And with strange aeons even death may die . . .'**

For many moments I pondered that weird passage and the even weirder couplet which terminated it; and the minutes ticked by in a solemn silence hitherto outside my experience at The Aspens.

It was the distant chime of the half-hour which roused me from my reverie to continue my reading of Brown-Farley's diary. I purposely put my face away from the mirror and leaned back in my chair, thoughtfully scanning the pages. But there were only one or two pages left to read, and as best I can remember the remainder of that disjointed narrative rambled on in this manner:

'10th. The nightmares on the *London* – all the way out from Alexandria to Liverpool – Christ knows I wish I'd flown. Not a single night's sleep. Appears the so-called "legends" are not so fanciful as they seemed. Either that or my nerves are going! Possibly it's just the echo of a guilty conscience. If that old fool Abu hadn't been so damned close-mouthed – if he'd been satisfied with the opium and brandy instead of demanding money – and for what, I ask? There was no need for all that rough-stuff. And his poxy waffle about "only wanting to protect me". Rubbish! The old beggar'd long since cleaned the place out except for the mirror... That damned mirror! Have to get a grip on myself. What state must my nerves be in that I need to cover the thing up at night? Perhaps I've read too much from the *Necronomicon*! I wouldn't be the first fool to fall for that blasted book's hocus-pocus. Alhazred must have been as mad as Nitocris herself. Yet I suppose it's possible that it's all just imagination; there are drugs that can give the same effects, I'm sure. Could it be that the mirror has a hidden mechanism somewhere which releases some toxic powder or other at intervals? But what kind of mechanism would still be working so perfectly after the centuries that glass must have seen? And why always at midnight? Damned funny! And those *dreams!* There is one sure way to settle it, of course. I'll give it a few more days and if things get no better, well – we'll have to wait and see.

'13th. That's it, then. Tonight we'll have it out in the open. I mean, what good's a bloody psychiatrist who insists I'm perfectly well when I know I'm ill? That mirror's behind it all! "Face your problems," the fool said, "and if you do they cease to bother you." That's what I'll do, then, tonight.

'13th. Night. There, I've sat myself down and it's eleven already. I'll wait 'til the stroke of midnight and then I'll take the cover off the glass and we'll see what we'll see. God! That a man like me should twitch like this! Who'd believe that only a few months ago I was steady as a rock? And all for a bloody mirror. I'll just have a smoke and a glass. That's better. Twenty minutes to go; good – soon be over now – p'raps tonight I'll get a bit of sleep for a change! The way the place goes suddenly quiet, as though the whole house were *waiting* for something to happen. I'm damned glad I sent Johnson home. It'd be no good to let him see me looking like this. What a God-awful state to get oneself into! Five minutes to go. I'm tempted to take the cover off the mirror right now! There – midnight! Now we'll have it!'

And that was all there was!

I read it through again, slowly, wondering what there was in it which so *alarmed* me. And what a coincidence, I thought, reading that last line for the second time; for even as I did so the distant clock, muffled somewhere by the city's mists, chimed out the hour of twelve.

I thank God, now, that he sent that far-off chime to my ears. I am sure it could only have been an act of Providence which caused me to glance round upon hearing it. For that still glass – that mirror which is quiet as the crystal pool of Yith-Shesh all the hours of day – *was still no longer!*

A *thing*, a bubbling blasphemous shape from lunacy's most hellish nightmare, was squeezing its flabby pulp out through the frame of the mirror into my room – *and it wore a face where no face ever should have been.*

I do not recall moving – opening my desk drawer and snatching out that which lay within – yet it seems I must have done so. I remember only the deafening blasts of sound from the bucking, silver-plated revolver in my clammy hand; and above the rattle of sudden thunder, the whine of flying fragments and the shivering of glass as the hell-forged bronze frame buckled and leapt from the wall.

I remember, too, picking up the strangely *twisted* silver

168

bullets from my Boukhara rug. And then I must have fainted.

The next morning I dropped the shattered fragments of the mirror's glass overboard from the rail of the Thames Ferry and I melted down the frame to a solid blob and buried it deep in my garden. I burned the diary and scattered its ashes to the wind. Finally, I saw my doctor and had him prescribe a sleeping-draft for me. I knew I was going to need it.

I have said the thing had a face.

Indeed, atop the glistening, bubbling mass of that hell-dweller's bulk there *was* a face. A *composite* face of which the two halves did not agree! *For one of them was the immaculately cruel visage of an ancient Queen of Egypt; and the other was easily recognizable – from photographs I had seen in the newspapers – as the now anguished and lunatic features of a certain lately vanished explorer!*

# AN ITEM OF SUPPORTING EVIDENCE

THE NEXT TWO stories were shorts written expressly for August Derleth's **Arkham Collector**. This slim magazine or 'house journal' didn't have room for long pieces, so Derleth liked to keep stories short and to the point.

But let's go back to a time twenty years earlier:

My father was a coal miner in a colliery on England's northeast coast, and he was also a very well-read, fascinating man with a keen and ever-thirsting mind. Museums drew him like a nail to a magnet, and some of his love of ancient civilizations and strange antiquities – his love of knowledge in general – naturally rubbed off on me. Sunderland had a fine museum, which we used to visit fairly regularly. And not far away, there stood Hadrian's Wall. I think we met Titus Crow there once, when we were walking under the wall.

Come to think of it, that might even have been the same day he stumbled across

**An Item of Supporting Evidence.**

It was the contents of a letter from Chandler Davies, the weird-artist, commenting upon the negative effect which my short story *Yegg-ha's Realm* had had on him, which determined me to invite him round to Blowne House. Not that I grieved to any great extent over Mr Davies' adverse comments – you can never please everyone – but I definitely disagreed with his expounded argument. He had had it that Mythological-Fantasy was 'out'; that the Cthulhu Mythos' fabled lands and creatures and Cimmeria's scintillating citadels and dark demons should have been allowed to die a sad but certain death along with their respective originators, and that constant culling from those tales – the brain children of my own, not to mention many another author's, literary progenitors – was weakening the impact of the original works. Nor, apparently, had my story – admittedly a Lovecraftian piece; set during the time of Rome's rule over England and involving the worship of an 'outside God' – irritated him in this respect alone. What seemed to have annoyed Mr Davies especially was the fact that I had portrayed 'so thoroughly unbelievable a God' as existing in such a well-known period of England's history that even an average student of our country's antiquities could hardly miss the obvious impossibility of my tale.

I was pleased that Mr Davies had written directly to

me and not to the letters section of *Grotesque*, in which magazine my tale had originally appeared, for then I would have been forced to take retaliatory measures which would undoubtedly have caused great tidal-waves of unwanted activity on many a scientific beach. Obviously the artist was not aware that all my stories have at least a tenuous basis in established fact, some more definitely than others, and that I have never chronicled anything which I believe could not possibly have happened or which has not, in some way or other, directly involved myself.

Anyway, Mr Davies accepted my invitation and braved the curious aura of foreboding which surrounds Blowne House to visit me one Sunday afternoon some weeks ago. It was the first time he had ever set foot inside my abode and I noted with satisfaction the way in which his eyes roved enviously over the contents of my amply stocked book-shelves.

Briefly fingering the spine of an original copy of Geoffrey's *People of the Monolith*, he remarked upon my extreme good fortune at owning so many scarce volumes and read off some of their titles as he scanned them. His short monologue included Feery's *Original Notes on the Necronomicon*, the abhorrent *Cthaat Aquadingen*, a literally priceless *Cultes des Goules* and many other similarly *outré* works including such anthropological source books as *The Golden Bough* and Miss Murray's *Witch Cult*. I made a point of bringing to his attention the fact that I also owned a translated copy of Lollius Urbicus' little known *Frontier Garrison*, circa AD 138, and took the book down from its shelf before pouring my guest a welcoming brandy.

'I take it that book contains the item of supporting evidence which you mentioned in your letter, Mr Crow?

That being the case I think it's only fair to warn you from the beginning that I can't put much stock in anything Urbicus says; though I'll admit that his description of the temple to Mithras at Barrburgh was pretty accurate.'

Appreciating the way in which my obviously erudite critic was shaping up, I countered his exploratory thrust by smiling and telling him: 'No, the book merely contains a few additional fragments of interest in connection with my actual *evidence* – which is of an entirely different nature.'

'I don't want you to get me wrong, Mr Crow,' he answered, taking out a cigarette and settling himself more comfortably in his chair in preparation for the more strenuous battle to come, 'as an entertainment your story was very good – excellent – and any casual reader of such tales must surely have experienced a definite shudder at some of the "shock" paragraphs which you so successfully employed; but to have set the thing in a period of which we're so historically and archaeologically "sure" – the same period, I note, in which old Urbicus scribbled his notes for that book of yours – was a mistake the story could well have done without. You see, I'm a collector – a *gourmet* of such tales, you could say – and while I don't wish to be offensive I must admit that blunders like yours irk me considerably . . .' He sipped at his brandy.

While Mr Davies had been speaking, I had carefully opened *Frontier Garrison* to a previously marked page and as soon as he was done I turned the book around and slid it over the table separating us so that he could read the selected paragraph. Smiling, he did so, though I thought his smile was just a trifle too sarcastic; and sure enough, when he was through, he closed the book with a flourish which indicated complete rejection.

'I have also read Plato on *Atlantis* and Borellus on, er, *revivication?* – No, Mr Crow, Lollius Urbicus' account of the death of Yegg-ha at the swords of a centuria of fear-frenzied Roman soldiers doesn't impress me at all. I'm sorry.'

'I rather fancy your dismissal of Plato and Borellus as a bit too perfunctory, Mr Davies! I can only suspect that your appraisal of their works, to say nothing of the work of Lollius Urbicus, is undertaken with the same attitude of mind with which the Inquisition viewed the work of Galileo Galilei; and, of course, if Sayce hadn't unearthed their remains all over Asia Minor and Northern Syria you'd probably still be denying that the Hittites ever existed!' I smiled.

'*Touché!*' he said. 'But now you're talking, Mr Crow! *Remains*, you said. Now, that's it *exactly!* After all, remains are proof! But tell me please – what remains are there to show that that abominable invention of Urbicus' ever existed?'

'You think he created Yegg-ha himself then?' I asked. 'You believe that the featureless, ten-foot-tall monstrosity he mentioned in his notes was purely a figment of his own imagination?'

'Oh, no. I wouldn't be so presumptuous. Urbicus probably got the idea from local legends or fairy tales. Later, rather than write off the ignominious loss of a half-centuria of soldiers to a barbarian attack, he attributed their annihilation to this giant, faceless God . . .'

'Hmmm – clever,' I answered, 'but how about the communal grave recently unearthed at Briddock Fort – with forty-eight fantastically mutilated Roman skeletons haphazardly piled one upon the other, some still encased in their armour, as if buried in great haste?'

That shook him a bit. 'I'd forgotten that,' he admitted.

'But for God's sake, man – there must have been thousands of small skirmishes which never got chronicled! You see, that's the whole point, Mr Crow; you talk about these things in exactly the same way in which you wrote about them in that damned story of yours – as though you believe in them conclusively! As though you actually believe that a great, murderous, lunatic thing was called up from hell by the barbarians to do battle with the Romans! As though you have definite proof – which you haven't. No, you shouldn't have done your story as an historical document at all. God only knows how many poor, deluded little lore-swallowers you'll have galloping all over Briddock and Housesteads, awesomely trembling at the thought that they're perhaps treading the same ground upon which the Romans did fearsome battle with the hideous Yegg-ha!'

While he sat there fuming I poured more brandy into his glass and grinned at him. 'Well, I've obviously made a literary enemy! I'm sorry about that because it was my intention to ask you to illustrate my next book. But anyway, tell me – have you ever seen that horrible, ten-foot chunk of granite statuary in the Roman Antiquities section of the British Museum?'

'Yes, I have; from Limestone Bank, I believe. A stubby-winged thing much similar to the God in your story, with defaced features and . . .' He checked himself. 'Just what are you getting at?'

'Try to think, Mr Davies – didn't you find it funny that the *features* of that statue were so cleverly, so *smoothly*, er, defaced? Why! If one looks at it at all closely it almost appears as though *it wasn't intended to have any features . . .*'

He choked over his brandy. I reached for his glass and

filled it again as he sputtered and coughed, dabbing at his lips with a handkerchief, getting himself under control.

'There you go again! Of all the prepos—'

'I've been unfair, Mr Davies.' I shut him off. 'I've kept you in suspense too long and you're losing your patience. Drink your brandy . . .'

'I beg your pardon?'

'Drink your brandy,' I repeated. 'You'll need it.' I opened my writing cabinet and took out an object cowled unconventionally in a tea-cosy. I balanced it upon the table. Then I pointed to the book in front of my bewildered visitor and said: 'Page thirty-four, second paragraph . . .' As Mr Davies fumblingly, suspiciously found the page and paragraph I stroked my item of supporting evidence beneath its tea-cosy cover.

Eventually he looked up from the book. 'It relates to a walk Urbicus took over the countryside shortly after his men allegedly disposed of your monster. Six of his best men went with him. So what?'

'He was looking for a place to bury something, and needed those men to carry it,' I explained. 'He wanted it hidden so that the barbarians wouldn't be able to use whatever powers of, er – what was that word you used? – *revivication* they might have possessed upon it.'

Mr Davies opened his mouth to stutter a denial but I cut him off. 'You see, I've examined the whole length of Hadrian's Wall in that area, between Housesteads and Briddock, and eventually I found the right spot. I'm quite a little archaeologist, you know, but even if I hadn't been, Urbicus' description,' – I nodded at the book which he had put down, – 'as with his description of the temple at Barrburgh, fitted the spot exactly. Surprisingly enough, the countryside hasn't changed all that much in eighteen centuries; all I had to do was look for the place where I would have put the body if I'd been Urbicus. It took me five weeks but I did eventually find it.'

'What on Earth are you talking—'

I lifted the tea-cosy and passed the football-sized item it concealed over the table for Mr Davies' incredulous inspection.

I made him promise to keep it to himself; I cannot say I fancy the idea of crowds of boffins disturbing my privacy, and I certainly would never part with that item of supporting evidence. Not only that but he promised to illustrate my next book.

There are many *outré* items in Blowne House; a weird, four-handed clock which ticks all out of rhyme, the *Cthaat Aquadingen* with its nameless binding, a crystal-ball which is so disturbing to look upon that I have to keep it locked away – and many others equally as strange as these. But I am particularly proud of my paperweight – though I will admit it does seem peculiar to put such an odd item to such a use. You see, it's a rather large, *socketless* skull . . .

With wire hooks screwed into them the wings make excellent coat-hangers.

# BILLY'S OAK

*THIS IS ANOTHER tale of an unconventional ghost. More I can't say . . .*

Having enjoyed a surprising measure of success with my latest book, *Here Be Witches!*; and, in the process of researching for that 'documentary' volume, having stumbled across various mentions of a certain 'black' book – the *Cthaat Aquadingen*, an almost legendary collection of spells and incantations purported to relate, among other things, to the raising of certain water-elementals – I was considerably put out to discover that the British Museum did not have a copy; or, if there was a copy at the museum, then for some reason the controllers of that vast establishment were reluctant to permit its perusal! Yet I especially desired to see a copy, in connection with a companion volume to *Here Be Witches!*, to be entitled *Forbidden Books!*, which my publisher was pressing me to start work upon.

It was this reluctance on the part of the Curator of the Rare Books Department to answer my inquiries with anything other than the most perfunctory replies which prompted me to get in touch with Titus Crow; a London-dwelling collector of obscure and eldritch volumes who, I had heard it rumoured, held a copy of the very book I wished to consult in his private library.

In prompt reply to a hastily scribbled letter Mr Crow invited me round to Blowne House – his residence on the outskirts of the city – assuring me that he did indeed own a copy of the *Cthaat Aquadingen* and that with one provision and on one condition I might be allowed to check through its contents. The provision was that any projected visit to Blowne House would have to be paid during the later hours of the evening; for, as he was currently engaged upon some studying himself, and because he was better able to concentrate at night, he was retiring very late and was rarely out of bed before noon. This, plus the fact that his afternoons were taken up by more mundane but nevertheless essential labours, left him only the evenings in which to work or entertain visitors. Not, as he was quick to explain, that he was given to entertaining visitors very often. In fact, had he not already acquainted himself with my earlier work he would have been obliged to pointblank refuse my proposal. Too many 'cranks' had already attempted the penetration of his retreat.

As the fates would have it, I chose a filthy night to call at Blowne House. The rain was coming down in sheets and great grey clouds hung heavy over the city in the lowering sky. I parked my car on the long driveway in front of Mr Crow's sprawling bungalow home, ran up the short path with my collar turned up against the downpour, and banged on the heavy door. During the space of the half-minute or so in which it took my host to answer my knock I got thoroughly soaked. As soon as I had introduced myself as being Gerald Dawson I found myself ushered inside, relieved of my dripping coat and soggy hat, and bustled through to Mr Crow's study where he bade me sit before a roaring fire to 'dry out'.

He was not what I had expected. He was tall and broad-shouldered and it was plain to see that in his younger days he had been a handsome man. Now, though, his hair had greyed and his eyes, though they were still bright and observant, bore the imprint of many a year spent exploring – and often, I guessed, discovering – along rarely trodden paths of mysterious and obscure learning. He was attired in a flame-red dressing-gown, and I noticed that a small, casual table beside his desk sported a bottle of the best brandy.

It was that which rested upon the desk itself, however, which mainly attracted my attention; for it was obviously the object of Mr Crow's studies; a tall, four-handed, hieroglyphed, coffin-shaped monstrosity of a clock, lying horizontally, face upwards, along the full length of the huge desk. I had noticed when he answered my knock that my host carried a book; and, as he placed this volume on the arm of my chair while he poured me a welcome drink, I was able to see that it was a well-thumbed copy of Walmsley's *Notes on Deciphering Codes, Cryptograms, and Ancient Inscriptions.* Apparently Mr Crow was attempting a translation of the fantastic hieroglyphics on the weird clock's face. Even as I got up and crossed the room to have a closer look at that device it was obvious to me that the intervals between its loud ticks were quite irregular; nor, I noticed, did the four hands move in consonance with any time-system with which I was at all familiar. I could not help but wonder just what chronological purpose so curious a timepiece served.

Crow saw the bewilderment on my face and laughed. 'It puzzles me to the same extent, Mr Dawson, but I shouldn't let it bother you. I doubt if anyone will ever truly understand the thing; every now and then I get the urge to have another bash at it, that's all, and then I'm at it for weeks at a time, getting nowhere! Still, you didn't come round here tonight to get yourself involved with de Marigny's clock! You're here to have a look at a book.'

I agreed with him and commenced to outline my plan for including a mention or two of the *Cthaat Aquadingen* in *Forbidden Books!* As I spoke he moved the occasional table from its position near his desk to a place nearer to where I had been seated beside the fire. This done he slid back a panel, hidden in the wall to one side of the fireplace, and took down from a dim shelf the very volume in which my interest was seated. Then an expression of extreme loathing crossed his face and he quickly put the book down on the table and wiped his hands on his dressing-gown.

'The, er, binding . . .' he muttered. 'It's forever sweating which is rather surprising, you'll agree, considering its donor has been dead for at least four hundred years!'

'Its *donor!*' I exclaimed, glancing in morbid fascination at the book. 'You don't mean to say that it's bound in . . .

'I'm afraid so! At least, *that* copy is.'

'My God! . . . Are there many copies then?' I asked.

'Only three that I know of – and one of the other two is here in London. I take it they wouldn't let you see it?'

'You're very shrewd, Mr Crow, and perfectly correct. No, I wasn't allowed to see the copy at the British Museum.'

'You'd have received the same answer if you'd asked for the *Necronomicon*,' he answered. I was taken completely aback.

'I beg your pardon? Don't tell me you believe there really is such a book? Why, I've been assured half-a-dozen times that this *Necronomicon* thing is purely a fiction; a clever literary prop to support a fictional mythology.'

'If you say so,' he blandly replied. 'But anyway, it's that book you're interested in.' He indicated the evilly-bound volume on the occasional table.

'Yes, of course,' I answered, 'but didn't you say something about a, well, a condition?'

'Ah! Well, I've taken care of that myself,' he said. 'I've had the two centre chapters – the more *instructive* ones – taken out and bound separately, just in case. I'm afraid you *can't* see them.'

'Instructive ones? In case?' I echoed him. 'I don't quite see what you mean?'

'Why, in case the thing should ever fall into the wrong hands, of course!' He looked surprised. 'Surely you must have wondered why those people at the museum keep their copies of such books under lock and key?'

'Yes; I imagine they're locked away because they're very rare, worth a lot of money!' I answered. 'And I suppose some of them must contain one or two rather *nasty* items; erotic-supernatural-sadistic stuff, I mean; sort of medieval Marquis de Sade?'

'Then you suppose wrongly, Mr Dawson. The *Cthaat Aquadingen* contains complete sets of working spells and invocations; it contains the *Nyhargo Dirge* and a paragraph on making the *Elder Sign*; it contains one of the *Sathlatta*, and four pages on Tsathogguan Rituals. It contains far too much – and if certain authorities had had their way even the three remaining copies would have been destroyed long ago.'

'But surely you can't *believe* in such things?' I protested. 'I mean, I intend to *write* of such books as though there's something damnably mysterious and monstrous about them – I'll have to, or I'd never make a sale – but I can't believe such things myself.'

Crow laughed at me, in a rather mirthless way. 'Can't you? If you'd seen the things I've seen, or been through some of the things I've been through, believe me you wouldn't feel so shocked, Mr Dawson. Oh, yes, I believe in such things. I believe in ghosts and fairies, in ghouls and genies, in a certain mythological "prop", and in the existence of Atlantis, R'lyeh, and G'harne.'

'But surely there's not one scrap of genuine evidence in favour of any of the things or places you've mentioned?' I argued. 'Where, for instance, can one be sure of meeting a – well – a ghost?'

Crow thought it over a moment and I felt sure I had scored a major victory. I just could not take it in that this so obviously intelligent man genuinely believed so deeply in the supernatural. But then, in defiance of what I had considered the unanswerable question, he said: 'You put me in the position of the ecclesiastical gentleman who once informed a small child of the existence of An-Almighty-God-Who-Is-Everywhere – and was then asked to produce him. No, I can't show you a ghost – at least, not without going to a lot of trouble – but I can show you a *manifestation* of one.'

'Oh, now come, Mr Crow, you . . .'

'No, seriously,' he cut me off. 'Listen!' He put a finger to his lips, signifying silence, and adopted a listening attitude.

The rain outside had stopped and there was only the sporadic patter of droplets draining from the tiles to disturb the silence of the room; that and the ticking of Crow's great clock. Then there came to my ears a quite audible, long drawn out, creaking sound – like straining timbers.

'You heard it?' Crow smiled.

'I heard it,' I answered. 'I've heard it half-a-dozen times while we've been talking. You've got unseasoned timber in your attic.'

'This house has very unusual rafters,' he observed. 'Teak – and seasoned well before the house was built.

188

And teak doesn't creak!' He grinned, obviously liking the sound of that last.

I shrugged. 'Then it's a tree straining in the wind.'

'Right, it is a tree, but it's not straining in the wind. If there was a wind up we'd hear it. No, that was a branch of "Billy's Oak", protesting at his weight.' He crossed to the window with its drawn curtains and inclined his head in the direction of the garden beyond. 'You missed our Billy when you wrote *Here Be Witches!*' he said. 'William "Billy" Fovargue – accused of wizardry – was hanged on that tree in 1675 by a crowd of fear-crazed peasants. He was on his way to trial at the time, but after the "lynching" the crowd testified they'd jumped the gun on Billy because he'd started a horrible incantation and weird shapes had begun to form in the sky – so they'd simply strung him up to prevent things from going any further . . .'

I got the idea. 'I see. So that sound is the branch from which he was hanged, still creaking with his weight two hundred and eighty years after the hanging?' I put as much sarcasm as possible into my reply.

Crow was quite unperturbed. 'That's right,' he answered. 'It got on the nerves of the previous owner of the house so much that he eventually sold the place to me. The owner before him nearly went crazy trying to discover the sound's source.'

I spotted Crow's mistake immediately. Something he had said did not ring quite true. 'Ah!' I pointed out. 'Now that's where your story falls down, Mr Crow. Surely he would've traced the sound to the oak?' I took his silence as acknowledgment of my cleverness and got to my feet, quickly crossing the room to where he stood by the drawn curtains. As I did so the creaking from the tree in the garden came again, louder.

'It's the wind in the oak's branches, Mr Crow,' I
assured him, 'and nothing else.'

As the eerie sound came yet again from beyond the
window I drew back the curtains and stared out into the
night.

I took a quick step backwards then, telling myself that
I must be seeing things. But that was just the point; I was
*not* seeing things. My mind suddenly whirled; but, after
a moment's thought, I burst into shaky laughter. The
clever devil. He had actually had me going there for a
moment. I turned to him in sudden anger and saw that
he was still smiling.

'So it is the rafters after all?' I blurted, my voice
cracking a little.

Crow kept right on smiling. 'No, it's not,' he said.
'That's what nearly drove that fellow I was telling you
about crazy. You see, when they built this house seventy
years ago, *they cut Billy's Oak down – so that its roots
wouldn't interfere with the foundations . . .'*

# DARGHUD'S DOLL

*BY THE TIME I got round to writing this next one, Titus Crow had already had dealings with ghosts, Cthulhu Mythos critters, 'Roman Remains,' and the like. Now I thought I'd try him out with sympathetic magic. So you see, it wasn't really Dawson who went to see him that day but me! And this is the story he told me:*

'So you're thinking of doing a book on basic magic, are you, Dawson?' Titus Crow broached the subject as soon as he had made me welcome with his customary offering of a glass of fine brandy. I glanced enviously about the occultist's marvellously appointed study, a room I had fortunately been able to view on a few rare previous occasions, before answering him.

'That's right, Crow, yes. In fact, with the help of a few good source-books, I've got quite a bit of it done already; but there's this one chapter that's giving me some difficulty.'

'Yes, I remember you mentioned it on the telephone – imitative magic, I believe you said?'

I nodded in agreement. 'Right. I know *why* it's supposed to work, and even *how* – but I'm damned if I can find more than two or three really well-documented cases. I mean, the theory of the thing is all well enough – but what about the facts?'

For a moment or two Crow thought about it, and the silence of the room was broken only by the occasional creak of branches from the nighted garden beyond the draped windows, and the oddly erratic ticking of a tall, four-handed, strangely hieroglyphed and coffin-shaped clock in one corner.

'Imitative or sympathetic magic,' he mused, frowning

193

as he cocked his head on one side in contemplation. 'Well, I'm afraid you're out of luck, Dawson. I do know of a few cases, yes, and one in particular which I suppose you could say is rather well authenticated – but you must realize that in many such cases there exists more than an element of chance. The simple truth is that unless the evidence is one hundred per cent conclusive . . . then the phenomena of imitative magic are usually purely coincidental.

'But anyway,' he quickly continued after a moment's pause, 'at a loss as I may be in that direction, I can probably supplement your list of source-books. Let me see now . . . Yes: you could try McPherson's *Primitive Beliefs in N.E. Scotland*, and Trachtenberg's *Jewish Magic and Superstitions*. Then you might find Oman's *Cults, Customs, and Superstitions of India* useful, or, perhaps, Dr E. Mauchamp's *La Sorcellerie au Maroc*. And then there's—'

'Hold on a minute there, Titus!' I cried, rudely breaking in on him. 'You changed the subject a bit fast there, didn't you? Come on, now, what about this "well-authenticated" case you mentioned? Is it something I shouldn't know about?'

'No, but . . . Well, you see, Dawson, I knew the people of the story personally, and . . .' He pursed his lips. 'If I did tell it, I'd have to alter the facts a bit, and the names of the characters. You see, Dawson? It would no longer be truly "authentic", now, would it? And after all, you're after *facts*; which in turn makes the telling of a disguised story rather pointless. Don't you agree?'

'Well, whether I can use it or not,' I answered in desperation, 'I've simply got to hear it now. I mean, you've got me going, Crow! You usually do get me going, and you very well know it. Now come on – how about the story?'

'As you wish,' he answered resignedly. 'But first let me fill your glass again.' He brought his chair over then, and I pulled mine a little closer to the fire; and in that strange, quiet room, with only the weird ticking of the great clock as a background to his voice, my host began the tale:

'It was all of nine years ago that Dr Maurice Jamieson went out to South Africa to visit his ailing brother, David, also a doctor, at his tiny hospital on the south shore of Lake Ngami.

'Now David Jamieson had had the so-called "missionary instinct" – a compassion, an urge to help underdeveloped peoples – ever since his boyhood. If his talents as a healer hadn't led him to medicine, then most probably he would have ended up in Africa anyway – wearing "The Cloth". As it was, in the fifteen years he'd been out there he had built himself a remarkable reputation with the natives of the region. He was looked upon by the various tribes almost as a god.

'David's trouble, his brother found when his landrover reached the hospital from Livingstone, was simply that he had been pushing himself too hard – and he'd been doing it for fifteen years. The man was quite simply run down, and Maurice Jamieson put him straight into one of his own beds in the hospital, ordering him to stay there and be looked after while he himself tended the hospital's primitive clientele.

'Well, apparently Jamieson's diagnosis of his brother's trouble had been perfectly correct, and the rest-cure had been applied none too soon. Within two or three days the frail, suntanned doctor developed a raging enteric fever, and it was plain that had he not taken to his bed when ordered the fever might well have knocked him down for good. His condition added considerably to the strenuous work already being done by his brother and the hospital's two trained native nurses. For you see, Dawson, David Jamieson's fever had not confined itself to him. This particularly nasty disease had been busy in the marshlands of the Okavango Basin, just across the narrow neck of Lake Ngami, since a time almost a week prior to the English doctor's arrival; and in ones and twos canoes containing sick natives had been crossing the lake to the hospital for some ten days.

'So things went for the first three weeks, and David Jamieson slowly recovered from his fever and began to put on weight again in his hospital bed. With most of the natives back on their feet and returned across the lake to their marshland villages, Dr Maurice Jamieson found he had a little more time to himself.

'Now the doctor had a hobby; he was something of an entomologist. Naturally, when first he decided to go out to his brother in Africa, he had seen the trip as a marvellous opportunity to add some tropical specimens to his collection. To this end he had taken with him certain items of entomological kit; tweezers and a butterfly-net, name-cards and a notebook – and, most important of all, a set of variously-sized moulds and the quick-drying artificial resin with which to fill them.

'This simple system was better by far than the old method of preservation and mounting, and the specimens thus encased could be examined minutely from all angles. Indeed, they were trapped as firmly as those prehistoric flies in amber which you can find in most museums, and when the resin was set it was as clear and hard as glass.

'In the evenings, when his work was done and the remaining patients had been properly bedded down for the night, Maurice Jamieson would get out into the large, enclosed gardens of the hospital and lose himself to the doubtless delightful diversions of "bug-hunting". He collected and categorized specimen after specimen, until the time came when his brother was almost well enough to be up and about again . . . Which was when the trouble started.

'You see, some of the natives effectively treated at the hospital had been M'bulus, possibly the most unfriendly and "uncivilized" of the local tribes, and hitherto they had never bothered to take their troubles to the "white Mganga". Their own Mganga, Darghud the witch-doctor, had always treated their ailments himself – and allegedly he was a man as well versed in native medicine as he was in Black Magic. This enteric disease, though, patently had the witch-doctor foxed. For a long time the chief of the M'bulus, Notka, who had long studied the benefits reaped by the other tribes, had been pressing for good relations with the hospital. Now Notka himself had gone down with the enteritis, against which Darghud's ministrations seemed of no earthly use. So the chief sent his eldest son and the Mganga Darghud across the lake to bring back some of the potent medicine of David Jamieson.

'Now this was the problem: David Jamieson, before his brother's arrival, had discovered the best treatment for the virulent enteric disease to be penicillin – with the result that only two shots of the medicine remained in the hospital's dispensary. Maurice Jamieson intended to use those shots on his brother, to finalize David's treatment, and he had one of the nurses explain the facts to the bone-rattling Mganga and to chief Notka's anxious son.

'Picture it, Dawson: Darghud, the painted savage, the

witch-doctor, sent like a messenger-boy by his chief, against his own wishes and heathen judgment, to beg healing juju from the white Mgangas – only to be perfunctorily refused and turned away! It was too much. Much more than that, however, it was the chance Darghud had been waiting for; the opportunity to defame the white men, the Great Mgangas, and perhaps even get rid of them!

'There in the hospital grounds, in front of the chief's son, Darghud puffed himself up in black rage, spitting on the ground at Maurice Jamieson's feet and flinging an itchy white powder in the face of the nurse-cum-interpreter. Before the astonished doctor could recover from his surprise (remember, Dawson, that to him the choice had been a simple, logical one; two shots could hardly help chief Notka across the lake, they wouldn't provide a sufficiently large dosage, but they were absolutely necessary in the completion of his brother's recovery), the Mganga passed him a great, wriggling beetle. Then Darghud stalked away, his two cringing, servile companions – the paddlers of his canoe – close on his heels.

'The black interpreter, when he'd managed to get the white powder out of his eyes, backed hurriedly away as soon as he saw the object of Dr Jamieson's puzzled scrutiny – the squirming, chitinous creature that he held in his hand – Darghud's great beetle!

'When Jamieson questioned the black's concern, he was told that the beetle was a "bad charm", designed to bring down evil on the person of its receiver. He advised the doctor to throw the thing far, far away – and then to pray most earnestly to God. Maurice Jamieson laughed at the suggestion, remarking that the beetle was of a sort he'd never seen before, and that he was certainly not going to throw it away; however, the nurse, by all means, could pray for him if he wished! Then he immediately went to his room and placed the beetle in a mould, pouring thick resin from a freshly opened bottle over its wriggling form. He left the whole to set and thought no more about it . . . until later.

'That evening, as usual, when the last few patients had been attended to for the night, Jamieson went into the gardens and had a look under the bushes to see if he could find any new bugs worth adding to his collection. His usual enthusiasm was lacking, however (a bit of a headache), and besides, there was that disturbing, rhythmic drumming from over the lake . . .

'When he went back to his room his first thought was of the beetle, the fetish-creature given him by Darghud. But the solid, clear-resin block in which the thing should now have lain dead and immobile, perfectly preserved and displayed forever, was barren of any sign of the insect! The only solution, the only answer to the puzzle, seemed to Jamieson to be that the beetle had somehow struggled out of the mould before the resin was properly set; something unprecedented in his experience. On the other hand (he told himself), it could be that the new bottle of resin was inferior, perhaps affected by the heat. After all, the stuff had been produced for use in rather cooler climes. The next morning, though, Jamieson did notice that all his other new specimens, locked in resin from the same bottle, had set as perfectly as any he ever treated in England.

'Three days later – during which time, incidentally, that unusual headache of Jamieson's, first felt on the evening of the beetle's disappearance, had constantly nagged him – his brother was up and about again. David Jamieson was paler than before, but chirpy and a lot more energetic, and so his bug-collecting brother decided it was time he took leave of the place. The heat seemed to be bothering him more and more; likewise, day and night, the insistent throb of drums from over the lake; his original enthusiasm for his brother's practice and the obscurity of the lakeside hospital had drastically fallen off. He put it all down to too much sun, and on the fourth morning after Darghud's visit he climbed back into the passenger seat of his guide's landrover to begin the long ride back to Livingstone. Five days later he was back in "Blighty" . . .

'Now I've explained, Dawson, how Dr Jamieson believed his continuing headache to be due to an overdose of the African sun; but why should the thing continue so *persistently* – worsening, in fact – in England? And ordinary remedies seemed of no use whatsoever.'

For a moment there was silence as Crow refilled our glasses. Then he sat back, took a sip of brandy, and carried on:

'Well, now that we've seen Maurice Jamieson safely returned to England, it might be as well to pick up the threads of the story back in Africa:

'It didn't take David Jamieson long, once his brother had left the little hospital, to begin wondering what was behind the damnable devil-drums pounding unceasingly from the other side of the lake. Nubo, the black male-nurse who had suffered Darghud's powder thrown in his face, was quick to supply the answer, telling the white Mganga all that had transpired at the time of the witch-doctor's visit.

'David Jamieson had been out in Africa long enough to appreciate the fact that there are plenty of things hidden away in dark corners about which the so-called "civilized world" knows very little; not the least of these being the power of primitive Black Magic. Also, he remembered now that his brother had first started to complain of his headache shortly after the incident with Darghud. Finally, of course, there was the drumming, which he recognized as being part of the ritual to propitiate injurious Black Magic! All in all, David Jamieson's knowledge was sufficient, at his earliest opportunity, to see him seated in a bark canoe between two trusted natives, skimming across Lake Ngami in what he hoped was the direction of the M'bulus' thorn- and marsh-bush bomas. He took with him some of a fresh supply of penicillin, just in from Livingstone.'

Crow paused again, frowning momentarily as he worked out the best way to relate the remainder of the story.

'Sorry to keep jumping about like this, Dawson, but I'm trying to tell the thing more or less chronologically. Let's see now – yes, we'd best go back to Maurice Jamieson in England.

'The doctor lived with his wife, Muriel, in a cottage just outside Brentwood where he had his practice; but within four days of his return it became plain that his recently contracted affliction was affecting his efficient control of that practice. The pounding headache – remarkably reminiscent in its sustained and regular *throb, throb, throb* of the drums across Lake Ngami – had worsened until its pain was so great it seemed to Jamieson that his head was slowly being crushed in a great vise. The next day he took to his bed, so terrible had the agony in his head become, and on the following morning he called in a fellow doctor to examine him. And yet, that same day, as mysteriously as it had waxed, Jamieson's headache waned and quickly disappeared. Altogether the thing had lasted two weeks.

'The next eight days passed uneventfully, and Maurice Jamieson had almost forgotten about the monstrous pains he had known in his head (which, I might add, he had been sure would be the death of him), when a heavily stamped parcel arrived airmail from Salisbury. The thing came with the morning mail, and Jamieson unwrapped it wonderingly to find a long, explanatory letter from his brother – and Darghud's doll.'

'A doll?' I cried, breaking in on Crow's narrative. 'Did you say Darghud's doll?'

'Yes, and I'll get on to that in a minute,' Crow continued, ignoring my rude outburst, 'but first a word about the parcel.

'Now that package was most odd; more like an entomologist's specimen-box than a parcel proper, with little ventilation holes – you know what I mean? And within the inner container, wrapped most carefully in cotton-wool and with only its head free, was the baked clay and straw doll; with slivers of blue glass for its eyes and with the top of its head painted red. I should mention here that Maurice Jamieson had red hair, and that his eyes were blue . . .

'The letter accompanying this *outré* object was no less extraordinary, explaining in detail all that David Jamieson had done since learning of his brother's confrontation with the witch-doctor. He had set out in his canoe three days after Maurice's departure, and it had taken him another three days to find the nomadic M'bulus; in the end the drums had led him to them. There in the marshlands he had treated the sick chief, bringing him back "miraculously" to renewed health in only a day or two. They're incredibly tough people, those marsh-dwellers.

'It was only then that the outpost doctor dared bring

up the question of Darghud and the devil-drums and what they meant. Shamefacedly, Notka told him that Darghud was "killing" the other white Mganga for refusing his request for help – but the chief was also quick to agree that the ritual could now be satisfactorily ended with no harm done. Darghud, disappointed and angry, was made to produce the doll – into the clay body of which he had ground the beetle containing the white Mganga's "aura" or essence – and also to call a halt to the drumming. Just how he had managed to "magic" the beetle out of the resin is something I don't suppose anyone will ever know.

'A cord had been twined about the doll's painted head, with two flat wooden discs the size of pennies attached at the temples. Every day Darghud had been turning the discs, tightening the cord, until eventually the head would have been quite squashed! Of course, Jamieson carefully removed the discs and cord immediately – and the point I make is this: *that at exactly the same time he freed the doll's head, five thousand miles away in England his brother's headache began to lift!*'

'Coincidence,' I said, feeling more than a little disappointed. It was, after all, a common enough tale.

'Coincidence? Perhaps – but there's more to come ...

'Of course, being a stoic sort of chap, Dr Maurice Jamieson came to the same conclusion as yourself, Dawson – nothing personal intended, you understand. He gave the doll to his wife and thought no more about it. Muriel, however, was an entirely different kettle of fish. She was a superstitious soul, and even if she did fancy that all this was just a bit too much like mumbo-jumbo – well, what harm in taking precautions?

'She'd got this idea right from the start, you see from the moment she saw Darghud's doll and learned the story behind it – for she simply didn't consider the little effigy of her husband to be *strong* enough! The doll was too frail; it wouldn't last a lifetime. And what if the thing really was, well, linked to Maurice in some way? What, she morbidly wondered, would be happening to her husband while Darghud's doll slowly disintegrated?

'Which was why, one night a short while later, she did what she did . . . And that was the end of that!' Crow snapped his fingers in sharp definition of finality.

I waited a moment and then said: 'Well, go on, Titus, finish it off. What did Muriel Jamieson do?'

Crow gazed at me a few seconds longer, sighed, and then continued: 'I thought you might have guessed it, Dawson . . .' He swirled the brandy round in the bottom of his glass.

'Well?' I prompted him.

He sighed again. 'Well, one hour after Muriel Jamieson attended to the doll, when she went to her husband's study with a cup of coffee, she found him dead at his desk. His face was blue, his eyes were bulging, and his tongue was lolling out.'

'Eh?' I jumped at his abrupt delivery, staring in unquiet fascination across the space between us. 'Dead? Like . . . that? But I thought you said that she was going to take some sort of precautionary measure? I don't follow you, Crow.'

Yet again my host sighed. 'I was hoping to spare myself the telling of the more unpleasant details,' he said.

'Well, come on, come on,' I was beginning to get impatient. 'How did he die? What was it all about?'

'You remember I told you how Jamieson's hobby was entomology, and how he used a type of quick-setting, artificial resin to—'

'My God!' I burst out, the horrible answer standing

out in my mind's eye with sudden, startling clarity.

'That's right,' Crow nodded his tawny head in grim affirmation. 'When Jamieson's doctor signed his death certificate, he said it was probably "a bug" Jamieson picked up in Africa – causing first the prolonged head-ache, then the fatal, terribly swift respiratory trouble ending in asphyxia. Funny that he should blame it on "a bug", eh?'

Crow paused, leaning over to top up my glass again before getting on with it. 'Quite naturally, Mrs Jamieson was a bit crazy for a good eighteen months after her husband's death – she more than half blamed herself, you see? And yet the final straw was not the doctor's death in itself. No, the thing that really put the cap on it all was what happened a few days *after* Jamieson died.'

'Eh? Something happened soon after his death?' I needlessly repeated the occultist's words.

'Yes,' he affirmed, quite matter-of-factly now that he had it almost all told. 'For it was then, in an agony of doubt and horror, that Muriel Jamieson took the doll in its resin coffin and burned it to ashes in the open-hearth fire in her living-room. The resin burned like celluloid. She figured "out of sight, out of mind", you know?

'And that evening, when the will was read, it was discovered that Maurice Jamieson had elected, in the event of his demise, *that the disposal of his body be carried out by cremation!*'

Somehow or other, I intend to use Crow's story!

# DE MARIGNY'S CLOCK

WAY BACK WHEN, before I was born, H. P. Lovecraft had written a story called **The Terrible Old Man**. The basic similarity between that tale and this present one didn't strike me until only very recently, but I suppose it's possible that I was subconsciously influenced sufficiently to write it 'after' H.P.L. Certainly the fate of the villains is . . . but that would be telling.

Something else in this story that you'll find in Lovecraft is that strange timepiece I call

**de Marigny's Clock.**

Any intrusions, other than those condoned or invited, upon the privacy of Titus Crow at his bungalow retreat, Blowne House, on the outskirts of London, were almost always automatically classified by that gentleman as open acts of warfare. In the first place for anyone to make it merely to the doors of Crow's abode without an invitation – often even *with* one – was a sure sign of the appearance on the scene of a forceful and dogmatic character; qualities which were almost guaranteed to clash with Crow's own odd nature. For Blowne House seemed to exude an atmosphere all its own, an exhalation of impending *something* which usually kept the place and its grounds free even from birds and mice; and it was quite unusual for Crow himself to invite visitors. He kept strange hours and busied himself with stranger matters and, frankly, was almost antisocial even in his most 'engaging' moments. Over the years the reasons for this apparent inhospitality had grown, or so it seemed to Crow, increasingly clear-cut. For one thing, his library contained quite a large number of rare and highly costly books, many of them long out of print and some of them never officially in print, and London apparently abounded with unscrupulous 'collectors' of such items. For another his studies, usually in occult matters and obscure archaeological, antiquarian or anthropological research, were such as required the most concentrated attention and personal involvement, completely precluding any disturbances from outside sources.

Not that the present infringement came while Crow was engaged with any of his many and varied activities – it did not; it came in the middle of the night, rousing him from deep and dreamless slumbers engendered by a long day of frustrated and unrewarding work on de Marigny's clock. And Titus Crow was not amused.

'What the hell's going on here? Who are you and what are you doing in my house?' He had sat bolt upright in bed almost as soon as the light went on. His forehead had come straight into contact with a wicked-looking automatic held in the fist of a most unbeautiful thug. The man was about five feet eight inches in height, thickset, steady on legs which were short in comparison with the rest of his frame. He had a small scar over his left eye and a mouth that slanted downward – cynically, Crow supposed – from left to right. Most unbeautiful.

'Just take it easy, guv', and there'll be no bother,' the thug said, his voice soft but ugly. Crow's eyes flicked across the room to where a second hoodlum stood, just within the bedroom door, a nervous grin twisting his pallid features. 'Find anything, Pasty?' the man with the pistol questioned, his eyes never leaving Crow's face for a second.

'Nothing, Joe,' came the answer, 'a few old books and a bit of silver, nothing worth our while – yet. He'll tell us where it is, though, won't you, chum?'

'Pasty!' Crow exclaimed. 'Powers of observation, indeed! I was just thinking, before hearing your name, what a thin, pasty creature you look – Pasty.' Crow grinned, got out of bed and put on his flame-red dressing-gown. Joe looked him up and down appraisingly. Crow

210

was tall and broad-shouldered and it was plain to see that in his younger days he had been a handsome man. Even now there was a certain tawniness about him, and his eyes were still very bright and more than intelligent. Overall his aspect conveyed an impression of hidden power, which Joe did not particularly care much for. He decided it would be best to show his authority at the earliest opportunity. And Crow obligingly supplied him with that opportunity in the next few seconds.

The jibe the occultist had aimed at Pasty had meanwhile found its way home. Pasty's retaliation was a threat: 'Lovely colour, that dressing-gown,' he said, 'it'll match up nicely if you bleed when I rap you on your head.' He laughed harshly, slapping a metal cosh into his open palm. 'But before that, you will tell us where it is, won't you?'

'Surely,' Crow answered immediately, 'it's third on the left, down the passage . . . *ugh!*' Joe's pistol smacked into Crow's cheek, knocking him sprawling. He carefully got up, gingerly fingering the red welt on his face.

'Now that's just to show you that we don't want any more funnies, see?' Joe said.

'Yes, I see,' Crow's voice trembled with suppressed rage. 'Just what do you want?'

'Now is that so difficult to figure out?' Pasty asked, crossing the room. 'Money . . . we want your money! A fine fellow like you, with a place like this–' the lean man glanced appraisingly about the room, noting the silk curtains, the boukhara rugs, the original erotic illustrations by Aubrey Beardsley in their rosewood frames – 'ought to have a good bit of ready cash lying about . . . we want it!'

'Then I'm sorry to have to disappoint you,' Crow told him happily, seating himself on his bed, 'I keep my money in a bank – what little I've got.'

'Up!' ordered Joe briefly. 'Off the bed.' He pulled Crow to one side, nodding to Pasty, indicating some sort of action involving the bed. Crow stepped forward as Pasty yanked back the covers from the mattress and took out a sharp knife.

'Now wait . . .' he began, thoroughly alarmed.

'Hold it, guv', or I might just let Pasty use his blade on you!' Joe waved his gun in Crow's face, ordering him back. 'You see, you'd be far better off to tell us where the money is without all this trouble. This way you're just going to see your little nest wrecked around you.' He waited, giving Crow the opportunity to speak up, then indicated to Pasty that he should go ahead.

Pasty went ahead!

He ripped open the mattress along both sides and one end, tearing back the soft outer covering to expose the stuffing and springs beneath, then pulling out the interior in great handfuls, flinging them down on the floor in total disregard of Crow's utter astonishment and concern.

'See, guv', you're a recluse – in our books, anyway – and retiring sorts like you hide their pennies in the funniest places. Like in mattresses. . . or behind wall-pictures!' Joe gave Pasty a nod, waving his pistol at the Beardsleys.

'Well for God's sake, just *look* behind them,' Crow snarled, again starting forward. 'There's no need to rip them off the walls.'

'Here!' Pasty exclaimed, turning an enquiring eye on the outraged householder, 'these pictures worth anything then?'

'Only to a collector – you'd never find a fence for stuff like that,' Crow replied.

'Hah! Not so stupid, our recluse!' Joe grinned, 'But

being clever won't get you anywhere, guv', except
hospital maybe ... Okay, Pasty, leave the man's dirty
pictures alone. You–' He turned to Crow, ' – your study;
we've been in there, but only passing through. Let's go,
guv'; you can give us a hand to, er, shift things about.'
He pushed Crow in the direction of the door.

Pasty was last to enter the study. He did so shivering,
an odd look crossing his face. Pasty did not know it but
he was a singularly rare person, one of the world's few
truly 'psychic' men. Crow was another – one who had
the *talent* to a high degree – and he sensed Pasty's sudden
feeling of apprehension.

'Snug little room, isn't it?' he asked, grinning cheerfully at the uneasy thug.

'Never mind how pretty the place is – try the
panelling, Pasty,' Joe directed.

'Eh?' Pasty's mind obviously was not on the job. 'The
panelling?' His eyes shifted nervously round the room.

'Yes, the panelling!' Joe studied his partner curiously.
'What's wrong with you, then?' His look of puzzlement
turned to one of anger. 'Now come on, Pasty boy, get a
grip! At this rate we'll be here all bleeding night!'

Now it happened that Titus Crow's study was the
pride of his life, and the thought of the utter havoc his
unwelcome visitors could wreak in there was a terrifying
thing to him. He determined to help them in their
abortive search as much as he could; they would not find
anything – there was nothing to find! – but this way he
could at least ensure as little damage as possible before
they realized there was no money in the house and left.
They were certainly unwilling to believe anything he said
about the absence of substantive funds! But then again,
to anyone not knowing him reasonably well – and few
did – Crow's home and certain of its appointments might

certainly point to a man of considerable means. Yet he was merely comfortable, not wealthy, and, as he had said, what money he did have was safe in a bank. The more he helped them get through with their search the quicker they would leave. He had just made up his mind to this effect when Pasty found the hidden recess by the fireside.

'Here!' The nervous look left Pasty's face as he turned to Joe. 'Listen to this.' He rapped on a square panel. The sound was dull, hollow. Pasty swung his cosh back purposefully.

'No, wait – I'll open it for you.' Crow held up his hands in protest.

'Go on then, get it open.' Joe ordered. Crow moved over to the wall and expertly slid back the panel to reveal a dim shelf behind. On the shelf was a single book. Pasty pushed Crow aside, lifted out the book and read off its title:

'The . . . what? . . . *Cthaat Aquadingen!* Huh!' Then his expression quickly turned to one of pure disgust and loathing. '*Ughhh!*' He flung the book away from him across the room, hastily wiping his hands down his jacket. Titus Crow received a momentary but quite vivid mental message from the mind of the startled thug. It was a picture of things rotting in vaults of crawling darkness, and he could well understand why Pasty was suddenly trembling.

'That . . . that damn book's *wet!*' the shaken crook exclaimed nervously.

'No, just sweating!' Crow informed. 'The binding is, er, human skin, you see. Somehow it still retains the ability to sweat – a sure sign that it's going to rain.'

'Claptrap!' Joe snapped. 'And you get a grip of yourself,' he snarled at Pasty. 'There's something about this place I don't like either, but I'm not letting it get me down.' He turned to Crow, his mouth strained and twisting in anger: 'And from now on you speak when you're spoken to.' Then carefully, practicedly, he turned his head and slowly scanned the room, taking in the tall bookshelves with their many volumes, some ancient, others relatively modern, and he glanced at Pasty and grinned knowingly. 'Pasty,' Joe ordered, 'get them books off the shelves – I want to see what's behind them. How about it, recluse, you got anything behind there?'

'Nothing, nothing at all,' Crow quickly answered. 'For goodness sake don't go pulling them down; some of them are coming to pieces as it is. *No!*'

His last cry was one of pure protestation; horror at the defilement of his collection. The two thugs ignored him. Pasty, seemingly over his nervousness, happily went to work, scattering the books left, right and centre. Down came the collected works of Edgar Allan Poe, the first rare editions of Machen's and Lovecraft's fiction; then the more ancient works, of Josephus, Magnus, Levi, Borellus, Erdschluss and Wittingby; closely followed by a connected set on oceanic evil: Gaston Le Fe's *Dwellers in the Depths*, Oswald's *Legends of Liqualia*, Gantley's *Hydrophinnae*, the German *Unter-Zee Ku!ten* and Hartrack's *In Pressured Places* . . .

Crow could merely stand and watch it all, a black rage growing in his heart; and Joe, not entirely insensitive to the occultist's mood, gripped his pistol a little tighter and unsmilingly cautioned him: 'Just take it easy, hermit. There's still time to speak up – just tell us where you hide your money and it's all over. No? Okay, what's next?' His eyes swept the now littered room again, coming to rest in a dimly lighted corner where stood a great clock.

In front of the clock – an instrument apparently of the

'grandfather' class; at least, from a distance of that appearance – stood a small occasional table bearing an adjustable reading-lamp, one or two books and a few scattered sheets of notepaper. Seeing the direction in which Joe's actions were leading him, Crow smiled inwardly and wished his criminal visitor all the best. If Joe could make anything of that timepiece, then he was a cleverer man than Titus Crow; and if he could actually *open* it, as is possible and perfectly normal with more orthodox clocks, then Crow would be eternally grateful to him. For the sarcophagus-like thing in the dim corner was that same instrument with which Crow had busied himself all the previous day and on many, many other days since first he purchased it more than ten years earlier. And none of his studies had done him a bit of good! He was still as unenlightened with regard to the clock's purpose as he had been a decade ago.

Allegedly the thing had belonged to one Etienne-Laurent de Marigny, once a distinguished student of occult and oriental mysteries and antiquities, but where de Marigny had come by the coffin-shaped clock was yet another mystery. Crow had purchased it on the assurance of its auctioneer that it was, indeed, that same timepiece mentioned in certain of de Marigny's papers as being 'a door on all space and time; one which only certain adepts – not all of this world – could use to its intended purpose!' There were, too, rumours that a certain Eastern mystic, the Swami Chandraputra, had vanished forever from the face of the Earth after squeezing himself into a cavity hidden beneath the panel of the lower part of the clock's coffin shape. Also, de Marigny had supposedly had the ability to open at will that door into which the Swami vanished – but that was a secret he had taken with him to the grave. Titus Crow had never been able to find even a keyhole; and while the clock weighed what it should for its size, yet when one rapped on the lower panel the sound such rappings produced were not hollow as might be expected. A curious fact – a curious history altogether – but the clock itself was even more curious to gaze upon or listen to.

Even now Joe was doing just those things: looking at and listening to the clock. He had switched on and adjusted the reading-lamp so that its light fell upon the face of the peculiar mechanism. At first sight of that clock-face Pasty had gone an even paler shade of grey, with all his nervousness of a few minutes earlier instantly returned. Crow sensed his perturbation; he had had similar feelings while working on the great clock, but he had also had the advantage of understanding where such fears originated. Pasty was experiencing the same sensations he himself had known when first he saw the clock in the auction rooms. Again he gazed at it as he had then; his eyes following the flow of the weird hieroglyphs carved about the dial and the odd move-ments of the four hands, movements coinciding with no chronological system of earthly origin; and for a moment there reigned an awful silence in the study of Titus Crow. Only the strange clock's enigmatic and oddly paced ticking disturbed a quiet which otherwise might have been that of the tomb.

'That's no clock like any I've ever seen before!' exclaimed an awed Joe. 'What do you make of *that*, Pasty?'

Pasty gulped, his Adam's apple visibly bobbing. 'I . . . I don't like it! It . . . it's shaped like a damned *coffin!* And why has it four hands, and how come they move like that?' He stopped to compose himself a little, and with the cessation of his voice came a soft whispering from beyond the curtained windows. Pasty's eyes widened and his face went white as death. '*What's that*?' His whisper was as soft as the sounds prompting it.

'For God's sake get a grip, will you?' Joe roared, shattering the quiet. He was completely oblivious to Pasty's psychic abilities. 'It's rain, that's what it is – what did you bleeding think it was, spooks? I don't know what's come over you, Pasty, damned if I do. You act as if the place was haunted or something.'

'Oh, but it is!' Crow spoke up. 'At least the garden is. A very unusual story, if you'd care to hear it.'

'We don't care to hear it,' Joe snarled. 'And I warned you before – speak when you're spoken to. Now, this . . . *clock!* Get it open, quick.'

Crow had to hold himself to stop the ironic laughter he felt welling inside. 'I can't,' he answered, barely concealing a chuckle. 'I don't know how!'

'You what?' Joe shouted incredulously. 'You don't know how? What the hell d'you mean?'

'I mean what I say,' Crow answered. 'So far as I know that clock's not been opened for well over thirty years!'

'Yes? S . . . so where does it p . . . plug in?' Pasty enquired, stuttering over the words.

'Should it plug in?' Crow answered with his own question. Joe, however, saw just what Pasty was getting at; as, of course, had the 'innocent' Titus Crow.

'Should it plug in, he asks!' Joe mimed sarcastically. He turned to Pasty. 'Good point, Pasty boy – now,' he turned back to Crow, menacingly, 'tell us something, recluse. If your little toy here isn't electric, and if you can't get it open – *then just how do you wind it up*?'

'I don't wind it up – I know nothing whatsoever of the mechanical principles governing it,' Crow answered. 'You see that book there on the occasional table? Well, that's Walmsley's *Notes on Deciphering Codes, Cryptograms and Ancient Inscriptions*; I've been trying for years merely to understand the hieroglyphs on the dial, let alone *open* the thing. And several notable gentlemen students of matters concerning things not usually apparent or open to the man in the street have opinionated to the effect that yonder *device* is not a clock at all! I refer to Etienne-Laurent de Marigny, the occultist Ward Phillips of Rhode Island in America, and Professor Gordon Walmsley of Goole in Yorkshire; all of them believe it to be a space-time machine – *believed* in the case of the first two mentioned, both those gentlemen now being dead – and I don't know enough about it yet to decide whether or not I agree with them! There's no money in it, if that's what you're thinking.'

'Well, I warned you, guv',' Joe snarled, 'space-time machine! – My God! – H. G. bloody Wells, he thinks he is! Pasty, tie him up and gag him. I'm sick of his bleeding claptrap. He's got us nervous as a couple of cats, he has!'

'I'll say no more,' Crow quickly promised, 'you carry on. If you can get it open I'll be obliged to you; I'd like to know what's inside myself.'

'Come off it, guv',' Joe grated, then: 'Okay, but one more word – you end up immobile, right?' Crow nodded his acquiescence and sat on the edge of his great desk to watch the performance. He really did not expect the thugs to do much more than make fools of themselves. He had not taken into account the possibility – the probability – of violence in the solution of the problem. Joe, as a child, had never had much time for the two-penny wire puzzles sold in the novelty shops. He tried them once or twice, to be sure, but if they would not go first time – well, you could usually *make* them go – with a hammer! As it happened such violence was not necessary.

Pasty had backed up to the door. He was still slapping his cosh into his palm, but it was purely a reflex action now; a nervous reflex action. Crow got the impression that if Pasty dropped his cosh he would probably faint.

'The panels, Pasty,' Joe ordered. 'The panels in the clock.'

'You do it,' Pasty answered rebelliously. 'That's no clock and I'm not touching it. There's something wrong here.'

Joe turned to him in exasperation. 'Are you crazy or something? It's a clock and nothing more! And this joker just doesn't want us to see inside. Now what does that suggest to you?'

'Okay, okay – but you do it this time. I'll stay out of the way and watch funnyman here. I've got a feeling about that thing, that's all.' He moved over to stand near Crow who had not moved from his desk. Joe took his gun by the barrel and rapped gently on the panel below the dial of the clock at about waist height. The sound was sharp, solid. Joe turned and grinned at Titus Crow. There certainly seemed to be *something* in there. His grin rapidly faded when he saw Crow grinning back. He turned again to the object of his scrutiny and examined its sides, looking for hinges or other signs pointing to the thing being a hollow container of sorts. Crow could see from the crook's puzzled expression that he was immediately at a loss. He could have told Joe before he began that there was not even evidence of jointing; it was as if the body of the instrument was carved from a solid block of timber – timber as hard as iron.

But Crow had underestimated the determined thug. Whatever Joe's shortcomings as a human being, as a safe-cracker he knew no peer. Not that de Marigny's clock was in any way a safe, but apparently the same principles applied! For as Joe's hands moved expertly up the sides of the panelling there came a loud click and the mad ticking of the instrument's mechanism went totally out of kilter. The four hands on the carven dial stood still for an instant of time before commencing fresh movements in alien and completely inexplicable sequences. Joe stepped nimbly back as the large panel swung silently open. He stepped just a few inches too far back, jolting the occasional table. The reading-lamp went over with a crash, momentarily breaking the spell of the wildly oscillating hands and crazy ticking of de Marigny's clock. The corner was once more thrown in shadow and for a moment Joe stood there undecided, put off stroke by his early success. Then he gave a grunt of triumph, stepped forward and thrust his empty left hand into the darkness behind the open panel.

Pasty sensed the *outsideness* at the same time as Crow. He leapt across the room shouting: 'Joe, Joe – for God's sake, leave it alone . . . *leave it alone!*' Crow, on the other hand, spurred by no such sense of comradeship, quickly stood up and backed away. It was not that he was in any way a coward, but he knew something of Earth's darker mysteries – and of the mysteries of other spheres – and besides, he sensed the danger of interfering with an action having origin far from the known side of nature.

Suddenly the corner was dimly illumined by an eerie, dappled light from the open panel; and Joe, his arm still groping beyond that door, gave a yell of utter terror and tried to pull back. The ticking was now insanely aberrant, and the wild sweeps of the four hands about the dial were completely confused and orderless. Joe had braced himself against the frame of the opening, fighting some unseen menace within the strangely lit compartment, trying desperately to withdraw his arm. Against all his effort his left shoulder abruptly jammed forward, into the swirling light, and at the same moment he stuck the barrel of his gun into the opening and fired six shots in rapid succession.

By this time Pasty had an arm round Joe's waist, one foot braced against the base of the clock, putting all his strength into an attempt to haul his companion away from whatever threatened in the swirling light of the now fearsome opening. He was fighting a losing battle. Joe was speechless with terror, all his energies concentrated on escape from the clock; great veins stuck out from his neck and his eyes seemed likely at any moment to pop from his head. He gave one bubbling scream as his head and neck jerked suddenly forward into the maw of the mechanical horror . . . and then his body went limp.

Pasty, still wildly struggling with Joe's lower body, gave a last titanic heave at that now motionless torso and actually managed to retrieve for a moment Joe's head from the weirdly lit door.

Simultaneously Pasty and Titus Crow saw something – something that turned Pasty's muscles to water, causing him to relax his struggle so that Joe's entire body bar the legs vanished with a horrible *hisss* into the clock – something that caused Crow to throw up his hands before his eyes in the utmost horror!

In the brief second or so that Pasty's efforts had partly freed the sagging form of his companion in crime, the fruits of Joe's impulsiveness had made themselves hideously apparent. The cloth of his jacket near the left shoulder and that same area of the shirt immediately beneath had been *removed*, seemingly *dissolved* or burnt away by some unknown agent; and in place of the flesh which should by all rights have been laid bare by this mysterious vanishment, *there had been a great blistered,*

*bubbling blotch of crimson and brown – and the neck and head*
*had been in the same sickening state!*

Surprisingly, Pasty recovered first from the shock. He
made one last desperate, fatal, grab at Joe's disappearing
legs – and the fingers of his right hand crossed the
threshold of the opening into the throbbing light beyond.
Being in a crouching position and considerably thinner
than his now completely vanished friend, Pasty did not
stand a chance. Simultaneous with Crow's cry, of horror
and warning combined, he gave a sobbing shriek and
seemed simply to dive headlong into the leering entrance.

Had there been an observer what happened next
might have seemed something of an anticlimax. Titus
Crow, as if in response to some agony beyond enduring,
clapped his hands to his head and fell writhing to the
floor. There he stayed, legs threshing wildly for some
three seconds, before his body relaxed as the terror of his
experience drove his mind to seek refuge in oblivion.

Shortly thereafter, of its own accord, the panel in the
clock swung smoothly back into place and clicked shut;
the four hands steadied to their previous, not quite so
deranged motions, and the ticking of the hidden
mechanism slowed and altered its rhythm from the
monstrous to the merely abnormal . . .

Titus Crow's first reaction on waking was to believe
himself the victim of a particularly horrible nightmare;
but then he felt the carpet against his cheek and, opening
his eyes, saw the scattered books littering the floor.
Shakily he made himself a large jug of coffee and poured
himself a huge brandy, then sat, alternately sipping at
both until there was none of either left. And when both
the jug and the glass were empty he started all over
again.

It goes without saying that Crow went nowhere near de Marigny's clock! For the moment, at least, his thirst for knowledge in *that* direction was slaked.

As far as possible he also kept from thinking back on the horrors of the previous night; particularly he wished to forget the hellish, psychic impressions received as Pasty went into the clock. For it appeared that de Marigny, Phillips and Walmsley had been right! The clock was, in fact, a space-time machine of sorts. Crow did not know *exactly* what had caused the hideous shock to his highly developed psychic sense; but in fact, even as he had felt that shock and clapped his hands to his head, somewhere out in the worlds of Aldebaran, at a junction of forces neither spatial, temporal, nor of any intermediate dimension recognized by man except in the wildest theories, the Lake of Hali sent up a few streamers of froth and fell quickly back into silence.

And Titus Crow was left with only the memory of the feel of unknown acids burning, of the wash of strange tides outside nature, and of the rushing and tearing of great beasts designed in a fashion beyond man's wildest conjecturing . . .

# NAME AND NUMBER

THIS PENULTIMATE TALE sprang from a personal interest in numerology, cryptography, and biblical prophecy. So many stories had been written about the antichrist, and I wanted to do it differently. Later, after Francesco Cova had published it in **Kadath**, his superb semi-professional magazine, he wanted to know how I'd worked it out. I told him I hadn't, that Titus Crow must take the credit himself.

Flippant? – you could say that – but it really is difficult to say how this one 'worked itself out'. It's one of those peculiar tales that has to be written backwards. Who was it said: 'You can prove anything with numbers'? And who, for that matter, asked, 'What's in a name?'

So here's Titus Crow posing a problem. Now put yourself in de Marigny's shoes and see how you make out. The clues are all there. Hey! – and no cheating!

# I

Of course, nothing now remains of Blowne House, the sprawling bungalow retreat of my dear friend and mentor Titus Crow, destroyed by tempestuous winds in a 'freak storm' on the night of 4 October 1968, but . . .

Knowing all I know, or knew, of Titus Crow, perhaps it has been too easy for me to pass off the disastrous events of that night simply as a vindictive attack of dark forces; and while that is exactly what they were, I am now given to wonder if perhaps there was not a lot more to it than met the eye.

Provoked by Crow's and my own involvement with the Wilmarth Foundation (that vast, august and amazingly covert body, dedicated to the detection and the destruction of Earth's elder evil, within and outside of Man himself, and working in the sure knowledge that Man is but a small and comparatively recent phe-nomenon in a cosmos which has known sentience, good and evil, through vast and immeasurable cycles of time), dark forces did indeed destroy Blowne House. In so doing they effectively removed Titus Crow from the scene, and as for myself . . . I am but recently returned to it.

But since visiting the ruins of Crow's old place all these later years (perhaps because the time flown in between means so very little to me?), I have come to wonder more and more about the *nature* of that so well-remembered attack, the nature of the very winds themselves – those twisting, rending, tearing winds – which fell with such intent and purpose upon the house and bore it to the ground. In considering them I find myself casting my mind back to a time even more remote, when Crow first outlined for me the facts in the strange case of Mr Sturm Magruser V.

Crow's letter – a single handwritten sheet in a blank, sealed envelope, delivered by a taxi-driver and the ink not quite dry – was at once terse and cryptic, which was not unusual and did not at all surprise me. When Titus Crow was idling, then all who wished anything to do with him must also bide their time, but when he was in a hurry –

*Henri,*
(said the note)
  *Come as soon as you can, midnight would be fine. I expect you will stay the night. If you have not eaten, don't – there is food here. I have something of a story to tell you, and in the morning we are to visit a cemetery!*
                                              *Until I see you –*
                                                      (signed)
                                                        *Titus.*

The trouble with such invitations was this: I had never been able to refuse them! For Crow being what he was, one of London's foremost occultists, and my own interest in such matters amounting almost to obsession – why, for all its brevity, indeed by the very virtue of that brevity – Crow's summons was more a Royal Command!

And so I refrained from eating, wrote a number of letters which could not wait, enveloped and stamped them, and left a note for my housekeeper, Mrs Adams, telling her to post them. She was to expect me when she saw me, but in any matter of urgency I might be contacted at Blowne House. Doubtless the dear lady, when she read that address, would complain bitterly to herself about the influence of 'that dreadful Crow person', for in her eyes Titus had always been to blame for my own deep interest in darkling matters. In all truth, however, my obsession was probably inherited, sealed into my personality as a permanent stamp of my father, the great New Orleans mystic Etienne-Laurent de Marigny.

Then, since the hour already approached twelve and I would be late for my 'appointment', I 'phoned for a taxi and double-checked that my one or two antique treasures were safely locked away; and finally I donned my overcoat. Half an hour or so later, at perhaps a quarter to one, I stood on Crow's doorstep and banged upon his heavy oak door; and having heard the arrival of my taxi, he was there at once to greet me. This he did with his customary grin (or enigmatic smile?), his head cocked slightly to one side in an almost inquiring posture. And once again I was ushered into the marvellous Aladdin's Cave which was Blowne House.

Now Crow had been my friend ever since my father sent me out of America as a child in the late thirties, and no man knew him better than I; and yet his personality was such that whenever I met him – however short the intervening time – I would always be impressed anew by his stature, his leonine good looks, and the sheer

weight of intellect which seemed invariably to shine out
from behind those searching, dark eyes of his. In his
flame-red, wide-sleeved dressing-gown, he might easily
be some wizard from the pages of myth or fantasy.

In his study he took my overcoat, bade me sit in an
easy chair beside a glowing fire, tossed a small log onto
ruddy embers and poured me a customary brandy before
seating himself close by. And while he was thus engaged
I took my chance to gaze with fascination and unfeigned
envy all about that marvellous room.

Crow himself had designed and furnished that large
room to contain most of what he considered important
to his world, and certainly I could have spent ten full
years there in constant study of the contents without
absorbing or even understanding a fifth part of what I
read or examined. However, to give a brief and
essentially fleshless account of what I could see from my
chair:

His 'Library,' consisting of one entire wall of shelves,
contained such works as the abhorrent *Cthaat Aquadingen*
(in a binding of human skin!), Feery's *Original Notes on
the Necronomicon* (the complete book, as opposed to my
own abridged copy), Wendy-Smith's translation of the
*G'harne Fragments*, a possibly faked but still priceless
copy of the *Pnakotic Manuscripts*, Justin Geoffrey's *People
of the Monolith*, a literally fabulous *Cultes des Goules*
(which, on my next birthday, having derived all he could
from it, he would present to me), the *Geph Transcriptions*,
Wardle's *Notes on Nitocris*, Urbicus' *Frontier Garrison*,
circa AD 183, Plato on *Atlantis*, a rare, illustrated, pirated
and privately printed *Complete Works of Poe* in three
sumptuous volumes, the far more ancient works of such
as Josephus, Magnus, Levi and Erdschluss, and a connected set of volumes on oceanic lore and legend which

included such works as Gantley's *Hydrophinnae* and Konrad von Gerner's *Fischbuch* of 1598. And I have merely skimmed the surface . . .

In one dim corner stood an object which had been a source of fascination for me, and no less for Crow himself: a great hieroglyphed, coffin-shaped monstrosity of a grandfather clock, whose *tick* was quite irregular and abnormal, and whose four hands moved independently and without recourse to any time-system with which I was remotely familiar. Crow had bought the thing in auction some years previously, at which time he had mentioned his belief that it had once belonged to my father – of which I had known nothing, not at that time.

As for the general decor and feel of the place:

Silk curtains were drawn across wide windows; costly boukhara rugs were spread on a floor already covered in fine axminister; a good many Aubrey Beardsley originals – some of them most erotic – hung on the walls in equally valuable antique rosewood frames; and all in all the room seemed to exude a curiously mixed atmosphere of rich, warm, Olde Worlde gentility on the one hand, a strange and alien chill of outer spheres on the other.

And thus I hope I have managed to convey something of the nature of Titus Crow and of his study – and of his *studies* – in that bungalow dwelling on Leonard's Heath known as Blowne House . . . As to why I was there –

'I suppose you're wondering,' Crow said after a while, 'just why I asked you to come? And at such an hour on such a chilly night, when doubtless you've a good many other things you should be doing? Well, I'll not keep you in suspense – but first of all I would greatly appreciate your opinion of something.' He got up, crossed to his desk and returned with a thick book of newspaper cuttings, opening it to a previously marked page. Most of the cuttings were browned and faded, but the one Crow pointed out to me was only a few weeks old. It was a photograph of the head and shoulders of a man, accompanied by the following legend:

Mr Sturm Magruser, head of 'Magruser Systems UK,' the weapons manufacturing company of world repute, is on the point of winning for his company a £2,000,000 order from the Ministry of Defence in respect of an at present 'secret' national defence system. Mr Magruser, who himself devised and is developing the new system, would not comment when he was snapped by our reporter leaving the country home of a senior Ministry of Defence official, but it has been rumoured for some time that his company is close to a break-through on a defence system which will effectively make the atom bomb entirely obsolete. Tests are said to be scheduled for the near future, following which the Ministry of Defence is expected to make its final decision . . .

'Well?' Crow asked as I read the column again.

I shrugged. 'What are you getting at?'

'It makes no impression?'

'I've heard of him and his company, of course,' I answered, 'though I believe this is the first time I've actually seen a picture of him – but apart from—'

'Ah!' Crow cut in. 'Good! This is the first time you've seen his picture: and him a prominent figure and his firm constantly in the news and so on. Me too.'

'Oh?' I was still puzzled.

'Yes, it's important, Henri, what you just said. In fact, I would hazard a guess that Mr Magruser is one of the world's least photographed men.'

'So? Perhaps he's camera shy.'

'Oh, he is, he is – and for a very good reason. We'll get to it – eventually. Meanwhile, let's eat!'

Now this is a facet of Crow's personality which did annoy me: his penchant for leaping from one subject to another, willy-nilly, with never a word of explanation, leaving one constantly stumbling in the dark. He could only do it, of course, when he knew that his audience was properly hooked. But in my case I do not expect he intended any torment; he merely offered me the opportunity to use my mind. This I seized upon, while he busied himself bringing out cold cuts of fried chicken from his kitchen.

## II

Sturm Magruser... A strange name, really. Foreign, of course. Hungarian, perhaps? As the 'Mag' in 'Magyar'? I doubted it, even though his features were decidedly eastern or middle-eastern; for they were rather pale, too. And what of his first name, Sturm? If only I were a little more proficient in tongues, I might make something of it. And what of the man's reticence, and of Crow's comment that he stood amongst the least photographed of men?

We finished eating. 'What do you make of the "V" after his name?' Crow asked.

'Hmm? Oh, it's a common enough vogue nowadays,' I answered, 'particularly in America. It denotes that he's the fifth of his line, the fifth Sturm Magruser.'

Crow nodded and frowned. 'You'd think so, wouldn't

you? But in this case it can't possibly be. No, for he changed his name by deed-poll after his parents died.' He had grown suddenly intense, but before I could ask him why, he was off again. 'And what would you give him for nationality, or rather origin?'

I took a stab at it. 'Romanian?'

He shook his head. 'Persian.'

I smiled. 'I was way out, wasn't I?'

'What about his face?' Crow pressed.

I picked up the book of cuttings and looked at the photograph again. 'It's a strange face, really. Pale somehow. . .'

'He's an albino.'

'Ah!' I said. 'Yes, pale and startled – at least in this picture – displeased at being snapped, I suppose.'

Again he nodded. 'You suppose correctly. . . All right, Henri, enough of that for the moment. Now I'll tell you what I made of this cutting – Magruser's picture and the story when first I saw it. Now as you know I collect all sorts of cuttings from one source or another, tidbits of fact and fragments of information which interest me or strike me as unusual. Most occultists, I'm told, are extensive collectors of all sorts of things. You yourself are fond of antiques, old books and *outré bric-à-brac*; much as I am, but as yet without my dedication. And yet if you examine all of my scrapbooks you'll probably discover that this would appear to be the most mundane cutting of them all. At least on the surface. For myself, I found it the most frightening and disturbing.'

He paused to pour more brandy and I leaned closer to him, fascinated to find out exactly what he was getting at. 'Now,' he finally continued, 'I'm an odd sort of chap, as you'll appreciate, but I'm not eccentric – not in the popular sense of the word. Or if I am,' he hurried on, 'it's of my choosing. That is to say, I believe I'm mentally stable.'

'You are the sanest man I ever met,' I told him.

'I wouldn't go that far,' he answered, 'and you may soon have reason for re-evaluation, but for the moment I *am* sane. How then might I explain the loathing, the morbid repulsion, the absolute shock of horror which struck me almost physically upon opening the pages of my morning newspaper and coming upon that picture of Magruser? I could not explain it – not immediately...' He paused again.

'Presentiment?' I asked. 'A forewarning?'

'Certainly!' he answered. 'But of what, and from where? And the more I looked at that damned picture, the more sure I became that I was onto something monstrous! Seeing him – that face, startled, angered, trapped by the camera – and despite the fact that I could not possibly know him, I *recognized* him.'

'Ah!' I said. 'You mean that you've known him before, under his former name?'

Crow smiled, a trifle wearily I thought. 'The world has known him before under several names,' he answered. Then the smile slipped from his face. 'Talking of names, what do you make of his forename?'

'Sturm? I've already considered it. German, perhaps?'

'Good! Yes, German. His mother was German, his father Persian, both nationalized Americans in the early 1900s. They left America to come here during McCarthy's Unamerican Activities witch-hunts. Sturm Magruser, incidentally, was born on 1 April 1921. An important date, Henri, and not just because it was April Fool's Day.'

'A fairly young man,' I answered, 'to have reached so powerful a position.'

'Indeed,' Crow nodded. 'He would have been forty-three in a month's time.'

'Would have been?' I was surprised by Crow's tone of finality. 'Is he dead then?'

'Mercifully, yes,' he answered, 'Magruser and his project with him! He died the day before yesterday, on 4 March 1964, also an important date. It was in yesterday's news, but I'm not surprised you missed it. He wasn't given a lot of space, and he leaves no mourners that I know of. As to his "secret weapon",' (and here Crow gave an involuntary little shudder), 'the secret has gone with him. For that, too, we may be thankful.'

'Then the cemetery you mentioned in your note is where he's to be interred?' I guessed.

'Where he's to be cremated,' he corrected me. 'Where his ashes are to be scattered to the winds.'

'Winds!' I snapped my fingers. 'Now I have it! "Sturm" means "storm" – it's the German word for storm!'

Crow nodded. 'Again correct,' he said. 'But let's not start to add things up too quickly.'

'Add things up?' I snorted. 'My friend, I'm completely lost!'

'Not completely,' he denied. 'What you have is a jigsaw puzzle without a picture to work from. Difficult, but once you have completed the frame the rest will slowly piece itself together. Now then, I was telling you about the time three weeks ago when I saw Magruser's picture.

'I remember I was just up, still in my dressing-gown, and I had just brought the paper in here to read. The curtains were open and I could see out into the garden. It was quite cold but relatively mild for the time of the year. The morning was dry and the heath seemed to beckon me, so that I made up my mind to take a walk.

After reading the day's news and after breakfast, I would dress and take a stroll outdoors. Then I opened my newspaper – and Sturm Magruser's face greeted me!

'Henri, I dropped the paper as if it were a hot iron! So shaken was I that I had to sit down or risk falling. Now I'm a fairly sturdy chap, and you can well imagine the sort of shock my system would require so to disturb it. Then as I sat down in my chair and stooped to recover the newspaper – the other thing.

'Out in the garden, a sudden stirring of wind. The hedgerow trembling and last year's leaves blowing across my drive. And birds startled to flight, as by the sudden presence of someone or thing I could not see. And the sudden gathering and rushing of spiralling winds, dust-devils that sucked up leaves and grit and other bits of debris and shot them aloft. Dust-devils, Henri, in March – in England – half-a-dozen of them that paraded all about Blowne House for the best part of thirty minutes! In any other circumstance, a marvellous, fascinating phenomenon.'

'But not for you?'

'No.' He shook his head. 'Not then. I'll tell you what they signified for me, Henri. They told me that just as I had recognized *something*, so I had been recognized! Do you understand?'

'Frankly, no,' and it was my turn to shake my head.

'Let it pass,' he said after a moment. 'Suffice it to say that there were these strange spiralling winds, and that I took them as a sign that indeed my psychic sense had detected something unutterably dangerous and obscene in this man Sturm Magruser. And I was so frightened by my discovery that I at once set about to discover all I could of him, so that I should know what the threat was and how best to deal with it.'

'Can I stop you for a moment?' I requested.

'Eh? Oh, certainly.'

'Those dates you mentioned as being important, Magruser's birth and death dates. In what way important?'

'Ah! We shall get to that, Henri,' he smiled. 'You may or may not know it, but I'm also something of a numerologist.'

Now it was my turn to smile. 'You mean like those fellows who measure the great pyramid and read in their findings the secrets of the universe?'

'Do not be flippant, de Marigny!' he answered at once, his smile disappearing in an instant. 'I meant no such thing. And in any case, don't be in too great a hurry to discredit the pyramidologists. Who are you to say what may or may not be? Until you have studied a thing for yourself, treat it with respect.'

'Oh!' was all I could say.

'As for birth and death dates, try these: 1889, 1945.'

I frowned, shrugged, said: 'They mean nothing to me. Are they, too, important?'

'They belong to Adolf Hitler,' he told me, 'and if you add the individual numbers together you'll discover that they make five sets of nine. Nine is an important number in occultism, signifying death. Hitler's number, 99999, shows him to have been a veritable Angel of Death, and no one could deny that! Incidentally, if you multiply five and nine you get forty-five, which are the last two numbers in 1945 – the year he died. This is merely one example of an ancient science. Now please, Henri, no more scoffing at numerology...'

Deflated, still I was beginning to see a glimmer of light in Crow's reasoning. 'Ah!' I said again. 'And Sturm Magruser, like Hitler, has dates which add up to forty-five? Am I right? Let me see: the 1st of the 4th 1921 – that's eighteen – and the 4th of the 3rd 1964. That's forty-five!'

Crow nodded, smiling again. 'You're a clever man, Henri, yes – but you've missed the most important aspect of the thing. But never mind that for now, let me get back to my story . . .

'I have said that I set about to discover all I could of this fellow with the strange name, the camera-shy manner, the weight of a vast international concern behind him – and the power to frighten the living daylights out of me, which no other man ever had before. And don't ask me how, but I knew I had to work fast. There wasn't a great deal of time left before . . . before whatever was coming came.

'First, however, I contacted a friend of mine at the British Museum, the Curator of the Special Books Department, and asked him to search something out for me in the *Necronomicon*. I must introduce you one day, Henri. He's a marvellous chap. Not quite all there, I fancy – he can't be to work in that place – but so free of vice and sin, so blindly naive and innocent, that the greatest possible evils would bounce right off him, I'm sure. Which is just as well, I suppose. Certainly I would never ask an inquiring or susceptible mind that it lay itself open to the perils of Alhazred's book.

'And at last I was able to concentrate on Magruser. This was about midday and my mind had been working frantically for several hours, so that already I was beginning to feel tired – mentally if not physically. I was also experiencing a singular emotion, a sort of morbid suspicion that I was being watched, and that the observer lurked somewhere in my garden!

'Putting this to the back of my mind, I began to make

discreet telephone inquiries about Magruser – but no sooner had I voiced his name than the feeling came over me again, more strongly than before. It was as if a cloud of unutterable malignity, heavy with evil, had settled suddenly over the entire house. And starting back from the telephone, I saw once again the shadow of a nodding dust-devil where it played with leaves and twigs in the centre of my drive.

## III

'Now my fear turned to anger. Very well, if it was war . . . then I must now employ weapons of my own. Or if not weapons, defences, certainly.

'I won't go into details, Henri, but you know the sort of thing I mean. I have long possessed the necessary knowledge to create barriers of a sort against evil influences; no occultist or student of such things worth his salt would ever be without them. But it had recently been my good fortune to obtain a certain – shall we call it "charm"? – allegedly efficacious above all others.

'As to how this "charm" happened my way:

'In December Thelred Gustau had arrived in London from Iceland, where he had been studying Surtsey's volcanic eruption. During that eruption, Gustau had fished from the sea an item of extreme antiquity – indeed, a veritable time-capsule from an age undreamed of. When he contacted me in mid-December, he was still in a high fever of excitement. He needed my skills, he said, to help him unravel a mystery "predating the very dinosaurs". His words.

'I worked with him until mid-January, when he

suddenly received an offer from America in respect of a lecture tour there. It was an offer he could not refuse – one which would finance his researches for several years to come – and so, off he went. By that time I had become so engrossed with the work I almost went with him. Fortunately I did not.' And here he paused to refill our glasses.

'Of course,' I took the opportunity to say, 'I knew you were extremely busy with something. You were so hard to contact, and then always at Gustau's Woolwich address. But what exactly were you working on?'

'Ah!' he answered. 'That is something which Thelred Gustau himself will have to reveal – which I expect he'll do shortly. Though who'll take him seriously, heaven only knows. As to what I may tell you of it – I'll have to have your word that it will be kept in the utmost secrecy.'

'You know you have it,' I answered.

'Very well . . . During the course of the eruption, Surtsey ejected a . . . a *container*, Henri, the "time-capsule" I have mentioned. Inside – fantastic!

'It was a record from a prehistoric world, Theem'hdra, a continent at the dawn of time, and it had been sent to us down all the ages by one of that continent's greatest magicians, the wizard Teh Atht, descendant of the mighty Mylakhrion. Alas, it was in the unknown language of that primal land, in Teh Atht's own hand, and Gustau had accidentally lost the means of its translation. But he did have a key, and he had his own great genius, and—'

'And he had you,' I smiled. 'One of the country's greatest paleographers.'

'Yes,' said Crow, matter-of-factly and without pride, 'second only to Professor Gordon Walmsley of Goole. Anyway, I helped Gustau where I could, and during the work I came across a powerful spell against injurious magic and other supernatural menaces. Gustau allowed me to make a copy for myself, which is how I came to be in possession of a fragment of elder magic from an age undreamed of. From what I could make of it, Theem'hdra had existed in an age of wizards, and Teh Atht himself had used this very charm or spell to ward off evil.

'Well, I had the thing, and now I decided to employ it. I set up the necessary paraphernalia and induced within myself the required mental state. This took until well into the afternoon, and with each passing minute the sensation of impending doom deepened about the house, until I was almost prepared to flee the place and let well alone. And, if I had not by now been certain that such flight would be a colossal desertion of duty, I admit I would have done so.

'As it was, when I had willed myself to the correct mental condition, and upon the utterance of certain words – the effect was instantaneous!

'Daylight seemed to flood the whole house; the gloom fled in a moment; my spirits soared, and outside in the garden a certain ethereal watchdog collapsed in a tiny heap of rubbish and dusty leaves. Teh Atht's rune had proved itself effective indeed . . .'

'And then you turned your attention to Sturm Magruser?' I prompted him after a moment or two.

'Not that night, no. I was exhausted, Henri. The day had taken so much out of me. No, I could do no more that night. Instead I slept, deeply and dreamlessly, right through the evening and night until the jangling of my telephone awakened me at 9 o'clock on the following morning.'

'Your friend at the Rare Books Department?' I guessed.

'Yes, enlisting my aid in narrowing down his field of research. As you'll appreciate, the *Necronomicon* is a large

volume – compared to which Feery's *Notes* is a pamphlet
– and many of its sections appear to be almost repetitious
in their content. The trouble was, I wasn't even certain
that it contained what I sought; only that I believed I had
read it there. If not–' and he waved an expansive hand in
the direction of his own more than appreciable occult
library, 'then the answer must be here somewhere –
whose searching out would form an equally frustrating
if not utterly impossible task. At least in the time
allowed.'

'You keep hinting at this urgency,' I frowned. 'What
do you mean, "the time allowed"?'

'Why,' he answered, 'the time in which Magruser must
be disposed of, of course!'

'Disposed of?' I could hardly believe my ears.

Crow sighed and brought it right out in the open: 'The
time in which I must kill him!' he said.

I tried to remain calm, tried not to seem too flippant
when I said, 'So, you had resolved to do away with him.
This was necessary?'

'Very. And once my enquiries began to produce results,
why, then his death became more urgent by the minute!
For over the next few days I turned up some very
interesting and very frightening facts about our Mr
Magruser, not the least of them concerning his phe-
nomenal rise from obscurity and the amount of power
he controlled here and abroad. His company extended
to no less than seven different countries, with a total of
ten plants or factories engaged in the manufacture of
weapons of war. Most of them conventional weapons –
for the moment. Ah, yes! And those numbers too, Henri,
are important.

'As for his current project – the completion of this
"secret" weapon or "defence system", in this I was to

discover the very root and nature of the evil, after which I was convinced in my decision that indeed Magruser must go!'

The time was now just after three in the morning and the fire had burned very low. While Crow took a break from talking and went to the kitchen to prepare a light snack, I threw logs on the fire and shivered, not merely because of the chill the night had brought. Such was Crow's story and his method of delivery that I myself was now caught up in its cryptic strangeness, the slowly strangling threads of its skein. Thus I paced the floor and pondered all he had told me, not least his stated intention to – murder? – Sturm Magruser, who now apparently was dead.

Passing Crow's desk I noticed an antique Family Bible in two great volumes, the New Testament lying open, but I did not check book or chapter. Also littering his desk were several books on cryptology, numerology, even one on astrology, in which 'science' Crow had never to my knowledge displayed a great deal of faith or interest. Much in evidence was a well-thumbed copy of Walmsley's *Notes on Deciphering Codes, Cryptograms and Ancient Inscriptions*, also an open notebook of obscure jottings and diagrams. My friend had indeed been busy.

Over cheese and crackers we carried on, and Crow took up his tale once more by hinting of the awesome power of Magruser's 'secret' weapon.

'Henri,' he began, 'there is a tiny island off the Orkneys which, until mid-1961, was green, lovely, and a sanctuary for sea birds. Too small and isolated to settle, and far too cold and open to the elements in winter, the place was never inhabited and only rarely visited. Magruser bought it, worked there, and by February '62—'

'Yes?'

'A dustbowl!'

'A dustbowl?' I repeated him. 'Chemicals, you mean?'

Crow shrugged. 'I don't know how his weapon works exactly, only what it produces. Also that it needs vast amounts of energy to trigger it. From what I've been able to discover, he used the forces of nature to fuel his experiment in the Orkneys, the enormous energies of an electrical storm. Oh, yes, and one other thing: the weapon was *not* a defence system!'

'And of course you also know,' I took a stab at it, 'what he intended to do with this weapon?'

'That too, yes,' he nodded. 'He intended to destroy the world, reduce us to savagery, return us to the Dark Ages. In short, to deliver a blow from which the human race would never recover.'

'But—'

'No, let me go on. Magruser intended to turn the world into a desert, start a chain reaction that couldn't be stopped. It may even have been worse than I suspected. He may have aimed at total destruction – no survivors at all!'

'You had proof?'

'I had evidence. As for proof: he's dead, isn't he?'

'You did kill him, then?'

'Yes.'

After a little while I asked, 'What evidence did you have?'

'Three types of evidence, really,' he answered, relaxing again in his chair. 'One: the evidence of my own five senses – and possibly that sixth sense by which I had known him from the start. Two: the fact that he had carried out his experiments in other places, several of them, always with the same result. And three—'

'Yes?'

'That too was information I received through government channels. I worked for MOD as a very young man, Henri. Did you know that? It was the War Department in those days. During the war I cracked codes for them, and I advised them on Hitler's occult interests.'

'No,' I said, 'I never knew that.'

'Of course not,' he replied. 'No man has *my* number, Henri,' and he smiled. 'Did you know that there's supposed to be a copy of the *Necronomicon* buried in a filled-in bunker just across the East German border in Berlin? And did you know that in his last hour Hitler was approached in his own bunker by a Jew – can you imagine that? – a Jew who whispered something to him before he took his life? I believe I know what that man whispered, Henri. I think he said these words: "I know you, Adolf Hitler!" '

'Titus,' I said, 'there are so many loose ends here that I'm trying to tie together. You've given me so many clues, and yet—'

'It will all fit, Henri,' he calmed me. 'It will fit. Let me go on . . .

'When I discovered that Magruser's £2,000,000 "order" from the MOD was not an order at all but merely the use of two million pounds' worth of equipment – and as soon as I knew what that equipment was – then I guessed what he was up to. To clinch matters there finally came that call from the British Museum, and at last I had all the information I needed. But that was not until after I had actually met the man face to face.

'First, the government "equipment" Magruser had managed to lay his hands on: two million pounds' worth of atomic bombs!'

## IV

'*What*?' I was utterly astonished. 'You're joking!'

'No,' he answered, 'I am not joking. They were to provide the power he needed to trigger his doomsday weapon, to start the chain reaction. A persuasive man, Magruser, Henri, and you may believe that there's hell to pay right now in certain government circles. I have let it be known – anonymously, of course – just exactly what he was about and the holocaust the world so narrowly escaped. Seven countries, Henri, and seven atomic bombs. Seven simultaneous detonations powering his own far more dreadful weapon, forging the links in a chain reaction which would spread right across the world!'

'But ... how ... when was this to happen?' I stammered.

'Today,' he answered, 'at ten o'clock in the morning, a little more than five hours from now. The bombs were already in position in his plants, waiting for the appointed time. By now of course they have been removed and the plants destroyed. And now too Britain will have to answer to the heads of six foreign powers; and certain lesser heads will roll, you may be sure. But very quietly, and the world as a whole shall never know.'

'But what was his purpose?' I asked. 'Was he a madman?'

He shook his head. 'A madman? No. Though he was born of human flesh, he was not even a man, not completely. Or perhaps he was more than a man. A force? A power ...

'A week ago I attended a party at the home of my friend in the MOD. Magruser was to be there, which was why I *had* to be there – and I may tell you that took a bit of arranging. And all very discreetly, mind you, for I could not let any other person know of my suspicions. Who would have believed me anyway?

'At the party, eventually I cornered Magruser – as strange a specimen as ever you saw – and to come face to face with him was to confirm my quarry's identity. I now knew beyond any question of doubt that indeed he was the greatest peril the world has ever faced! If I sound melodramatic, Henri, it can't be helped.

'And yet to look at him . . . any other man might have felt pity. As I have said, he was an albino, with hair white as snow and flesh to match, so that his only high points seemed to lie in pallid pulses beating in his throat and forehead. He was tall and spindly, and his head was large but not overly so; though his cranium did display a height and width which at one and the same time hinted of imbecility and genius. His eyes were large, close together, pink, and their pupils were scarlet. I have known women – a perverse group at best – who would call him attractive, and certain men who might envy him his money, power and position. As for myself, I found him repulsive! But of course my prejudice was born of knowing the truth.

'He did not wish to be there, that much was plain, for he had that same trapped look about him which came through so strongly in his photograph. He was afraid, Henri, afraid of being stopped. For of course he knew that someone, somewhere, had recognized him. What he did not yet know was that I was that someone.

'Oh, he was nervous, this Magruser. Only the fact that he was to receive his answer that night, the go-ahead from the ministry, had brought him out of hiding. And he did receive that go-ahead, following which I cornered him, as I have said.'

'Wait,' I begged him. 'You said he knew that someone had recognized him. How did he know?'

'He knew at the same moment I knew, Henri, at the very instant when those spinning winds of his sprang up in my garden! But I had destroyed them, and fortunately before he could discover my identity. Oh, you may be sure he had tried to trace me, but I had been protected by the barriers I had placed about Blowne House. Now, however, I too was out in the open . . .'

'But I still can't see how the British government could be tricked into giving him a handful of atomic bombs!' I pressed. 'Are we all in the hands of lunatics?'

Crow shook his head. 'You should know by now,' he said, 'that the British give nothing for nothing. What the government stood to gain was far greater than a measly £2,000,000. Magruser had promised to deliver a power-screen, Henri, a dome of force covering the entire land, to be switched on and off at will, making the British Isles totally invulnerable!'

'And we believed him?'

'Oh, there had been demonstrations, all faked, and it had been known for a long time that he was experiment-ing with a "national defence system". And remember, my friend, that Magruser had never once stepped out of line. He was the very model of a citizen, a man totally above suspicion who supported every welfare and charity you could name. Why, I believe that on occasion he had even funded the government itself; but for all this he had not the means of powering his damnable weapons. And now you begin to see something of the brilliance of the man, something of his fiendishness.

'But to get back to what I was saying: I finally cornered

him, we were about to be introduced, I even stuck out my hand for him to shake, and –

'At that very moment a window blew in and the storm which had been blowing up for over an hour rushed into the room. Rushing winds, Henri, and fifty ladies and gentlemen spilling their drinks and hanging onto their hats – and a whirling dervish of a thing that sucked up invitation cards and flowers from vases and paper napkins and flew *between* Magruser and myself like . . . like one of hell's own devils!

'How his pink eyes narrowed and glared at me then, and in another moment he had stepped quickly out of my reach. By the time order was restored Magruser was gone. He had rushed out of the house to be driven away, probably back to his plant outside Oxford.

'Well, I too left in something of a hurry, but not before my friend had promised not to tell Magruser who I was. Later, Magruser did indeed call him, only to be fobbed off with the answer that I must have been a gatecrasher. And so I was safe from him – for the moment.

'When I arrived home my telephone was ringing, and at first I was of a mind not to pick it up – but . . . it was the information I had been waiting for, a quotation from the Mad Arab himself, Abdul Alhazred.' Here Crow paused to get up, go to his desk, rummage about for a second or two and return with a scrap of paper. He seated himself once more and said: 'Listen to this, Henri:

"Many and multiform are ye dim horrors of Earth, infesting her ways from ye very prime. They sleep beneath ye unturned stone; they rise with ye tree from its root; they move beneath ye sea, and in subterranean places they dwell in ye inmost adyta. Some there are long known to man, and others as yet unknown, abiding ye terrible latter days of their revealing. One such is an evil born of a curse, for ye Greatest Old One, before He went Him down into His place to be sealed therein and sunken under ye sea, uttered a cry which rang out to ye very corners of ye All; and He cursed this world then and forever. And His curse was this: that whosoever inhabit this world which was become his prison, there should breed amongst them and of their flesh great traitors who would ever seek to destroy them and so leave ye world cleared off for ye day of His return. And when they heard this great curse, them that held Him thrust Him down where He could do no more harm. And because they were good, they sought to eradicate ye harm He had willed, but could not do so. Thus they worked a counter-spell, which was this: that there would always be ones to know the evil ones when they arose and waxed strong, thus protecting ye innocents from His great curse. And this also did they arrange: that in their fashion ye evil ones would reveal them-selves, and that any man with understanding might readily dispose of such a one by seizing him and saying unto him, 'I know you,' and by revealing his number . . ."

'And in the end it was as simple as that, Henri . . .

'Late as the evening had grown, still I set about to strengthen those psychic or magical protections I had built about Blowne House. Also, I placed about my own person certain charms for self-protection when I was abroad and outside the safety of these stout walls; all of which took me until the early hours of the morning. That day – that very day – Sturm Magruser would be collecting his deadly detonators, the triggers for his devilish device; and in my mind's eye I pictured a vehicle pulling up at some innocuous-seeming but well-guarded and lethally supplied establishment, and the driver showing a pass, and documents being signed in triple-triplicate and the subsequent very careful loading of seven heavy crates.

'There would be a pair of executive jets waiting on the private runway inside Magruser's Oxford plant, and these would take six of the atomic bombs off to their various destinations around the globe. And so it can be seen that my time was running down. Tired as I was, worn down by worry and work, still I must press on and find the solution to the threat.'

'But surely you had the solution?' I cut in. 'It was right there in that passage from Alhazred.'

'I had the means to destroy him, Henri, yes – but I did not have the means of delivery! The only thing I could be sure of was that he was still in this country, at his centre of operations. But how to get near him, now that he knew me?'

'He knew you?'

Crow sighed. 'My face, certainly, for we had now met. Or almost. And if I knew my quarry, by now he might also have discovered my name and particulars. Oh, yes, Henri. For just as I have my means, be sure Magruser had his. Well, obviously I could not stay at Blowne House, not after I realized how desperate the man must be to find me. I must go elsewhere, and quickly.

'And I did go, that very night. I drove up to Oxford.'

'To Oxford?'

'Yes, into the very lion's den, as it were. In the morning I found a suitable hotel and garaged my car, and a little later I telephoned Magruser.'

'Just like that?' Again I was astonished. 'You tele-phoned him?'

'No, not just like that at all,' he answered. 'First I ordered and waited for the arrival of a taxi. I dared not use my Mercedes for fear that by now he knew both the car and its number.' He smiled tiredly at me. 'You are beginning to see just how important numbers really are, eh, Henri?'

I nodded. 'But please go on. You said you phoned him?'

'I tried the plant first and got the switchboard, and was told that Mr Magruser was at home and could not be disturbed. I said that it was important, that I had tried his home number and was unable to obtain him, and that I must be put through to him at once.'

'And they fell for that? Had you really tried his home number?'

'No, it's not listed. And to physically go near his estate would be sheer lunacy, for surely the place would be heavily guarded.'

'But then they *must* have seen through your ruse,' I argued. 'If his number was ex-directory, how could you possibly tell them that you knew it?'

Again Crow smiled. 'If I was the fellow I pretended to be, I would know it,' he answered.

I gasped. 'Your friend from the ministry! You used his name.'

'Of course,' said Crow. 'And now we see again the importance of names, eh, my friend? Well, I was put through and eventually Magruser spoke to me, but I knew that it was him before ever he said a word. The very sound of his breathing came to me like exhalations from a tomb! "This is Magruser," he said, his voice full of suspicion. "Who is speaking?"

' "Oh, I think you know me, Sturm Magruser," I answered. "Even as I know you!"

## V

'There was a sharp intake of breath. Then: "Mr Titus Crow," he said. "You are a most resourceful man. Where are you?"

' "On my way to see you, Magruser," I answered.

' "And when may I expect you?"

' "Sooner than you think. I have your number!"

'At that he gasped again and slammed the 'phone down; and now I would discover whether or not my preliminary investigation stood me in good stead. Now, too, I faced the most danger-fraught moments of the entire business.

'Henri, if you had been Magruser, what would you do?'

'Me? Why, I'd stay put, surrounded by guards – and they'd have orders to shoot you on sight as a dangerous intruder.'

'And what if I should come with more armed men than you? And would your guards, if they were ordinary chaps, obey that sort of order in the first place? How could you be *sure* to avoid any encounter with me?'

I frowned and considered it. 'I'd put distance between us, get out of the country, and—'

'Exactly!' Crow said. 'Get out of the country.'

I saw his meaning. 'The private airstrip inside his plant?'

'Of course,' Crow nodded. 'Except I had ensured that I was closer to the plant than he was. It would take me fifteen to twenty minutes to get there by taxi. Magruser would need between five and ten minutes more than that . . .

'As for the plant itself – proudly displaying its sign, *Magruser Systems, UK* – it was large, set in expansive grounds and surrounded by a high, patrolled wire fence. The only entrance was from the main road and boasted an electrically operated barrier and a small guard-room sort of building to house the security man. All this I saw as I paid my taxi fare and approached the barrier.

'As I suspected, the guard came out to meet me, demanding to know my name and business. He was not armed that I could see, but he was big and heavy. I told him I was MOD and that I had to see Mr Magruser.

' "Sorry, sir," he answered. "There must be a bit of a flap on. I've just had orders to let no one in, not even pass-holders. Anyway, Mr Magruser's at home."

' "No, he's not," I told him, "he's on his way here right now, and I'm to meet him at the gate."

' "I suppose that'll be all right then, sir," he answered, "just as long as you don't want to go in."

'I walked over to the guard-room with him. While we were talking, I kept covert watch on the open doors of a hangar spied between buildings and installations. Even as I watched, a light aircraft taxied into the open and mechanics began running to and fro, readying it for flight. I was also watching the road, plainly visible from the guard-room window, and at last was rewarded by the sight of Magruser's car speeding into view a quarter-mile away.

'Then I produced my handgun.'

'What?' I cried. 'If all else failed you planned to shoot him?'

'Not at all. Oh, I might have tried it, I suppose, but I

doubt if a bullet could have killed him. No, the gun had another purpose to serve, namely the control of any merely human adversary.'

'Such as the security man?'

'Correct. I quickly relieved him of his uniform jacket and hat, gagged him and locked him in a small back room. Then, to make absolutely certain, I drove the butt of my weapon through the barrier's control panel, effectively ruining it. By this time Magruser's car was turning off the road into the entrance, and of course it stopped at the lowered barrier. There was Magruser, sitting on my side and in the front passenger seat, and in the back a pair of large young men who were plainly bodyguards.

'I pulled my hat down over my eyes, went out of the guard-room and up to the car, and as I had prayed Magruser himself wound down his window. He stuck out his hand, made imperative, flapping motions, said, "Fool! I wish to be in. Get the barrier—"

'But at that moment I grabbed and held onto his arm, lowered my face to his and said, "Sturm Magruser, I know you – and I know your number!"

' "What? What?" he whispered – and his eyes went wide in terror as he recognized me.

'Then I told him his number, and as his bodyguards leapt from the car and dragged me away from him, he waved them back. "Leave him be," he said, "for it's too late now." And he favoured me with such a look as I shall never forget. Slowly he got out of the car, leaning heavily upon the door, facing me. "That is only half my number," he said, "but sufficient to destroy me. Do you know the rest of it?"

'And I told him the rest of it.

'What little colour he had drained completely from

him and it was as if a light had gone out behind his eyes. He would have collapsed if his men hadn't caught and supported him, seating him back in the car. And all the time his eyes were on my face, his pink and scarlet eyes which had started to bleed.

' "A very resourceful man," he croaked then, and, "So little time." To his driver he said, "Take me home . . ."

'Even as they drove away I saw him slump down in his seat, saw his head fall on one side. He did not recover.'

After a long moment I asked, 'And you got away from that place?' I could think of nothing else to say, and my mouth had gone very dry.

'Who was to stop me?' Crow replied. 'Yes, I got away, and returned here. Now you know it all.'

'I know it,' I answered, wetting my lips, 'but I still don't understand it. Not yet. You must tell me how you—'

'No, Henri.' He stretched and yawned mightily. 'The rest is for you to find out. You know his name and you have the means to discover his number. The rest should be fairly simple. As for me: I shall sleep for two hours, then we shall take a drive in my car for one hour; following which we shall pay, as it were, our last respects to Sturm Magruser V.'

Crow was good as his word. He slept, awakened, breakfasted and drove – while I did nothing but rack my brains and pore over the problem he had set me. And by the time we approached our destination I believed I had most of the answers.

Standing on the pavement outside the gardens of a quiet country crematorium between London and Oxford, we gazed in through spiked iron railings across plots and

257

head-stones at the pleasant-seeming, tall-chimneyed building which was the House of Repose, and I for one wondered what words had been spoken over Magruser. As we had arrived, Magruser's cortege, a single hearse, had left. So far as we were aware, none had remained to join us in paying 'our last respects'.

Now, while we waited, I told Crow, 'I think I have the answers.'

Tilting his head on one side in that old-fashioned way of his, he said, 'Go on.'

'First his name,' I began. 'Sturm Magruser V. The name Sturm reveals something of the nature of his familiar winds, the dust-devils you've mentioned as watching over his interests. Am I right?'

Crow nodded. 'I have already allowed you that, yes,' he said.

'His full name stumped me for a little while, however,' I admitted, 'for it has only thirteen letters. Then I remembered the "V", symbolic for the figure five. That makes eighteen, a double nine. Now, you said Hitler had been a veritable Angel of Death with his 99999. . . which would seem to make Magruser the very Essence of Death itself!'

'Oh? How so?'

'His birth and death dates,' I reminded. 'The 1st April 1921, and 4th March 1964. They, too, add up to forty-five, which, if you include the number of his name, gives Magruser 9999999. Seven nines!' And I gave myself a mental pat on the back.

After a little while Crow said, 'Are you finished?' And from the tone of his voice I knew there was a great deal I had overlooked.

## VI

I sighed and admitted: 'I can't see what else there could be.'

'Look!' Crow said, causing me to start.

I followed his pointing finger to where a black-robed figure had stepped out onto the patio of the House of Repose. The bright wintry sun caught his white collar and made it a burning band about his neck. At chest height he carried a bowl, and began to march out through the garden with measured tread. I fancied I could hear the quiet murmur of his voice carrying on the still air, his words a chant or prayer.

'Magruser's mortal remains,' said Crow, and he automatically doffed his hat. Bare-headed, I simply stood and watched.

'Well,' I said after a moment or two, 'where did my calculations go astray?'

Crow shrugged. 'You missed several important points, that's all. Magruser was a "black magician" of sorts, wouldn't you say? With his demonic purpose on Earth and his "familiar winds", as you call them? We may rightly suppose so; indeed the Persian word "magu" or "magus" means magician. Now then, if you remove Magus from his name, what are you left with?'

'Why,' I quickly worked it out, 'with R, E, R. Oh, yes and with V.'

'Let us rearrange them and say we are left with R, E, V and R,' said Crow. And he repeated, 'R, E, V and R. Now then, as you yourself pointed out, there are thirteen letters in the man's name. Very well, let us look at—'

'Rev. 13!' I cut him off. 'And the family Bible you had on your desk. But wait! You've ignored the other R.'

Crow stared at me in silence for a moment. 'Not at all,' he finally said, 'for R is the *eighteenth* letter of the alphabet. And thus Magruser, when he changed his name by deed-poll, revealed himself!'

Now I understood, and now I gasped in awe at this man I presumed to call friend, the vast intellect which was Titus Crow. For clear in my mind I could read it all in the eighteenth verse of the thirteenth chapter of the Book of Revelations.

Crow saw knowledge written in my dumbfounded face and nodded. 'His birthdate, Henri, adds up to eighteen – 666, the Number of the Beast!'

'And his ten factories in seven countries,' I gasped. 'The ten horns upon his seven heads! And the Beast in Revelations rose up *out of the sea!*'

'Those things, too,' Crow grimly nodded.

'And his death date, 999!'

Again, his nod and, when he saw that I was finished: 'But most monstrous and frightening of all, my friend, his very name – which, if you read it in reverse order–'

'Wh-what?' I stammered. But in another moment my mind reeled and my mouth fell open.

'*Resurgam!*'

'Indeed,' and he gave his curt nod. 'I shall rise again!'

Beyond the spiked iron railings the priest gave a sharp little cry and dropped the bowl, which shattered and spilled its contents. Spiralling winds, coming from nowhere, took up the ashes and bore them away...

# THE BLACK RECALLED

CROW HAS GONE, *dweller now in Elysia. Nothing now remains of him in this earth.*

*Or does it . . . ?*

'Do you remember Gedney?' Geoffrey Arnold asked of his companion Ben Gifford, as they stood on the weed-grown gravel drive before a shattered, tumbled pile of masonry whose outlines roughly suggested a once-imposing, sprawling dwelling. A cold November wind blew about the two men, tugging at their overcoats, and an equally chilly moon was just beginning to rise over the near-distant London skyline.

'Remember him?' Gifford answered after a moment. 'How could I forget him? Isn't that why we chose to meet here tonight – to remember him? Well, I certainly do – I remember fearing him mightily! But not as much as I feared this chap,' and he nodded his head toward the nettle- and weed-sprouting ruin.

'Titus Crow?' said Arnold. 'Yes, well, we've all had reason to fear him in our time – but moreso after Gedney. Actually, it was Crow who kept me underground all those years, keeping a low profile, as it were. When I picked up the reins from Gedney – became "chairman" of the society, so to speak, "donned the Robes of Office" – it seemed prudent to be even more careful. Let's face it, we hadn't really been aware that such as Crow existed. But at the same time it has to be admitted that old Gedney really stuck his neck out. And Crow . . . well, he was probably one of the world's finest headsmen!'

'Our mutual enemy,' Gifford nodded, 'and yet here we pay him homage!' He turned down the corners of his mouth and still somehow summoned a sardonic grin. 'Or is it that we've come to make sure he is in fact dead, eh?'

'Dead?' Arnold answered, and shrugged. 'I suppose he is – but they never did find his body. Neither his nor de Marigny's.'

'Oh, I think it's safe to say he's dead,' Gifford nodded. 'Anyway, he's eight years gone, disappeared, and that's good enough for me. *They* took him, and when *they* take you . . . well, you stay taken.'

'They? The CCD, you mean? The Cthulhu Cycle Deities? Well, that's what we've all suspected, but—'

'Fact!' Gifford cut him short. 'Crow was one of their worst enemies, too, you know . . .'

Arnold shuddered – entirely from the chill night air – and buttoned the top button of his coat just under his chin. Gifford took out and lighted a cigarette, the flame of his lighter flickeringly illuminating his own and Arnold's faces where they stood in what had once been the garden of Blowne House, residence of the white wizard, Titus Crow.

Arnold was small, thin-faced, his pale skin paper-thin and his ears large and flat to his head. He seemed made of candle wax, but his eyes were bright with an unearthly mischief, a malicious evil. Gifford was huge – bigger than Arnold remembered him from eight years earlier – tall and overweight; his heavy jowls were pock-marked in a face lined, roughened and made coarse by a life of unnatural excesses.

'Let's walk,' the smaller man finally said. 'Let's see, one last time, if we can't somehow resolve our differences, come to an agreement. I mean, when all's said and done, we do both serve the same Master.' They turned away from the ruined house, whose stone chimney stack, alone intact, poked at the sky like a skeleton finger. Beyond the garden, both lost in their own thoughts, they followed a path across the heath.

Arnold's mind had returned again to that morning eight years ago when, greatly daring, he had come to Leonard's-Walk Heath and passed himself off as a friend and colleague of Crow, actually assisting the police in their search of the ruins. For on the previous night Blowne House had suffered a ferocious assault – a 'localized freak storm' of unprecedented fury – which had quite literally torn the place to pieces. Of Titus Crow and his friend Henri-Laurent de Marigny, no slightest trace; but of the occultist's books and papers, remains aplenty! And these were the main reason Geoffrey Arnold was there, the magnet which had lured him to Blowne House. He had managed to steal certain documents and secrete them away with him; later he had discovered among them Crow's notes on The Black, that manifestation of Yibb-Tstll which years earlier Crow had turned back upon Arnold's one-time coven-master, James D. Gedney, to destroy him.

Yibb-Tstll, yes . . .

Ben Gifford's mind also centred upon that dark, undimensioned god of lightless infinities – his mind and more than his mind – and he too remembered James Gedney and the man's use and misuse of black magic and powers born of alien universes. Powers which had rebounded in the end.

In those days Gifford and Arnold had been senior members of Gedney's cult or coven. And they had prospered under the man's tutelage and had shared his ill-gotten gains as avidly as they had partaken of his dark rites and demoniac practices. For Gedney had been no mere dabbler; his studies had taken him to all the world's strange places, from which he rarely returned empty-handed. All the lore of elder earth lay in books, Gedney had claimed, and certainly his occult library had been second to none. But his power sprang from the way in which he *understood* and *used* those books.

It was as if, in James Gedney, a power had been born to penetrate even the blackest veils of myth and mysticism; an ability to take the merest fragments of time-lost lore and weave them into working spells and enchantments; a masterly erudition in matters of linguistics and cryptography, which would unlock for him even the most carefully hidden charm or secret of the old mages, those wizards and necromancers long passed into dust, whose legacy lay in Gedney's decades-assembled library.

And uppermost in Gedney's itinerary of research and study had been the pantheon of Cthulhu and the star-spawned Old Ones, lords and masters of this Earth in its prime, before the advent of mere man and before the dinosaurs themselves. For in those ages before memory Cthulhu and his spawn had come down from strange stars to a largely inchoate, semi-plastic Earth and built their cities here, and they had been the greatest magicians of all!

Their 'magic,' according to Gedney, had been simply the inconceivable science of alien abysses, the knowledge of dark dimensions beyond the powers of men even to perceive; and yet something of their weird science had found its way down all the eons.

That would seem, on the surface, purely impossible; but Gedney had an answer for that, too. The CCD were not dead, he had claimed. Men must not forget Alhazred's conjectural couplet:

> *'That is not dead which can forever lie,*
> *And with strange aeons even death may die.'*

– and Teh Atht's much less cryptic fragment:

> *'Where weirdly angled ramparts loom,*
> *Gaunt sentinels whose shadows gloom*
> *Upon an undead hell-beast's tomb –*
> *And gods and mortals fear to tread;*
> *Where gateways to forbidden spheres*
> *And times are closed, but monstrous fears*
> *Await the passing of strange years –*
> *When that will wake which is not dead . . .*

– in which the reference was surely to Cthulhu himself, dreaming but undead in his house in R'lyeh, ocean-buried in vast and pressured vaults of the mighty Pacific. Something had happened in those eon-hidden prehistoric times, some *intervention* perhaps of Nature, perhaps of alien races more powerful yet, whose result had been a suppression or sundering of the CCD; and they had either fled or been 'banished' into exile from a world already budding with life of its own.

The regions in which the 'gods' of the cycle had interred themselves or had been 'prisoned' (they could never really die) had been varied as the forms they themselves had taken. Cthulhu was locked in sunken R'lyeh; Hastur in the star-distant deeps of Hali; Ithaqua the Wind-Walker confined to icy Arctic wastes where, in five-year cycles, to this very day he is still known to make monstrous incursions; and so on.

Yet others of the cycle had been dealt with more harshly: the Tind'losi Hounds now dwelled beyond Time's darkest angles, locked *out* from the three sane dimensions; and Yog-Sothoth had been encapsulated in a place bordering all time and space but impinging into neither facet of the continuum – except should some foolhardy wizard call him out! And Yibb-Tstll, too – he also had his place . . .

But if these gods or demons of the conjectural Cthulhu Mythology were largely inaccessible to men, certain manifestations of them were not. Masters of telepathy, the CCD had long discovered the vulnerable minds of men and insinuated themselves into the dreams of men. On occasion such dreamers would be 'rewarded', granted powers over lesser mortals or even elevated to the priesthood of the CCD. In ancient times, even as now, they would become great wizards and warlocks. And James Gedney had been one such, who had collected all the works of wizards gone before and learned them, or as much of them as he might. Titus Crow had been another, but where Gedney's magic had been black, Crow's had been white.

Looking back now, Gifford could see that it had been inevitable that the two must clash. Clash they had, and Darkness had lost to Light. And for a little while the world had been a cleaner place . . .

'Do you remember how it all came to a head?' Gifford asked. 'Crow and Gedney, I mean?'

The moon was fully up now, its disk silvering distant spires, turning the path to a night-white ribbon winding its way across the heath. And the path itself had grown narrower, warning that perhaps the two had chosen the wrong route, which might well peter out into tangles of gorse and briar. But they made no effort to turn back.

'I remember,' said Arnold. 'Gedney had discovered a way to call an avatar of Yibb-Tstll up from hell. "The Black," he called it: putrid black blood of Yibb-Tstll, which would settle upon the victim like black snow, thicker and thicker, suffocating, destroying – and leaving not only a lifeless but a *soulless* shell behind. For the demon was a soul-eater, a wampir of psyche, of id!' He shuddered, and this time not alone from the chill of the night air. And his eyes were hooded where they glowed for a moment upon the other's dark silhouette where it strolled beside him. And in his mind he repeated certain strange words or sounds, a conjuration, ensuring that he had the rune right.

'Your memory serves you well,' said Gifford. 'He'd found a way to call The Black, all right – and he'd used it. I saw Symonds die that way, and I knew there had been others before him. People who'd crossed Gedney; and of course The Black was a perfect murder weapon.'

Arnold nodded in the moonlight. 'Yes, it was . . .' And to himself: . . . *And will be again!*

'Do you recall the actual machinery of the thing?' Gifford asked.

*Careful* – something warned Arnold – *careful!* He shrugged. 'Something of it. Not much.'

'Oh, come now!' Gifford chided. 'Eight years as leader of your coven, and far more powerful now than Gedney ever was, and you'd tell me you never bothered to look into the thing? Hah!' And to himself: *Ah, no, friend Arnold. You'll have to do better than that. Squirm, my treacherous little worm, squirm!*

'Something of it!' Arnold snapped. 'It involves a card, inscribed with Ptetholite runes. That was the lure, the scent by which The Black would track its victim,

269

Gedney's sacrifice. The card was passed to the victim, and then ... then ...'

'Then Gedney would say the words of the invocation,' Gifford finished it for him. 'And The Black would come, appearing out of nowhere, black snowflakes settling on the sacrifice, smothering, drowning, sucking out life and soul!'

Arnold nodded. 'Yes,' he said. 'Yes ...'

They had come to the end of the path, a bank that descended to a broad, moonlit expanse of water rippled by the light wind. 'Hah!' Gifford grunted. 'A lake! Well, we'll just have to retrace our steps, that's all. A waste of time – but still, it allowed us a little privacy and gave us the chance to talk. A lot has happened, after all, since I went off to America to start a coven there, and you stayed here to carry on.'

They turned back. 'A lot, yes,' Arnold agreed. 'And as you say, I am far more powerful now than ever Gedney was. But what of you? I've heard that you, too, have had your successes.'

'Oh, you know well enough that I've prospered,' Gifford answered. 'My coven is strong – stronger, I suspect, than yours. But then again, I am its leader.' He quickly held up a hand to ward off protests. 'That was not said to slight you, Arnold. But facts speak for themselves. It wasn't idle chance that took me abroad. I went because of what I knew I'd find there. Oh, we divided Gedney's knowledge, you and I – his books – but I knew of others. And more than mere books. There are survivals even now in old New England, Arnold, if a man knows where to seek them out. Cults and covens beyond even my belief when I first went there. And all of them integrated now – under me! Loosely as yet, it's true, but time will change all that.'

'And you'd integrate us, too, eh?' the smaller man half-snarled, rounding on his companion. 'And you even had the nerve to come here and tell me it to my face! Well, your American influence can't help you here in England, Gifford. You were a fool to come alone!'

'Alone?' the other's voice was dangerously low. 'I am *never* alone. And you are the fool, my friend, not I.'

In their arguing the two had strayed from the path. They stumbled on awhile in rough, damp turf and through glossy-leaved shrubbery – until once more the stack of an old chimney loomed naked against the moon. And now that they had their bearings once more, both men reached a simultaneous decision – that it must end here and now.

'Here,' said Arnold, 'right here is where Gedney died. He gave Crow one of his cards, called The Black and loosed it upon the man.'

'Oh, Crow had set up certain protections about his house,' Gifford continued the tale, 'but they were useless against this. In the end he had to resort to a little devilishness of his own.'

'Aye, a clever man, Crow,' said Arnold. 'He knew what was writ on Geph's broken columns. The Ptetholites had known and used Yibb-Tstll's black blood, and they'd furnished the clue, too.'

'Indeed,' Gifford mocked, 'and now it appears you know far more than you pretended, eh?' And in a low tone he chanted:

*'Let him who calls The Black*
*Be aware of the danger –*
*His victim may be protected*
*By the spell of running water,*
*And turn the called-up darkness*

271

*Against the very caller . . .'*

Arnold listened, smiled grimly and nodded. 'I looked into it later,' he informed. 'Crow kept records of all of his cases, you know? An amazing man. When he found himself under attack he heeded a certain passage from the *Necronomicon*. This passage:

' " . . . from the space which is not space, into any time when the Words are spoken, can the holder of the Knowledge summon The Black, blood of Yibb-Tstll, that which liveth apart from him and eateth souls, that which smothers and is called Drowner. Only in water can one escape the drowning; that which is in water drowneth not . . ."

'It was easy,' Arnold continued, '– for a man with nerves of steel! While yet The Black settled on him in an ever thickening layer, he simply stepped into his shower and turned on the water!'

Backing away from Arnold, Gifford opened his mouth and bayed like a great hound. 'Oh, yes!' he laughed. *'Yes!* Can't you just picture it? The great James Gedney cheated like that! And how he must have fought to get into the shower with Crow, eh? For of course Crow must have given him his card back, turning The Black "against the very caller . . ." And Crow fighting him off, keeping him out of the streaming water until The Black finished its work and carried Gedney's soul back to Yibb-Tstll in his place. Ah! – what an *irony!'*

Arnold too had backed away, and now the modern magicians faced each other across the rubble of Blowne House.

'But no running water here tonight, my friend,'

Arnold's grin was ferocious, his face a white mask in the moonlight.

'What?' Gifford's huge body quaked with awful mirth. 'A threat? You wouldn't dare!'

'Wouldn't I? Your left-hand coat pocket, Gifford – that's where it is!'

And as Gifford drew out the rune-inscribed card, so Arnold commenced to gabble out loud that nightmarish invocation to summon Yibb-Tstll's poisoned blood from a space beyond all known spaces. That demented, droning, cacophonous explosion of sounds so well rehearsed, whose effect as its final crescendo reverberated on the heath's chill night air immediately began to make itself apparent – but in no wise as Arnold had anticipated!

'Fool, I named you,' Gifford taunted across the rubble of Blowne House, 'and great fool you are! Did you think I would ignore a power strong enough to snuff out a man like Gedney?' As he spoke his voice grew louder and even deeper, at the last resembling nothing so much as a deep bass croaking. And weird energies were at work, drawing mist from the earth to smoke upward in spiralling wreaths, so that the tumbled remains of the house between the two men now resembled the scene of a recent explosion.

Arnold backed away more yet, turned to run, tripped over moss-grown bricks and fell. He scrambled to his feet, looked back – and froze!

Gifford was still baying his awful laughter, but he had thrown off his overcoat and was even now tearing his jacket and shirt free and tossing them to the reeking earth. Beneath those garments –

– *The gross body of the man was black!*

Not a Negroid black, not even the jet of ink or deepest ebony or purest onyx. Black as the spaces between the farthest stars – black as the black blood of Yibb-Tstll himself!

'Oh, yes, Arnold,' Gifford boomed, his feet in writhing mist while his upper torso commenced to quiver, a slithering blot on normal space. 'Oh, yes! Did you think I'd be satisfied merely to skim the surface of a mystery? I had to go deeper! Control The Black? Man, I *am* The Black! Yibb-Tstll's priest on Earth – his High-Priest, Arnold! No longer born of the dark spaces, of alien dimensions, but of me! I am the host body! And you dare call The Black? So be it . . .' And he tore in pieces the rune-written card and pointed at the other across the smoking ruins.

It seemed then that darkness peeled from Gifford, that his upper body erupted in a myriad fragments of night which hovered for a moment like a swarm of midnight bees – then split into two streams which moved in concert *around* the outlines of the ruins.

Geoffrey Arnold saw this and had time, even in his extreme of utter terror, to wonder at it. But time only for that. In the next moment, converging, those great pythons of alien matter reared up, swept upon him and layered him like lacquer where he stood and screamed. Quickly he turned black as the stuff thickened on him, and his shrill screams were soon shut off as the horror closed over his face.

Then he danced – a terrible dance of agony – and finally fell, a bloated blot, to the mist-tortured earth. For long seconds he jerked, writhed and twisted, and at last lay still.

Benjamin Gifford had watched all of this, and yet for all that he was a devotee of evil had gained little pleasure from it. Wizard and necromancer though he was, still he knew that there were far greater sources of evil. And for

Great Evil there is always Great Good. The balance is ever maintained.

Now Gifford stopped laughing, his mouth slowly closing, the short hairs rising at the back of his neck. He sniffed like a hound at some suspicious odour; he sensed that things were far from right; he questioned what had happened – or rather, the *way* it had happened – and he grew afraid. His body, naked now and slenderer far than when The Black shrouded him, shivered in the spiralling mists.

Those mists, for example: he had thought them part of Arnold's conjuring, a curious side-effect. But no, for Arnold was finished and still the reeking, strangely twisting mists poured upward from the ruins of the old house. The ruins of Titus Crow's old house . . .

And why had The Black chosen to split and deflect around that smoking perimeter of ruin? Unless –

'No!' Gifford croaked, the dark iron vanished now from his voice. 'No, that can't be!' It could *not* be . . . could it?

No slightest vestige of life remained in Arnold now. The Black lifted *en masse* from his body where it lay contorted in death's rigors, lifted like a jagged hole torn in normal space and paused, hovering at the edge of the ruins of Blowne House. And slowly that cloud of living evil formed into two serpents, and slowly they retraced their paths around the ruins.

Menacing they were, in their slow, *sentient* approach. And at last Gifford thought he knew why. Crow was long gone but the protections he had placed about Blowne House remained even now, would stay here until time itself was extinct and all magics – black and white – gone forever. The place was a focal point for good, *genius loci* for all the great benevolent powers which through all the ages men have called God! And those powers had not waned with Crow's passing but had fastened upon this place and waxed ever stronger.

To have called The Black here, now, in this place was a blasphemy, and the caller had paid in full. But to have *brought* The Black here – to have worn it like a mantle, to have been Yibb-Tstll's priest – that were greater blasphemy far. This place was sacrosanct, and it would remain that way.

'*No!*' Gifford croaked one last time, an instant before The Black fell upon him. Priest no more, be was borne under . . .

\* \* \*

When the mists ceased their strange spiralling the ruins of Blowne House lay as before, silvered under a cleansing moon. Except that now there were corpses in the night. Pitiful shapes crumpled under the moon, where morning would find them chill as the earth where they lay.

But the earth would have a soul . . .